PRAISE FOR *THE SHANGHAI WIFE*

'A superb debut, conjuring all the mayhem of pre-revolutionary China through the eyes of a young Australian woman. I hope Emma Harcourt writes many more!'

Paul Ham, historian, author and journalist

'With extraordinary historical and sensory detail, Emma Harcourt brings the world of early twentieth century Shanghai to contemporary readers. Into this lush and complex setting comes a young woman straining against convention. In Annie, Harcourt has created a dynamic and vivid character, a woman both conflicted and courageous, a woman readers will fall in love with.'

Kathryn Heyman, author of *Storm and Grace*

'Emma's book is lyrical and beautiful ... she has written a love story as dangerous and exotic as the worlds she describes.'

Caroline Overington, author and journalist

'An immersive tale of illicit love set in Shanghai during the Chinese anti-Imperialist movement of 1925. Propels you straight to the streets of 1920s Shanghai.'

Nicole Alexander, author

Photo: Nicholas Purcell

Emma Harcourt has worked as a journalist for over 25 years, in Australia, the UK and Hong Kong. In 2011, she completed the Faber Academy Writing a Novel course and *The Shanghai Wife* was born. Emma lives in Sydney with her two daughters and she has a son who lives in London. She is currently working on her second novel.

The Shanghai Wife

Emma Harcourt

First Published 2018
First Australian Paperback Edition 2018
ISBN 978 148924914 2

THE SHANGHAI WIFE
© 2018 by Emma Harcourt
Australian Copyright 2018
New Zealand Copyright 2018

Published by
HQ Fiction
An imprint of Harlequin Enterprises (Australia) Pty Ltd.
Level 13, 201 Elizabeth St
SYDNEY NSW 2000
AUSTRALIA

A catalogue record for this book is available from the National Library of Australia www.librariesaustralia.nla.gov.au

Printed and bound by CPI Group (UK) Ltd, Croydon CR0 4YY

For Oliver, Clare & Zoe and for my intrepid grandmother, Ilma Hilda Harcourt.

AUTHOR'S NOTE

This novel is a work of fiction, although it takes as its inspiration my grandmother's story. She was born and died in Australia but as a young woman she lived in Shanghai in 1925–26 with her husband, my grandfather, who captained boats on the Yangtze River.

My grandfather, Captain A V Harcourt, wrote a navigational account of the river and I used this excellent resource when writing the river section of the book: *Yangtse-kiang, The Great River of China*, 1930. I am indebted to a number of other books on Shanghai in the 1920s, especially Hanchou Lu's *Beyond The Neon Lights* (University of California Press, 2004), Robert Bickers' *Empire Made Me* (Penguin Books, 2004) and George Wang and Betty Barr's *Shanghai Boy Shanghai Girl* (Old China Hand Press, 2002).

While all the characters in this book are fictitious, the story is set around real historical events, although as a novelist I have taken some liberty with the dates and details of those events.

For more information please see the historical note at the end of this book.

CHAPTER ONE

The Yangtze River, April 1925

The water was as still as the early morning air. Annie stood alone on the starboard deck, impatient to sail beyond the river's bend. She threw her arms wide 'til she held the entire view of the distant shoreline and waters in her grasp and stretched her neck with the glorious sensation of freedom which the Yangtze voyage offered. A sudden wind sent dark green eddies whirling across the river's glassy surface and Annie watched the shifting colours move towards her before feeling the breeze swirl deliciously through her hair. Less than a year ago she'd been stuck on her father's farm, now she lived in China. Beyond the rocky shoreline, farmers with bullocks tilled the rice paddies. Annie kicked off her shoes and rolled up the trousers she planned on wearing as often as possible, now there was no one to judge. Without her nylons, her bare feet felt clean and cool. She wiggled her toes triumphantly. There were no Shanghai rules here. A shudder from the engine room signalled they would soon be underway and Annie turned to watch the receding view of the river. She belonged on this working boat as a guest of the Captain, her husband. The air was cold and fresh; she took in a deep, cleansing breath. Finally, Annie felt she could stop running.

It had taken a day to sail beyond the crowded, commercial section of the river that ran from the Bund all the way around Pudong Point. She'd watched steamships power away from them, amazed at how the large vessels managed to avoid the junks that dipped and bobbed in the churned-up waters. Huge billboards dotted the shoreline, advertising cigarettes, tiger balm, even chewing gum. There had been British gunboats positioned out from the Point, a potent reminder of the unrest. But now, with the violence of Shanghai behind her, and rural scenery on either side of the shoreline, it felt like a real river journey.

The passageway smelt of damp carpet and fuel as Annie made her way to her cabin. The ship pitched forward and she felt a thrill of excitement as she fell onto the bunk bed, her feet touching the end where she lay. From the open porthole, the smell of cold water breezed through and briefly disguised the dank that pervaded every inch of her small cabin. Annie pulled off her trousers and shirt and let the cool of the river breeze ruffle her slip.

Opposite the bed, a wash basin stood on a small table against the wall. A stalk of plum blossoms sat in a jar; a gesture from one of the crew. The shiny bolts that kept her bunk locked to the floor glinted as the sun slipped into the room.

The river boat was considered substantial by professional standards. But Annie couldn't help comparing it to the splendid American passenger liners they'd passed as they sailed away from the Bund and into the Whangpoo River. Beside those, this working vessel was endearingly drab and small. But Annie wasn't bothered by the conditions onboard; this ship was her chance to experience the Yangtze and see something of the real China beyond the cloying social scene of the International Settlement. Even though she'd only been in Shanghai for six months, she was ready to escape.

One deck ran the length of the boat, coming to a point at the stern where a bench allowed for contemplation of the receding waters. There were no deck chairs, no cover from the sun. Annie slept in one of two staterooms—Alec had the other. There were no double berths on board. A thin passageway snaked from bow to stern of the interior. To one side a mess served as dining hall and recreation area for Alec and the crew. On the other was the captain's saloon which served as Annie's lounge. The crew slept in a tight room of bunks below the waterline close to the bilge.

Annie sat up at the sound of the door opening and was surprised to see Alec with a cup of tea. He dipped his head through the doorway and she couldn't help smiling. Such a big man was not made for these river boats. The tea was hot and black. He bowed gallantly as he placed it on the small table and Annie smiled at his playful theatrics.

'How on earth do you manage in these small spaces?' She dangled her feet off the end of the bunk, laughing.

'With a lot of bruises,' Alec smiled ruefully, grabbing hold of the bed as the ship keeled unexpectedly.

'What about seasickness?'

'Don't forget I've spent a lot more time than you on the water. You'll get your sea legs soon enough.' He towered over her as he spoke, one hand pressed to the roof of her cabin to steady himself, the other planted on her bed. 'In the meantime, hold onto the bulkheads when you move around and try not to hurt yourself, blossom.' Annie felt his gaze travelling up her body. The skin on her forearms prickled; she still wasn't used to such cool directness.

In truth, she hadn't planned to marry anyone; she'd just wanted to get away from home and be someone other than Annabelle Samuels. The future her father talked about, as the only family left to him—it wasn't for her. Leaving the Macleay Valley was the most exciting thing she'd ever done.

It was only once the ship had sailed far beyond Sydney's headland, with the ocean's constant swell beneath them, that Annie realised she had no idea what to do when they docked in Hong Kong. All her energy had gone into leaving home. She'd stood on deck watching the vast spread of water roll out in limitless waves to strange, unknown coastlines. The view didn't change for days, but each morning, Annie stopped and looked out across the sea, contemplating her future. Until the day Alec Brand, First Officer, came into her sights. He'd risked his position protecting her from the unwanted attention of a lewd passenger, and after that, he became her regular companion, watching Annie as she played quoits on the promenade deck, or offering a blanket for her knees when the shadows crept over her deckchair. He described the work that was taking him to China, the city as he'd been told. He grew as a romantic male lead right there and then; Shanghai, navigating ships up and down the Yangtze, a home, a purpose, belonging. Annie married him two weeks after arriving in Hong Kong, and they left for Shanghai the very next day. The boat's engine rumbled again and Annie's attention was back in the small cabin. Alec shifted his feet in response to the thudding vibrations.

'She's getting into her stride.' He peered out of the porthole eagerly and called to someone on deck. The muscles in his neck strained with anticipation. Annie heard footsteps and imagined the crew leaping to attention at her husband's orders.

'It's time I got back to the bridge.' Alec turned to her but he didn't move. Annie was conscious of the strap of her slip, which had loosened off her shoulder. The room was quiet. Then Alec reached out and hooked his finger under the ribbon of silk before dropping it back into place. 'Beautiful,' he murmured.

Annie shifted on the bed. 'You'd better give me some privacy to change my clothes if you want me to join you anytime soon.' She reached past him for her dressing gown and wrapped it around her shoulders. 'Don't take long, blossom.' His words echoed from the passageway. Alec had started calling her blossom from their first day as husband and wife but Annie didn't feel like a dainty little flower. She looked down at her slim gold wedding band as she reached for her trousers and thought back to the intimate ceremony in Hong Kong's cathedral only six months previously. It had been as simple and unadorned as her ring and Annie had been relieved not to have to think about trousseaus and wedding breakfasts. She'd just wanted to be married and get on the boat for China. She'd dismissed the fact that Alec was shadowy; they would get to know each other with time, and she'd felt safe in the half-light of their early companionship, when neither revealed too much. Only now she wondered if those shadows would always linger between them.

She ran a brush through her hair and slid her feet into the flat, canvas boat shoes Alec had insisted she purchase. At least her ring fit snugly. Annie stretched on tippy toes to see her reflection in the one mirror mounted above the wash basin. She didn't bother with lipstick or rouge. There was only Alec, after all, and it was a relief not to pretty herself up. It still surprised Annie when she caught sight of herself these days, so different to the girl from the farm in the Macleay Valley. Thank goodness she'd met Connie.

Connie, who shared a cabin with her on the boat to Hong Kong, helped Annie cut her long brown hair into a fashionable bob. She pulled out a pair of scissors big enough to shear a sheep. Annie hung her head over the sink and watched her dark hair fall helplessly into the bowl.

When she looked up it was a different girl staring back. Her face seemed leaner, her eyes stood out with flecks of hazel and dark green she'd never noticed before and they were larger, brighter. She saw for the first time how clear her skin was.

Connie gave her the silk dress that showed her legs. The hemline stopped just below her calves, so the skirts didn't get caught between her legs in the ship's wind. The waistline sat on her hips. Annie felt modern. For dinner one night, Connie suggested lipstick, a flapper headband, a feather. Annie had never worn anything so outrageous. She wasn't expecting to be beautiful.

Now here she was on another boat trip, only this time accompanying her husband up the Yangtze. She had to pinch herself to believe it as she walked along the slim passageway which led to the deck.

When they first arrived in Shanghai, Annie wanted to join Alec on the river, but he wouldn't take her; a working boat was no place for a lady. Yet he'd changed his mind, or rather, Shanghai had changed his mind for him.

He'd clasped both Annie's hands, she could still picture the way he'd looked at her. 'Finally, you will see my river.' His plans had been sealed by the early arrival of the summer high tides which meant Alec could begin the lucrative run shipping fuel to towns in the upper section of the river. His expression had been more open than she'd ever seen. Annie held to the bulkhead as the ship inclined slightly. This was her chance to see Alec in his world and hopefully they'd find the closeness she longed for.

The brightness of the late afternoon was a shock after the dusky interior of her cabin. It felt glorious to let the sun's heat seep into her skin. How far she'd come indeed!

She stayed on deck until the dusk drew in and Alec joined her. He reached an arm around her waist when she began to sway, firm as a tree trunk, and she moved closer to balance herself against him. In the fading light they watched small boats move about on the water, firing up lanterns that served as night markers across the channel. Only when the last lantern was lit and the dark river was softened by each small beacon's glow did they retire inside.

'That's her safely lit for the night,' Alec said, motioning to the river.

He held the hatch, whistling a tune softly as he let her pass. She breathed in the smoky sweetness of cigars as she brushed past him and took his hand as they walked to the saloon.

'I feel so much more at ease here. Why do you think that is?' She leant into his shoulder.

'No lists to tick off, no schedule, it's freedom.'

Yes, she thought. Free of Shanghai's overbearing social strictures and the Club ladies who enforced them. For a moment her mind wandered to Shanghai's latest unrest. There had been violent protests before they left; labourers demanding better wages had stopped work and were joined by students in street riots, the clashes with police fuelled by the underground gangs who armed the protestors with knives and guns in a bid to gain influence and a bigger patch of territory for their own illegal businesses. The city pulsed with a nervous energy but they would not hear any updates until they reached the next major port at Nanking. Annie reminded herself to focus on the journey, not the city she'd left behind. The night air cooled her cheeks as the river curved ahead, bearing her silently forward.

Dinner would be brought in shortly. Only one place was set, Alec ate with the crew. There was a knock and a coolie entered with two glasses of sherry. She took the glass and was glad for the soft tingle of alcohol. Alec pulled the curtains across the porthole, and came back to join her.

'Don't make me sit on my own; I would really prefer to eat with you.'

'It's not just me you know, the whole crew dines together. I didn't think you would enjoy hobnobbing with the coolies?'

'We're not in Shanghai now.'

'Too true, my love, and I trust these men with my life.'

With that he took her hand and, tucking her arm into his own with a quick squeeze, he led her along the passageway to the galley. His palm was warm and familiar.

A large, wooden rectangular table filled the room. There were more chairs than men, pushed in tightly to make room to pass. Alec said something in Chinese, a long, breathlessly connected set of sounds. Chairs scraped back as a space was made for Annie to the right of the captain's place at the head of the table. Whatever he said, they responded quickly.

A bowl of soup, with chunks of pork and a few floating green stalks was placed in front of her. It smelt strongly of steam and the sweet spice of ginger. A large terrine of boiled rice sat in the middle of the table with a soup ladle stuck directly into the centre.

A man spoke to Alec, nodding politely at Annie before leaving. Her husband understood, indeed he looked completely at ease with the conversation. Another man across the table said something. Alec replied in Chinese. She recognised his expression, the nodding and agreement, all familiar conversational tactics of her husband. But the speaking in Chinese was absolutely unexpected.

'Do they all speak to you in Chinese?'

'There are only so many phrases I need to know, and everything works a lot faster if there's no tongue-twisting around English.'

'What did he say?'

'He's going to relieve the man on watch so he can have his food.'

'Goodness me!'

'Annie, really, it's part of the daily rituals on board.'

'It may very well be, but my husband translating for me is not a regular occurrence. What a dark horse you are! In Shanghai you only ever speak English.'

'And that's as it should be. What would our friends think if they knew I conversed with my crew like a coolie? I don't have a problem with Shanghai etiquette. But this ship is my domain and on board I do what I please.'

'You are full of surprises Alexander Brand.'

'I'll have to dream up some more if surprises make you look at me like that.' She felt his hand gently rest on her knee. He motioned to the bowl that had been placed in front of her and raised his own spoon.

'Eat up, blossom. I can't vouch for the taste but it will keep the wolves from the door.' He leant in, so close she felt his breath on her neck, and whispered softly. 'Though not your husband.'

Butterflies tingled in Annie's stomach. She concentrated on eating, sensing her husband's presence stronger and fuller than ever.

The next day feathery tendrils of silky fog hung in the air. It was mid-morning but they weren't moving. Annie stepped cautiously, curiously, out onto the deck. The ship was shrouded in mist. A smoky hue of light was visible across the distance and it reminded her of the night beacons. But now, between that light and where she stood, Annie couldn't tell if there was water or land. She rubbed the goosebumps on her arms as her shoulders shivered. In fact, she couldn't tell where the edge of the deck stopped. She breathed out slowly, listening to the dense stillness around her. A ship's foghorn bellowed, long and deep, signalling its position. The sound lingered like a lonely echo, cushioned by the fog, while powdery spots of mist grazed her cheeks.

She turned her head to one side and frowned at a different, unusual noise floating across the foggy air. It rose slowly in volume as though moving towards her through the opaqueness. As the sound grew closer she heard crowing and squawking. She instinctively raised her hands for protection, thinking a flock of birds was about to land on her head. With it came a pungent smell like wet, fouled wool. She looked up and around, but couldn't see anything through the fog's dense cover.

She stumbled forwards. Her shoes slipped on the damp boards. She grabbed something. It was the cold, wet railing. A gust of air billowed up the side of the ship and whipped her hair back from her face. A splash of waves against the ship's side broke the fog and she found herself leaning into the misty drop to the water and the river's deep.

Then she heard voices and the deck lit up from a frame of light as the hatch to the bridge opened. Alec appeared. His white shirt was bright against the darkness. He looked tall with his captain's hat firmly placed centre, brim dipped low, on his head. Even his black shoes shone with authority. He clapped another fellow on the back as he looked out into the fog. They were laughing while behind him other men in the room cheered.

'Alec?'

He saw her then, and immediately stepped out to help. 'Annie, what on earth are you doing here? I thought you were resting?'

'A girl could die of boredom in that cabin.' Despite her words, she felt a little wobbly. 'I thought I'd get some fresh air.' His arms were warm round her back as he took her into the bridge and sat her down.

'This weather is very normal, nothing to worry about.' He dropped his voice and gave her a serious smile. 'We often hit fog between Shanghai and Chinkiang. It's like losing your sight, tricky navigation.'

'Then why are you all laughing?'

'Out of relief, blossom. Did you hear anything outside just now?'

'Yes, in fact I did—very strange noises.'

'That would be the local chicken boats, stuffed to the rafters with crates of fowl. They make an awful din but they're our saviours in these conditions. Those fellows know this river better than anyone; most of them have been running the same course since they joined their father's boats as boys. If we're lucky enough to hear the crowing of cockbirds we know we're not far off course. And the message just reached me from the watch that there's a din of crowing like you wouldn't believe!'

The fog stayed with them until lunchtime. Annie heard the coolies' bare feet running along the deck as they checked the water depth blindly with long poles. She stayed on the bridge with Alec, watching the dull light of the fog shift and swirl, and it felt like theirs was the only boat in all the world sailing along the Yangtze.

The next day they were due to pass the city of Chinkiang and Annie wanted to watch from the deck. She had read that the city was picturesque, enclosed by an old stone wall. The ship moved slowly, allowing her to watch as the huge wood and iron gates of Chinkiang were opened wide for the day. A line of people snaked out along the path, some pushing barrows, some carrying scythes, others leading bullocks. All of them wore peaked straw hats so that Annie saw in their silhouette a miniature mirror of the distant hill tops.

But as the shoreline came into closer view, she saw filth and flotsam washed against the banks with each small wave. A dead dog's bloated stomach bobbed above the water. Children wearing only the bottomless pants abhorred by foreigners moved about, prodding the water, occasionally lifting something of value from the dirty mess.

The sight didn't shock Annie; she'd seen similar in Shanghai, but it reminded her that there was little romance in living on this river. She'd been lulled by their languid progress into a gentler vision of this country. But the Yangtze was a working river, which Alec continually reminded her, and for him, the summer months were the busiest. The river levels rose and that meant the larger cargo ships travelled the full route of the Yangtze, from Shanghai to Hankow, and on to Ichang in the middle section and finally Chungking in the upper Yangtze. These months Alec transported fuel regularly to Chungking. He was gone for months, depending on the conditions. Often the ship was delayed in shallow sections requiring coolies on shore to painstakingly drag the vessel slowly along with ropes strapped around their bodies and attached to the boat. Or Alec would be forced to stop and take action against bandits who shot at his ship from rocky outcrops when they were in the upper section of the river. But there were also days of calm sailing along the wide, brown waters which Alec described to Annie as extraordinary, the natural beauty of the landscape unsurpassed by anything he'd seen. Now these would be shared memories.

Afternoons were languid and uneventful as they made the run through a wide expanse of open river. Annie walked the deck and watched the scenery. Everything slowed with the rhythm of the river. A stork flew off the bank, its thin legs hung gracefully below long curved wings. The shadow of its extended neck floated on the water's surface. Another took off, and another, 'til soon the sky was full of their angled airborne shapes, like floating paper cut-outs. She watched them turn towards the horizon.

A spray of water caught her on the cheek and Annie raised her face to the cool sensation. The wind changed direction and pushed through the sleeves of her shirt so that they billowed and flapped about her arms.

'That's Little Orphan Rock. You can see the Buddhist Temple on its southern face.'

She hadn't heard Alec approach. In front of them a bulbous rock rose like a breaching whale from the river's flat surface. Built into one side were a series of temple buildings, their slanted roofs dipping towards the water. Right at the tip of the rock sat a single temple with an air of isolated distinction.

'I imagine that's a very hard temple to reach.'

'Yes, indeed.'

They passed Nanking a day later. The dock bustled with activity, while bicycles and automobiles jostled on the road. The sound of a few car horns reached Annie across the wind. A community existed in Nanking that rivalled Shanghai. She'd heard the parties were as gay as their own. One of Alec's friends had recently transferred up to Nanking and travelled there by rail, the last link to Shanghai. She stayed on the deck through the morning as the uneven bend of Nanking's stone wall receded.

Annie looked forward to the evenings, when Alec joined her. She chose a pair of wide, linen trousers, their pale green colour a compliment to her darker eyes. Her hair fell loose and a thin band of turquoise drops sat snug around her neck. But the material clung about her uncomfortably and she wished the temperature would drop. When the wind died, every inch of the ship became a humid oven. She joined Alec on deck in a light cotton dress instead.

'Those hills in the distance are getting closer.'

She looked up into his face. The line of his jaw was relaxed and his eyes glistened with the water's reflected dark. *This is what he looks like happy*, she thought.

'My goodness, Annie, they're a sight up close. I've never seen such steep cliffs drop right down to the river's edge. They're like thunderbolts thrown to earth and lodged there for good.' Alec shook his head and slipped his arm around her shoulder.

'How long before we reach them?'

'In a day or so the gorges will come into view. I need my wits about me. It's a different beast altogether, travelling the upper Yangtze.' He turned to her, and gently tucked an unruly curl behind her ear. 'I've been considering what to do and I've decided I can't keep you with us. It's too dangerous for a woman. I'm sorry, blossom, but when we reach Ichang at the foot of the gorges you'll be getting off.'

'For goodness sake, Alec, I've come all this way, don't make me go home now, just when it's getting interesting.'

'I wish I could, but it's too dangerous. Trouble is closer than I thought. Pirates aren't usually active for at least another month which would give us time to make it north to Chungking. But this year the crops have failed, people are hungry, and that means more to gain for the devils who attack us. What's more, the warlords are stirring things up, and news of the student unrest in Shanghai has reached the remoter port towns. Everyone's nervous. I'm not hearing anything good from my contacts in Nanking.

'So I've sent a telegram ahead to the Merchant Service Club in Ichang. I have contacts there and I've stayed at the Club in the past. It has adequate accommodation and a dining room. The president's wife will meet us at the docks and she'll chaperone you until the TS *Ah-Kwang* arrives. It should only be a matter of days. The *Ah-Kwang's* going direct to Shanghai; it's a passenger steamer so you'll have a faster run than on this old cargo ship.' Annie shook her head with frustration.

'My love, I can't afford to let you continue travelling with us, not if it puts you in danger.' Alec reached for her but Annie shrugged out of his embrace. The pit of her stomach swirled.

'What about you? The danger is as real for you as I!'

'I'll take on armed guards at Ichang as usual, and don't forget doing the final run above Ichang gets me that automatic bonus. We deal with this sort of thing on the river frequently. It's just not the place for a woman, especially my wife.'

'It might be worse back in Shanghai. We left the city to be safe, now you want to send me back. I don't understand?' She turned away. An uneven piece of wood dipped and bobbed in the current and Annie watched til the wood was a small thing in the huge river, too far for her to make out if it was still moving. Shanghai had certainly changed since they'd arrived the previous winter. Armed guards now stood on street corners and no dance hall stayed open beyond midnight. It was difficult to find a party where the conversation wasn't all about the Communists and the nationalist

Kuomintang. It was why Alec had insisted she join him on the Yangtze.

'You don't need to understand.' Alec pulled Annie around to face him. 'What's important is that you trust me; I'm your husband, after all. But if it helps stop that frown, then I'll tell you. I picked up a copy of the *North China Daily News* in Nanking. Reports of home are rather good. It appears detectives have broken a significant gang ring in the city which was operating out of an opium den at the back of a local tearoom. They arrested the leader and his men.'

'I don't understand how this makes the city any safer. Everyone knows Shanghai has a dark side full of gangs, and that most of the laneways house opium dens and worse.'

'This is the Green Gang we are talking about, the biggest and strongest underworld organisation in Shanghai with local rings of operatives who report up a chain of command which we don't even know the full extent of. If the police have broken the gang's central powerbase and confiscated a significant haul of weapons and ammunition, then this will have a huge impact on their ability to operate. The paper says the gang will flounder without its leader and likely dissolve into petty disputes as factions compete to take over. It's a big win for the municipal police and the city will be quieter now.'

'But—I'll worry less if we stay together. If this ship is your domain, then keep me with you; protect me here, like you said you would.'

'I've made my decision, as I said, it's just too dangerous.' Alec took her hands as he often did. 'Everything is arranged and settled.' He spoke calmly.

'But you're leaving me, again?'

'Don't be ridiculous. I'll be home a month after you.'

A painful band tightened in Annie's chest as she stared out at the river's dark. 'Being here together is bringing us closer, don't you see that? If you send me home now, I'll be all alone.'

'Annie, my love, you won't be alone in Shanghai. We have so many friends to keep you company.'

'Don't you hear me, Alec? I don't want to go back to Shanghai. I want to stay with you.'

'But you love Shanghai, blossom. We have a good life there, with a decent house; it may not be as grand as some, but it's good enough, isn't it? We dine at the Club, we entertain, and you even have servants to take care of you. I don't understand.'

'I don't care about any of that, it's all just decoration. But this journey is about us. You told me I'd finally see your river.'

'Annie, my love, I'm doing the best I can. Everything is arranged and I will not change it now. It's just too danger-ous. Enjoy the quiet of Ichang. I believe they have a bridge club and an excellent tiffin.'

'Good god, Alec, is that what you think of me?' She caught her breath on his name and turned away quickly so he wouldn't see her tears.

Annie couldn't sleep that night. She pushed the sheet down to her toes in the hope some breeze would relieve the heat that pressed on every inch of her body. Was she wrong to expect more from her husband? She'd been so caught up in the notion of being his wife that Annie hadn't consid-ered how, or indeed if, they would work together as a cou-ple. Now she'd seen this fuller version of him it felt utterly cruel to cut short her stay on the boat and their chance of closeness. She thought about what he had said and shook her head. Maybe what they had was enough for Alec.

She got up and ran her hands under the tap, the cold water flashed on her cheeks like ice. Leaving her father hadn't changed anything; she had no more control over her life now, the only difference was that she took care of a husband. Yet marriage was the job she said yes to. She wanted to scream, and tell the girl in the mirror that everything would be all right. Only she knew it wouldn't change anything, and stared ruefully back, willing herself to keep going.

The porthole was open and the night's quiet noises drifted through to keep her company—the odd splash of a fish jumping, creaks and groans from the body of the ship as it sat at anchor, and the distant sound of bats calling out in the dark. She hadn't set foot on land for three weeks and she wasn't sure how many more days until they reached Ichang, but Annie's journey back to Shanghai had begun.

There was one last major port before Ichang, at Hankow where they stopped to take on supplies. Sampans and junks filled the channel that ran between two cities on either side of the river. Hankow was close by them on the left bank, while on the opposite far bank was Wuchang, capital of Hupeh Province. Tea factories crowded the shoreline and Annie breathed in the strong smell of tannin as she watched the crowded river from the deck.

A long, wooden junk with sails that split the air in two triangular flashes of white pushed up against the side of a departing ship. Annie could hear shouting from someone standing at the head of the junk beneath an arched dome of matting. A woman appeared, gesticulating to her five oarsmen to get as close to the side of the bigger vessel as possible.

Annie watched in amazement as the junk safely manoeuvred through the churning waters of Hankow Channel, attached to the larger ship. The woman then shrilly called her men to move off, and the junk slipped into the distant river depths once more. The foreign ship had been oblivious to the whole affair.

CHAPTER TWO

Four days later, Annie held tight to the railings as they bumped hard against the company pontoon at Ichang. The river's swell sucked water down and under the hull. Men threw lines to the coolies on board to secure the ship. The air smelt of fumes and sewage, no more the open river. She held a lavender-scented handkerchief to her nose and watched as they came up against the moorings.

A ladder was being lowered and the air had been still since they'd docked. A line of jetties marked the distance between the ship and the shore. In a few short steps she'd be back amongst the Club ladies. In her mind she pictured a nosy English matron sent to chaperone her and smoothed the skirts of her dress in readiness. The short day-gloves felt tight; it had been weeks since she'd worn them. Beneath her the ship groaned as it pushed against the pontoon. It sounded like a lament to her freedom.

'There you are!' Alec pushed towards her past the coolies who were busy loading fresh supplies. 'Everything packed and ready?'

One of the coolies dropped a bag of tea and it sunk helplessly under water. 'That'll be a day's wages,' Alec swung round and barked at the man.

Annie looked at him with resignation. Here was the Shanghai husband she recognised.

'It's going to be just fine here, blossom. It's for the best.'

On the grassy verge beside the roadway she kissed him goodbye. His lips were tangy and dry. She rested her head against his chest and listened to the reassuring thud of his heartbeat. The crunch of car wheels in the loose stones made Annie turn and squint through the sunlight. The dust caught in her throat. An older woman stepped out, her white hair neatly curled in a thick bun at the nape of her neck. Her long grey skirt touched the toes of her shoes as she walked. The laced shoes themselves were so clean and polished Annie thought they must be new. Her smile was warm and friendly.

'You must be Captain and Mrs Brand?'

'Yes.'

'How do you do. I'm Ilma Pitt. Let's get you back to town and out of this sun, shall we, Mrs Brand?'

Alec pulled Annie aside and took her hands.

'I must go.' Behind them the ship pulled at its lines as waves splashed against the uneven rocks that fortified the bank.

'Make sure you have enough adventures for both of us.' Annie whispered before reaching up and kissing him once, softly.

'I'll be focused on getting back to you.'

'No you won't be, but I understand; you've a job to do. Just don't forget me.'

'A little bit of water won't make me forget my wife. We're going to be just fine, Annie.' He squeezed her hands tightly before letting go.

'Be careful,' she called.

Ten minutes later he was standing on deck. She waved but her arm stopped in mid-air, like a question mark. Mrs Pitt waited patiently beside her. She couldn't go just yet, not until Alec waved goodbye. But the distance between Annie and the world of the ship was already insurmountable.

They sat in silence as the car rumbled through the sand and dirt streets. Annie ran her hands over the soft leather. It felt luxurious after the starkness of the ship's interiors. She watched the flat sprawling expanse of land and houses flash past. There was little traffic but a line of bullocks ambled along the dusty path that doubled as a road and slowed their progress. Annie listened to the steady thud of their hooves in the dirt as they edged around the beasts, and continued onto the simple town centre. Then the car engine died. They'd stopped outside a dressmaker's shop.

'This will only be brief. I do hope you don't mind. Back shortly.' With that Mrs Pitt disappeared into the store. The car door clipped softly shut. Annie shifted on the leather seat for comfort. A few locals peered into the automobile and Annie smiled at them. There was none of the noise or chaos of Shanghai. She pulled at her gloves, stretching the material up her wrists.

An entirely unexpected vision came into view. Mrs Pitt was wearing a long traditional red smock, with loose-fitting pants that brushed against the ground. Her European shoes had been replaced with soft embroidered slippers. The bun in her hair was unpinned, and now hung in a long white plait down her back. It was very Chinese and a complete surprise.

She nodded to the driver who didn't acknowledge the change in his mistress as he started the engine. Mrs Pitt looked relaxed.

'You're probably too shocked to speak, am I right? Not sure what to make of this old lady? I promised my husband I would wear something suitable to meet you off the ship, and I did. Job well done I'd say, Fred! But really, Mrs Brand, you have to agree this weather is not made for our style of dress. It's just plain sense to take a lead from our hosts. And these lovely things were waiting to be collected. I feel so much fresher now.'

With that she pulled out a delicate paper fan. The ivory and jade bangles on her arm clinked in applause. Annie had to admit she looked cool and comfortable. The style suited her tall, lean shape, and was kind to her age. She must have been at least sixty.

'Don't worry Mrs Brand; we still serve tiffin in Ichang.' There was a cheeky glint in her eyes which Annie liked; it was so very far removed from what she'd anticipated.

'I'm not worried, Mrs Pitt. A little surprised, I'll admit.'

'Well I hope that's a good thing.'

'Yes, it is, absolutely.'

The car pulled up outside a plantation-style house, modest by Shanghai standards but Annie surmised this was grand for Ichang. As they made their way through the corridor of the Club house, a few ladies stopped to greet them. They all ignored the fact that Mrs Pitt was dressed like a local, despite their own elaborate display of high collars and stockings. Mrs Marsden, the officious wife of the president of Alec's club back in Shanghai, would certainly not put up with such flagrant disregard for all things European. Yet Mrs Pitt strode ahead as though she were at home. Indeed, it turned out she lived upstairs in rooms provided for the president.

Annie rested in her room through the lunch hour. Her shoes lay discarded on the floor, her gloves thrown across the commode. The soft mattress was a treat after her bunk on the ship. She closed her eyes with a deep sigh. The smell of Yardley's Old English Lavender soap soothed her. Clearly some foreign goods were considered irreplaceable, even for the eccentric Mrs Pitt.

Later that afternoon Annie joined Mrs Pitt in the garden for tea. A small table was set for the two women away from the social hub of the ladies' lounge. Somehow she'd guessed that Annie would prefer not to be amongst company. Or perhaps it was Mrs Pitt who avoided the Club tiffin room.

They sat side-by-side, chairs backed up against a thick tree trunk for shade. Its branches spanned out above their heads in a canopy of lush green. Annie looked up as she leant back in her comfortable chair. A bright spot of light played on her arm where the sun's rays found a gap through the branches. She passed her hand through the sunlight, feeling the momentary warmth move from her arm to the skin of her hand and back again. The servants moved around them discreetly, placing tea things on the table.

Mrs Pitt leant over and squeezed Annie's arm.

'It's so nice to have a new face with us, if only for a few days.'

The gesture was kindly and Annie warmed to the older woman.

'Thank you, Mrs Pitt. You're very kind to take me in. I do hope it hasn't put you out in any way?'

'Not at all, I'm pleased to have a young thing to liven us up.'

'I'm not sure I can do that, but I'm very happy to be here. Have you lived in Ichang for long?'

'Yes indeed, a very long time. My husband retired here five years ago. Running this club keeps him busy and it's our home.'

The servants retreated inside. Annie still felt the occasional motion in her head as though she was rolling with the river's swell. She leant back and closed her eyes.

'By the way, please call me Ilma. You can see I don't stand on the usual ceremony.' She chuckled and poured them both another cup of tea. The sweet, warm liquid relaxed Annie's muscles. It had been a long time since she felt the maternal care of anyone, but this old lady stirred a child's need inside her. She rubbed her arm where Ilma had squeezed it and shifted in the oversized cane chair, feeling about ten years old as she held her teacup out for a refill.

'You look a little pale my dear, are you feeling all right?'

'It's the river still in my limbs making me sway, such an odd sensation when you get back on solid ground. I'll be fine, thank you. This tea is helping no end.

'You have a beautiful home here Ilma. It feels like a secret oasis, hidden away from censure.'

'Yes, isn't it splendid?'

'If you don't mind me asking, what does Ichang society think of your unorthodox dress?'

'It's simple, really. My husband is the most adored man in Ichang, so they put up with me. He runs the Club brilliantly, is always available to make up a set for bridge, stocks the best brandy, funds the local paper hunts and we've never lost a servant to anything other than age. I bask in the glow of his perfection.'

'It seems to me he's a lucky man to have you.'

'Well, there you're wrong. It is I who am the lucky one. My Fred is a genuinely good man, bless him. He loves me. And even though it might mean on occasion he finds himself defending the eccentricities of his wife, for Fred, that is a far better choice than trying to change me. I wouldn't have stuck around if he had tried. And the man is intelligent enough to realise that.'

Ilma shook the teapot in the air and a servant quickly appeared. Annie listened to her talking to the old man.

'Your number one son all better?'

'Very well, very well.'

'Good, good.' Ilma patted the man's arm warmly. Then she turned back to their conversation, as though it was perfectly acceptable to be asking a servant if his son had recovered from an illness. She leant in conspiratorially.

'It drives the younger members mad when I talk to the servants like old friends.' The tea sloshed from the side of her cup as she laughed. Annie felt a kindred spirit in Ilma.

'Why didn't you go home to England when your husband retired?'

'We're too old to go home now, and frankly, too set in our ways. We both wanted to stay, no children to worry about. Where is home for you, Annie?'

'Shanghai.'

'Ah, the metropolis; we spent a few months in Shanghai many years ago but it got too big for my liking.'

Ilma put down her teacup and sat back comfortably. Annie noticed how thin she was, the bony point of an elbow resting on the arm of the chair. Heavy ivory teardrops hung low in her ears, dragged down by years of wearing earrings. They sat in silence for a while. Annie closed her eyes and enjoyed the familiar smell of moist manicured lawns. There was a lovely quiet too, without the constant noise of a ship's engine.

She must have fallen asleep. Ilma was still sitting beside her, though the tea things had disappeared and someone had tucked a cotton blanket around her. It was like a sanctuary, she thought to herself, snuggling into the deep roll of her cane chair. Ilma hadn't noticed she was awake which allowed Annie time to watch her companion smooth her hair and tuck a few loose strands behind her ears. There were flecks of pale grey amongst the white. Annie noticed how her hair caught the sun and shimmered as Ilma slowly loosened the strands and began to rebraid the plait.

'Perhaps you'd prefer a quiet dinner in your room tonight? I can arrange it, and then tomorrow I'd like to show you something of our countryside, if I may? The ship will be here in another day, and you'll be off to Shanghai. But before you go will you join me on a little expedition?'

'Yes, I'd like that. I've always enjoyed exploring.'

A cold rush of air thrilled through Annie; it was exciting to be up so early, with the world cast in a sepia shroud of pre-dawn anticipation. A few staff moved quietly about loading supplies onto a donkey for the day's outing. Ilma came to stand beside Annie, a thin cigarette held tightly in her teeth. The gravel drive crunched beneath her boots.

'Ready?'

Annie nodded. They both mounted waiting sedan chairs. Annie's back pressed into the hard wood. It was an unceremonious means of transport and she took a while to adjust. The awkward walking rhythm of her two bearers pushed her body about in the seat like a rolling ball. Ahead, her first bearer dipped and bobbed with the bounce of the long wooden poles that stretched through and back to the man at her rear. Already she saw red marks where her weight bore into his shoulders.

But the first breeze of the day caught in her curls and breathed lightness into her mood. She left her hat off, ever hopeful of more breezes. Beneath her, the chair creaked as they set off at a steady gait.

In front, Ilma's head bobbed in motion. Both sedans moved to the side as a wagon cart loaded with crates of fowl rumbled past. The road was barely wide enough to fit the wagon. It scraped against a wall on the far side, and the driver shouted angrily at the sedan bearers. Then they were on their way once more and the street dissolved into a dirt path that opened out into countryside.

Annie exhaled and settled. Now they'd left the town she could see the sky, with its broad, blue expanse. She waved to Ilma as they passed each other. Some children ran out of a house and beside the sedans for a stretch, sticks flapping like flags about their heads. Annie threw coppers to them.

The constant movement became a lulling rhythm and her eyelids drooped despite the uncomfortable chair.

The stillness woke her. She licked her lips, aware of how dry her mouth felt. They'd stopped by the side of a hill. Ilma was already stretching out her arms and leaning into her back.

'Pit stop, my dear.'

They shared a water flask. The cool drink flushed down Annie's throat pleasantly. A farmer and ox worked a field just below them, the plough kicking back small chunks of mud and grass. The smell of churned earth carried across the breeze.

Ilma walked over to the bearers who were sitting on their haunches against some rocks. One lit the cigarette in Ilma's outstretched fingers and she turned to rejoin Annie. The men waited a respectful distance from them. Their bare chests were shiny with sweat.

'How much further will we travel?'

'We're halfway there. From now the path gets steeper. If you look back, you can see where we've come from.' Ichang sat in the distance below them. Annie shielded her eyes and squinted into the sunlight. Faraway, the river splintered into channels like the veins on the old lady's wrists.

The bearers clicked their tongues and the women turned away from the view and climbed once more into the sedan chairs. Their pace slowed considerably as the path followed the turn of a hill. The sensation of dipping backwards was exhilarating as the men shifted their weight into the steeper climb. Each tree, each rock, was new and undiscovered and Annie strained to see beyond the bend of every approaching turn. To one side the path dropped away steeply. On the other, trees grew precariously out of the slope. It smelt of scented wood and leaves. Above Annie's head, swallows darted about in the open space.

The bearer in front stumbled and Annie gasped. The muscles across his shoulders pinched tightly as he corrected the weight of the chair. Ilma's hand shot up in a wave; she was fine. They paused while the bearer found his footing. Then the coolies resumed the slow, cautious climb along the gravelly path. Annie held on tightly. But within minutes they'd rounded a bend into a flat patch of grass and rubble. A simple stone temple sat into the mound of the hill. The summit peaked above the temple's dome. Annie was relieved to see there was nowhere further to climb.

She jumped down from the chair; it was good to stand on solid ground again. Something rustled amongst the rocks, sounding loud in the silence of the clearing. The men moved away and pulled out a table and chairs from the packing on the donkey. They set about preparing lunch.

Ilma came to stand beside Annie.

'How are you feeling, dear?'

'Like an explorer who's just discovered a new mountain. This is so beautiful and untouched. I feel honoured that you've brought me here.'

'It's one of my favourite spots.' Ilma hooked her arm through Annie's and walked with her to the temple. 'Come and have a look inside.'

The entrance was cut up in rocky uneven edges where the bricks had tumbled from the walls. Two long, narrow steps led into a plain room with a dirt floor, open to the elements. The pointed roof swooped out at each corner in a tidal surge.

It took a few moments to see clearly after the brightness outside. Annie closed her eyes and opened them again, to see Ilma lighting a joss stick. The incense burned in pots of dirt to the sides of a long, low table that ran the width of the room. After the freshness of the hillside, the temple air cloyed at Annie's throat.

On the table was a row of six porcelain gods. The statues all sat cross-legged and were draped in intricately painted robes with long beards. One had his arm raised above his head, the other arm reaching across his chest. Between his legs sat a drum. Another looked directly ahead, his hands in a prayer position.

On the ground was a set of fraying mats. Ilma stuck her incense into one of the pots and moved beside Annie. The small head fired up briefly then dropped to a glow. As they turned to go, one of the bearers moved silently past them to crouch on a mat. The soles of his feet were dark with dust and indented with stones. There were marks where the wooden pole had dug into his shoulder. Annie wondered if he had a wife at home waiting to rub oil into his skin and prepare him for another day of carrying foreigners.

The dining chairs at the picnic table could have been straight from her home, mused Annie as she relaxed into one. The lunch was simple but delicious. Ilma dismissed the bearers to their own food and the two women sat companionably with cold drinks and sandwiches. Annie noticed the men had pots of rice and vegetables they unpacked from neatly tied cloth bindings. She considered the bottles of cold sarsaparilla on the table, wet with condensation from their packing of iceblocks.

'Would you mind if I offer these to the men? I think they could do with a cold drink more than us?'

'By all means, my dear, go ahead.'

Annie handed the drinks to one of the men. 'That made them smile,' she said as she returned to the table. 'Thank you for bringing me here, Ilma. It's so peaceful.'

'It must be a relief to be out of Shanghai.'

'I can't deny it was good to get away. But my husband says things in the city have calmed down since we left. As I understand it, there've been some big arrests including a gang leader and that will make a significant difference to the strength of the local gangs. They're always trying to conflate tensions between the Chinese and ourselves. It's madness, but hopefully not after these arrests. Hence my early return.' Annie tried to keep the regret out of her voice; she knew she wasn't telling Ilma the full story.

'We get news infrequently, but the last visitors told us Shanghai feels like a warzone with barricades and curfews and police everywhere. Workers protesting against low wages is not something that would have happened in my day. But I suppose the new Communist fad is filling their uneducated heads with foolish notions.'

'It's more serious than a fad. Two policemen were killed in a riot recently at a cotton warehouse down river from Pudong Point. The workers refused to disband and there was a gunfight. Frightening business.'

'Goodness, did they find who shot them?'

'I really don't know if they've got the killers or not, although they've arrested a large group from the protest;

most of them weren't even workers, they were students and they will be tried for the deaths.'

'It's those Communists getting in their heads; so young and foolish, what a waste.'

Annie found it liberating talking so freely about politics with Ilma. Such conversations scared her European friends in Shanghai. But no one took the time to investigate what it actually meant to be a Communist. What if they just wanted a better life; wasn't the same yearning for more from life the reason she'd run away to Shanghai? She didn't feel threatened, she felt angry. No one cared about the Chinese and Japanese students who now sat in prison cells awaiting trial. No one wrote about the bodies left like fallen leaves in the street until their compatriots came to pile them into carts.

'We're a long way from the streets of Shanghai now and as Alec said, with the recent arrests of gang members and all their guns off the street, hopefully the whole thing has calmed down. It doesn't stop me worrying about my friends and home though.' Beyond Ilma, Annie could see an eagle hovering high, probably scouting some small animal.

'It's good to know where home is, my dear. It grounds you, makes you stronger. Look at me, funny old thing that I am—many would say I'm halfway round the world from my home in England. I know how people talk, but I don't care. I've got Fred and we have a home and community in Ichang and with those foundations I can suffer any fool's criticism.

'Shanghai is such a big city these days, full of gossip and intrigue.' Ilma threw bread crumbs into the grass as she spoke. They scattered like seedlings in the wind. 'Many Ichang folk leave for Shanghai, thinking they will find work and be able to send money home to their families. But more often than not their families never hear from them again. There are rumours that the river boatmen in this region are connected to a gang in Shanghai and they are the culprits, enticing the poor and ignorant to join them in the city. If only we could convince them to stay here. I'm part of the local branch of the Moral Welfare League. We try to help the villagers find work locally so they have a reason to stay, but we've not been very successful. They don't much care for meddling *gweilos*. I see more and more young men with the tattooed mark of their gang membership. The older generation believe it is an insult to your ancestors to blemish the body and I quite agree. But these young, ignorant men parade their new membership around in the streets like cuckolds.'

'I suppose everyone is entitled to want for a better life. But I doubt they will find it in the city.' For the briefest moment Annie's mind turned to her father waking to an empty house, but she shook the image from her head.

'The more you tell me, the more I'm glad to be well away from the place.'

A donkey whinnied in objection to the weight of its load as the bearers hauled the chairs into their straps in readiness for the journey back down the mountain. Annie breathed in deeply before arranging herself in the sedan. She wanted to hold onto the crisp smell of pine trees and clean air. Soon she'd be back in Shanghai where the strongest smell was often the night soil carts. Annie closed her eyes and made herself a promise that she'd be different when she returned; she'd make more effort to discover the real Shanghai and experience life in the city beyond the Club gates.

By mid-afternoon the following day Annie was ready to board the TS *Ah-Kwang*. She kissed Ilma on both cheeks, letting her lips linger a moment on the papery skin. Then she turned and watched the building recede as the car drove out of the driveway towards the docks and the ship that would take her home.

CHAPTER THREE

Shanghai, May 1925

The waters churned and rolled around them as the TS *Ah-Kwang* manoeuvred to its anchor spot in the Whangpoo. Annie looked across to the distant outline of the Bund with its distinctively lit promenade skipping in the evening light. Her skin prickled with the cool air and with unexpected nerves that flashed about inside her at the sight of Shanghai. She remembered Alec's parting words to her in Ichang; she hoped everything would be fine.

The sea spray splashed her hair and cheeks as Annie held onto the edge of the small boat which ferried passengers from the ship to the wharfs. She wrapped a scarf around her neck and scanned the crowds on the docks. Alec had arranged for a friend to meet Annie and escort her home. Chow was the maître d'hôtel of the Shanghai Maritime

Club and the local man they trusted the most. Annie waved madly when she saw him at the back of the throng, conspicuously tall and elegant in his western driving coat and cap. He dipped his head in response and she motioned that she was coming to him.

It was only a few months since her first real conversation with Chow—one that didn't involve an order for drinks, Annie mused as she pushed through the crowds on the dock towards him. Chow had approached her one cold afternoon as she sat in a cane chair in the Club garden under a shady puzzle of leaves and branches, pleased to be alone with her paper and a blanket wrapped around her legs. She was reading an opinion piece and felt his solicitous presence hovering at a professional distance to one side. When he stepped forward she asked him what he thought of the political situation. Her mind was so focused on the racist nonsense she was reading that the question came out in a tumble, leaving her instantly regretting having asked it in the excruciating minutes of silence that followed. Chow folded the linen cloth he always carried over his arm into a neat square and laid it on his empty tray. He didn't speak and seemed to look beyond Annie. She thought he was ignoring her. But then his eyes swung back and she saw the hesitation in his look, unguarded, as though he wanted her to sense his dilemma. But she couldn't change the status quo: in the Club, his job was to serve her. She could talk to him though, and hope that he understood this was her way of evening the balance. He cleared his throat softly, making a raspy coughing sound that seemed to announce his imminent voice. Then he asked her to explain, quietly, confidently, what she thought a Communist was; what such a person stood for. She didn't expect to be challenged. But his question made her feel like a truer version of herself. No men in her own world talked to Annie like that.

'Welcome home, Mrs Brand.' Chow took her bag and stood back to let her lead the way. 'How was your trip?' He was forced to shout over the noise and chaos on the wharf.

'Too short for my liking but my husband insisted I return.'

'How is Captain Brand?'

'He's where he wants to be—along the upper Yangtze somewhere. It will be a few weeks before we have him home.'

'During which time there will be many social events to distract you.'

'Really, Chow, what do you know that I don't?'

'Mrs Marsden has taken over the Club in the lead-up to the May Ball. Your return will not escape her attention. I fear she is more insufferable than ever.'

Annie laughed. 'At least some things never change.' She ducked her head to get into the car that was waiting by the curb.

It was peaceful driving home, after the constant noise of the ship's engine. They turned off Nanking Road at the junction with Chekiang Road, past the Sincere Department Store's five floors of shopping heaven. On the opposite side of the road was its competitor—the Italianate Wing On Department Store. Annie knew these Chinese department stores well, they were cheaper than Hall & Holtz or Lane Crawford, and she enjoyed shopping like a local.

The streets flashed by in a palate of bright colours. Annie wound down the window and breathed in the smells of hot pavements and gasoline. 'Have there been any developments since the gang arrests?'

'You heard about this?'

'It's why I'm home. Alec read about the arrests in a newspaper he picked up in Nanking and suddenly Shanghai was a safer port than keeping me onboard in the upper Yangtze. I'd rather be exploring the river, even if there are pirates.'

'Captain Brand would only do what is best for you. The newspaper report was correct; the arrests will have an impact, though I do not think it will be as long-lasting as your Commissioner of Police would have us believe. It will take more than a few high profile arrests to stop the gangs in Shanghai. There is a web of many secret societies, who work together and against each other, as it suits them. Someone will easily step up to replace the imprisoned leader. These gangs are part of an age-old system that runs deep in our culture. But I wish the commissioner luck.' Chow smiled and shrugged his shoulders.

'But the gangs are not the only news in Shanghai right now,' he continued. 'Did Captain Brand not hear about what has happened to the gaoled student protestors?'

Annie shook her head.

'The trial of the protestors finished, the judge ruled against them.'

'What does that mean?'

'There will be more protests now, and more violence. The foreign judge made his decision with only an imperial ear. The students are to be detained indefinitely; I do not know how they will survive with no hope of freedom. I myself was handed a leaflet in the street just earlier today that called for a day of action. The foreign powers are fools not to realise the situation will escalate into violence.'

'Alec mentioned nothing of this.'

Chow flicked a ring around on his finger. 'I suspect he will be reading it in the paper he collects from the next port.'

The conversation reminded Annie why she always looked forward to seeing Chow. He made her feel intelligent and his otherness was intriguing. She hoped she had enough interesting things to say and, when they found a moment for conversation, that he would give her his full attention. He always did and she came to know the shift in his stance from servant to man, as he softly cleared his throat and, voicing his own opinions, moved out of silhouette and into flesh and blood.

Chow paused and Annie saw the sweep of his gaze to the street beyond the window.

'Chow, you're worrying me. Is everything all right?'

'There are people in Shanghai who will use this judgement to stir up more trouble. They want to show the foreign powers they will not be deterred by this decision, that it has made them stronger. I believe the situation is going to get very bad indeed.

'Had Captain Brand been aware of this news I do not believe he would have sent you home. You must take extra care, Mrs Brand.'

The car pulled up outside Annie's house. She shivered as a cold night wind licked about her. The afternoon had disappeared too quickly. A perfectly rounded moon filled the patch of night sky in her line of sight; its circular rim glowed opalescent. She wondered where Alec and the ship were spending the night.

'Thank you for meeting me off the ship, Chow. I'm sure the police will keep these gangs in check; I saw constables on every corner as we drove home.'

'I do not mean to alarm you, Mrs Brand. I will be at your service until Captain Brand returns.' He nodded goodbye and Annie turned and followed her house boy inside.

They were lucky to get the house in the International Settlement at such short notice. Alec wired ahead from Hong Kong explaining his changed circumstances and requested a house for a married couple. She told him she'd be happy in an apartment, but Alec was determined his new wife would have a proper home. The house was close to the Club and not too far from the Bund for Annie. It wasn't one of the large, imposing mansions she visited in the French Concession, but for Annie the neat, attached brick building, with its latched front gate, formal lounge room as well as her favourite sunroom, was just how she imagined a married couple's home to be.

The evening light sneaked through the windows as Annie wandered around her house. Her body swayed slightly and so she stopped every now and then to right herself. It was only an hour ago she'd disembarked at the Quai de France wharf, and the river's swell still hung in her legs. She stamped her feet, annoyed at the feeling of imbalance.

In the bedroom she moved about, hanging up her trousers, folding handkerchiefs. All the while, she was aware of Alec's slippers watching her from their place beside the bed. On the river, she'd discovered that her husband was a genuine, hard-working man who treated his crew with respect. Understanding this side of Alec made his city habits less annoying, and she felt like she'd seen the true man for the first time.

After eating a light supper alone, Annie went through her post. Amongst the letters and invitations waiting to be opened was an embossed card from Mrs Marsden inviting her to a luncheon for the May Ball committee later that week. Annie stuck the rest of the mail in her dresser, fed up with opening it; lunch with Mrs Marsden was the last thing she felt like.

She spent the next morning returning the house to its lived-in state; pulling off the dust covers from the chairs and sofas and shaking out the cushions. All the windows needed to be opened to blow away the stale smell of confined air in the rooms. The house boy was busy beside her, and there was an easy silence between them as they worked. Soon the rooms would regain their formality and order, just as Alec liked. Annie sat to catch her breath. The smell of jasmine floated through the open window. It was delicious and enticing.

She'd been cooped up inside all morning. Chow's advice from the previous day still rang in her ears. But she couldn't stay indoors all day, and if she walked her usual route to the Bund, and stayed on the main streets, then there was little risk. She'd like to see for herself what was happening, and she needed to move after weeks on board the ship.

As Annie set off, she passed a Sikh policeman patrolling her street and stopped to chat with him briefly. His presence reassured her. The constable waved Annie on as she crossed the road. The Settlement had certainly changed since she and Alec left those weeks ago. Annie walked through police fence lines and past armed men she recognised as bank tellers only the previous month. But it was reassuring to see so many of the Municipal Police around. As she got closer to the Bund she saw barricades across the main buildings too.

Summer in Shanghai was going to be very interesting with this as a backdrop.

As she walked moisture pooled on her skin, ready to trickle into the dark corners of her body. She wriggled a little, trying to dislodge the sweat tickling her back. But Annie liked the blanketing warmth that accompanied the early onset of summer: her body drank up the sun and her bones stretched with the sensation of it. The increased police measures hadn't stopped others from promenading along the Bund either, Annie thought as she passed a set of pretty parasols. Underneath the appendages, European women sweated in silk stockings and gloves.

A bicycle-peddler shouted and waved one hand at her as she stepped out into the street. The wind rushed up her back as he sped past. The smell of the Whangpoo was strong at the Bund end of Nanking Road. Day-tripping passenger boats lined the carpeted jetties, tied elegantly to wrought-iron railings. Spirals of steam floated in the air above the boats. Rows of rickshaws waited patiently for business, lined up along the walkway like hovering creatures in small hats. At the waterline, a few small wooden boats, one end capped with reed roofing, attempted to berth, while drying clothes flapped on washing lines strung across these river homes. A policeman frequently pushed a boat off with his foot, and the peasant owner moved around from the Grand Canal to Soochow Creek to join the mass of other boats that crowded the banks.

Behind Annie, the recently completed Hongkong and Shanghai Banking Corporation building sat huge and complacent. A ring of barbed wire threaded solidly across the splendid portico where armed police stood to attention.

Annie turned aside from the war-like image and looked out to the open water where white streaks patterned behind a ship. Her eyes hurt a little from staring. The weight of her satchel dug into her shoulder. She stood ever so still to enjoy the feeling of her mind concentrating on something so visual. She could almost feel the blood moving inside her veins.

Once, during a school test, she stopped writing mid-sentence, put her pencil down and sat still. Her eyes watched the clock tick through each minute that she wasn't writing. She became aware of the throb of her own pulse in the side of her neck, then the throb of blood moving down her legs and through her arms. There was something sensual about it. Until the anxious need to finish the paper overwhelmed her and she picked up the pencil. But she enjoyed the tingling in her body and it became the dangerous thing she did in tests. She was noticed by teachers, sitting still and upright, while everyone else was bent over scribbling feverishly.

She shifted her weight from leg to leg and walked on, wishing she'd brought a parasol with her as she passed another group of women shaded from view. Many of Shanghai's expatriate community would escape the worst of the summer heat to Mokanshan Mountain. The hill resort was only a day's journey south of Shanghai and it was a tradition to relocate to the cooler hills but everyone knew the other, unspoken reason that year was the political unrest.

The audacity of the protesting workers and students had rattled the foreign powers. Yet the threat was laughed off by the members of the Municipal Council as they relaxed over cigars and cognac in the Long Bar; it was all merely typical, harmless behaviour of uneducated natives. Until it became

clear the illiterate poor were being recruited by the burgeon-
ing new Communist Party which had joined forces with
some of the gangs in Shanghai to grow its influence quickly,
all in the shadow of the Bund's very European profile. Annie
stopped again to watch the tide lap against the stone wall.
Small waves pushed into the holes in the bricks and were
sucked out again to meet the incoming surge. A rush of
air scooped under her skirts as a Chinaman ran past, close
enough for her to smell the musty damp of his shirt. He
stopped suddenly right there before her, head bent forward,
panting heavily, a drop of sweat trickling down the long
smooth length of his forehead. He held a woman's purse
close to his chest. Two constables were fast approaching.

The Chinaman shouted something Annie didn't understand and the policemen quickly barrelled into him,
knocking the man to the ground. The noise was like a
smack across her face, a shock so unexpected she couldn't
move. A tight vein in the man's neck bulged as he lay pressed
against the pavement. One of the constables looked up at
her momentarily, and nodded. It was an unexpected gesture
of respect and she felt the heat swell in her chest. She took a
step backwards and immediately felt the closeness of others
behind her: a crowd had quickly formed around the scene,
jostling to see. Annie was pushed and shoved about by the
throbbing pressure of the spectators. Someone leant against
her heavily and she lost her balance, tripping over another
man's feet as she fell.

The sound of the policeman's wooden truncheon hitting
the man's head cut through the babbling noise of the crowd.
Annie saw him strike once, twice. She tried to get up, but the

crowd pressed in, swaying with emotion as the policeman hit the thief again. A trickle of bright red blood leaked from the man's ear. The rank smell of urine clung in Annie's throat.

Her ankle throbbed and her palms stung. It was hard to breathe. Through the maze of legs she saw the policeman haul the thief up. Then someone was shouting above her and pushing people back. Arms reached down and lifted her shoulders.

She looked into the grinning face of a local boy. He was only about twelve years old yet he had the strength of a man. She instinctively pulled away from him, and the boy instantly dropped his hold and held his hands up to show he meant no harm. He smiled and nodded at her scared expression, revealing an awkward smile; his front teeth were tightly packed together by the couple either side. Beyond that it was all pale and lumpy gum. Annie stumbled and winced with the pain of her ankle and the boy offered her his arm to lean on. She realised she needed his help. He pointed to the Happy Joy Tearoom across the road from the Bund.

'Yes, thank you. That's a good idea.' He looked at her blankly so she nodded instead.

A group of young men passed noisily close and Annie felt herself stiffen; she leant into the boy heavily and pulled her hat further down. He patted her arm proudly, as though he were escorting her to a ball, not across the road. His finger-nails were dark with dirt.

The Bund was crowded now. Children scampered in between foreign tourists in their cream panama suits and labourers pushing wheelbarrows. Rickshaw drivers touted for business or squatted beside their vehicles. The smell of salty water mixed with ocean diesel. A man jostled through the crowds, trying to keep his produce from spilling out of the buckets balanced at either end of a wooden pole weighted behind his shoulders. The constant noise of car horns and bicycle bells throbbed in Annie's ears.

A traffic warden blew his whistle sharply as a tram rumbled past. The boy helped Annie across the metal tramlines which gleamed in the heat. But the street's noise shut off the moment the door of the tearoom closed. As she looked around, the tightness in Annie's shoulders eased. The tables and chairs were all a dark chocolate brown colour, ornately carved, with red and gold silk covers. The boy hovered by the door. Annie pulled out a chair from an empty table and sat heavily. She was in too much pain to wait for propriety.

'Madaahm, Mrs Brand, here, here. Hello.'

Annie looked across the room. Chow was sitting alone, waving to her. He wore the loose-fitting, wide-legged trousers and cropped shirt of his countrymen. He walked over quickly.

'You are hurt?' He looked from her to the boy and raised his eyebrows.

The boy spoke quickly. Annie couldn't understand what he said but Chow remained quiet for a few minutes. Annie rubbed her ankle.

'You have had quite an afternoon of excitement I hear? Just as well this young man was able to assist you.'

'I know you said not to walk on my own, Chow, but I took the main road and it is broad daylight. This was just unfortunate timing. The man was a common thief, probably stealing to feed his family; nothing more sinister or dangerous.'

Chow's forehead creased in a frown. 'How does your ankle feel now?'

'It's sore, but it will be fine once I get home and rest. I would like to thank this boy for helping me, but he doesn't speak English. Can you tell him how grateful I am?'

'This is someone I know, in fact. His name is Li Qiang and he recently started in the kitchens at the Club. He says he recognised you.'

'I don't think I've seen him before?'

'But he has seen you. He likes to spy on the guests sometimes, looking through doors when no one will notice him. It's a silly exercise which I am constantly reprimanding him for, but I understand his fascination with the clothes and glamour of the foreign ladies.'

'How can I thank him properly? What do you suggest?'

'He would be grateful for a few coppers.'

Annie shook the boy's hand and gave him the money. He seemed unperturbed by the attention his presence was receiving. Faces turned to look at the foreign woman with the two Chinamen. A few ladies frowned at Annie. It made her skin bristle with indignation.

The boy had turned to leave and Chow was following him out. How wrong it seemed. Annie quickly followed Chow and tapped him on the shoulder.

'Would you stay and have tea with me?'

'I already have a table inside, Mrs Brand. I was just walking Li Qiang out. But I would be honoured if you would join me?' He chuckled softly.

'Well, now. Thank you, Chow. I would be delighted.' Annie hobbled over to where Chow held a chair back for her.

'I am here to try a new tea. It is a mixture of English and a local variety, mild but perfumed. I have been asked for it at the Club by the ladies. I heard that this tearoom is serving the blend.'

As he spoke a waiter placed a small stoneware teapot on the table in front of Chow, with a single teacup. Chow said something quietly and the man disappeared, returning minutes later with a second teacup.

'Does the blend meet Club standards?' Annie asked.

'It must meet my standards first and I am undecided. Won't you tell me what you think?' Chow poured some tea into a cup for Annie and held it out for her to take. She sipped self-consciously.

'It is like drinking bubble bath—not to my taste at all!' She grimaced dramatically and laughed. Chow leant over his teacup and breathed in the steam a moment, wafting it to him with his hands. Then he raised the cup to his lips and drank. 'The flavour is delicate and hovers in my throat a moment. It is not too strong; I taste the perfume in the drenched leaves.' He nodded to Annie.

'Now, close your eyes and taste again.'

Even though Annie felt a little foolish she took up the teacup again and closed her eyes.

'Let the tea's steam wet your nostrils before you drink, the flavour is in the smell.'

Annie breathed in deeply. 'Yes, I smell rose buds, no ... liquorice.'

'Now, drink.' Annie's eyes were still closed and even though she knew Chow was sitting on the opposite side of the table, his voice sounded so soft and close she felt the skin on her forearms tingle. She sipped and the hot tea infused her mouth. She blinked and smiled.

'Mmm, better, I like it.'

Chow sat back, satisfied. 'Then it is decided. I will purchase the blend for the Club.'

'You are very dedicated to your job.'

'It is serving tea, Mrs Brand. That is all.'

They both laughed. Annie was aware the table of women from the Club seated nearby were staring. She saw them lean in and share a whispered exchange. They were probably shocked; Mrs Alec Brand, taking tea with a Chink.

'Would you like a top-up?' Annie smiled at Chow as she leant over and rested her hand on his arm briefly before sliding his teacup towards her. Her hand shook slightly as she poured.

'I'm sorry, Chow; the morning has unravelled me more than I expected.'

'Please, Mrs Brand, you have no need to apologise.'

'I saw so many police and barricades when I was walking this morning. Do we really need that much protection?'

'Since the trial of the students I've seen many anti-foreign posters and pamphlets floating about. I do not know what will happen but if there are extra police on the streets then it might discourage protests.'

'Yes, I've seen one of these posters. Do the Chinese really call us foreign devils?' Annie bit her lip as Chow's expression darkened.

'Yes, and with good reason. If you had been here when the first foreigners arrived and seen the travesty of our exploitation you might understand why we use the term.'

'You hate us?'

'Hate is a very strong word.'

'Then how would you describe it, Chow?'

'I believe that it is easier to control by force than agreement.'

'So you do hate us?'

Chow shook his head. 'I also believe we are all just citizens. The demonstration at the factory last week was only peaceful students rallying for better wages for their fellow countrymen, for a better China. Yet the police dealt with the poor chaps as though they were a violent mob. Chinese politics does not have to be the beginning of something terrible. What if it is the end of something wrong instead?' They sat in silence.

Chow took a sip of tea, taking his time to replace the cup on its gold-rimmed saucer, and when he looked up at Annie he was smiling again. She watched him. Such incendiary talk by a Chinaman was considered criminal and Chow could lose his job, yet here he was talking candidly to her.

'I know there's a lot I don't understand about your city and the local politics, but I do want to learn. I'm not like those women over there,' she raised her eyebrows and nodded in the direction of the table of Club ladies. 'Every morning when I leave my house and I'm hit by the noise and the smells and all the people, I think how lucky I am to be here. I don't want to live like them, distanced from the people on the street and uninterested in what lies beyond the Settlement.'

'You certainly stand out from the other Club ladies.'

'I hope that's a good thing?'

Chow nodded. The silence hung between them. Annie's skin began to tingle and the blood throbbed in her veins.

She felt that dangerous thrill alive in her again and she was back in the classroom, mid-test, pencil raised but not writing. It was disconcerting.

'Please allow me to escort you home, Mrs Brand. It will be safer, and your ordeal has upset you.'

Annie stood a little too quickly. Chow reached out a hand as she winced on her sore ankle and she grasped it without thinking. She felt the eyes of the other patrons upon them.

'There you go, Mrs Brand,' he said, taking a respectful step back so she was forced to walk in front and away from him. A waiter held the door but Annie didn't see him there as she walked out into the afternoon sunlight. Her palm still throbbed where Chow had held it.

Before long they were moving through tree-lined, residential streets in the Concession. Chow tapped the little finger on his left hand against his knee and a brown-green ring slipped around as he did. 'What an unusual colour.' Annie watched him twist it in his fingers and noticed a flash of tattoo ink on his skin. His nails were pale and opalescent.

'This jade belonged to my grandfather. Would you like to feel how smooth it has become with age?' Chow offered the ring to Annie. A flush of heat rose in her cheeks as the cool, light weight of it tickled her hand.

'It's beautiful.'

'It's a connection to family; I'm honoured to wear it.'

'It makes me melancholy to think of things I don't have from home.' Annie turned away and looked out to where the street moved quickly along. Her hands were bare except for the simple gold wedding band that still shone with newness. She had no idea where the few pieces of jewellery that belonged to her mother ended up; perhaps they were still waiting to be found in the drawer at home.

She didn't regret leaving all her possessions behind when she left home that lifetime ago; it was easier to travel light as she moved anonymously through the small towns and countryside of her childhood. But really, that was an excuse; she couldn't bear any reminders of the life she was about to abandon.

The rickshaw driver coughed loudly to signal their arrival and Annie realised Chow was standing on the street, holding out his hand, looking up at her expectantly.

CHAPTER FOUR

Annie loitered over breakfast. Her ankle was still sore and bruised two days after she'd fallen in the street and she was annoyed at herself for getting caught up in the arrest of the thief. She was very grateful for Li Qiang's help. She'd be more careful today and take the car to the Club for bridge.

She flicked through the morning newspaper as she sipped on her daily coffee. The steam tickled her nostrils. She'd finally taught the cook how to brew a decent cup, and now she enjoyed one each morning. The headlines continued to report on the incarceration of the student protestors. The trial may have finished but it would still be weeks before the students received their sentence. In the meantime, they languished in the Nanking Road gaol while the police gathered information about who was behind the protests, focusing all their attention on the Communists. Annie didn't know how much to believe. Chow had implied the papers were biased, which she agreed with. Yet, there were few alternative sources of reliable information.

The Club library had a larger selection of newspapers and journals so Annie decided to go early and take a look. Bridge started at eleven so if she got going soon, she'd have a good hour to spend in the library before cards.

She hurried up the imposing steps of the Shanghai Maritime Club, stopping to marvel at the high ceilings, as though they needed all that open space above their heads to breathe. It was designed to resemble a grand English country manor house, which helped foreigners feel at home. At least a dozen local families could live in the entrance hall alone.

Annie went straight through to the library, running her hand over the meticulously ironed *North China Daily News* where it lay waiting to be read as she looked around at the multitude of book spines, tightly stacked together like a tapestry woven across the shelves. She looked for the journals and newspapers. The latest edition of *Country Life* and *Ladies' Companion* were stacked on a rosewood coffee table. They were in pristine condition which meant they must just have arrived on the ship from London. But Annie ignored them, pulling out a Commerce Council journal from a shelf instead. She flipped through the first pages to an article about the protest. The few hours during the demonstration had become, in this sensational retelling, a nightmare of brandished scythes battering the windows and lascivious eyes whose wanton owners were intent on only one purpose. The report called it a Communist plot. She let the crackling paper drop back to the desk with frustrated resignation and resumed her search, hoping to find a piece that was less biased. But there were no magazines, newspapers or journals which gave a different view.

Annie sat for a while, disappointed there was not a more measured account of the local politics to be found. Her hand rested briefly on the long deep mahogany table, one of many that fitted the room in symmetrical elegance, like rows of bed-ridden old men in an ordered cluster. Annie liked the library; it smelt of books and the silence was soothing. She pushed her chair back and felt the weight of wood and leather. Of course she could not find an alternative viewpoint in the library; here everyone agreed with the official position. Annie couldn't imagine Admiral Marsden, the president of the Club, allowing a pro-Chinese perspective to be read by any of his members. He was, after all, a sitting member of the Municipal Council.

Admiral Marsden was known for his experience with danger, having been through the Great War; twice wounded, once gassed, and with an artificial eye to show for it. He absolutely believed it was this experience which tipped his election to president of the Shanghai Maritime Club and not, as Annie ruefully believed, because his father had been master of the hunt in Leicestershire and hence he was an excellent horseman. The Shanghai Paper Hunt trophy had graced the glass cabinet in the gentlemen's smoking lounge for the past two years. Annie checked the time on the wall clock and closed the library door quietly as she hurried to cards.

Bridge was played in the smaller lounge, where Annie found ladies catching up on the latest gossip and family news before the proceedings commenced. There was a flurry of activity as women prepared themselves for the start of games. Mrs Marsden, their convenor, issued instructions to the servants on what time they would break for tea. Annie looked around for Chow, assuming he'd be supervising the tiffin, before moving to join her partner Flora. There seemed to be more tables in the room than usual but she found Flora seated and waiting. Annie patted her bridge partner encouragingly on the back. Flora was a slow and nervous player, and Annie felt for the poor girl who suffered terribly under Mrs Marsden's critical eye.

A hush descended on the room, as players settled into their seats and prepared to receive their cards. Mrs Marsden welcomed the assembly, with plain instructions on timings and etiquette. She repeated herself each week without fail. The wall clock ticked in sympathy as Annie accepted her cards from Mrs Sargeant. Poor Flora pursed her lips and stared at Annie. Mrs Marsden interjected.

'Oh do get a wiggle on Flora; we'd all like to get to the tea before it's cold.'

The other players at their table nodded in agreement. Around them, games were underway as the sound of sharpened pencils scratched scores on paper. Behind them china clinked as the tea service was prepared.

Tiffin was served through the French doors, which when pushed wide open doubled the length of the room. One end was filled with bridge tables; the other was clear, except for a long pair of trestle tables set up across the far wall, dressed in linen and decadently flush with cakes. The door swung inwards and servants entered. The smell of freshly brewed tea began to circle. Annie watched a young man saunter through in a uniform that drowned him with its size. Flecks of perspiration dotted his forehead as he walked towards the table, balancing a steaming, full silver teapot on a tray. She recognised him when he smiled. It was Li Qiang who had helped her in the street. His toothy grin was hard to miss.

Annie waved but he wasn't looking her way, he was staring at the loaded platter of sandwiches. One of the more senior staff shouted at him and he turned too quickly. As he did the tray he was carrying dipped precariously to one side and even though he did his very best to save it, the teapot slid off and clattered to the floor.

The ladies all stared regally at the startled boy, a ripple of necks turned in perfect unison. Mrs Marsden rose quickly to her feet.

'You clumsy, stupid boy, what a mess! Chow, where are you?' she shouted loudly and very quickly Chow appeared. 'Why on earth is this dirty little chit serving tea? Get him out of my sight and clean this up immediately.'

Annie was on her feet, pushing her way through the tables to get to where Li Qiang stood rooted to the spot. But Chow quickly ushered him out of the room. She turned to Mrs Marsden.

'It was an accident. We all saw it.' Her voice was high and agitated. Then she swung round to the tables of women, expecting to hear someone agree with her, but there was silence. 'He didn't deserve such harsh words.'

Mrs Marsden looked at Annie with the full force of her English pride. 'Mrs Brand, as you are only newly arrived in Shanghai, I will forgive your indiscretion. Unless one has been brought up with servants it's impossible to know how to deal with them.' Then she turned to the astonished women. 'Make some room so Mrs Brand can return to her table.'

Annie felt her blood boil. She couldn't think for the heat that flared inside her but she walked steadily back to her chair through the silent stares with her head held high. When she sat she turned all her attention to helping poor

Flora who struggled with her hand and by the end they had not done too badly. Annie couldn't wait to leave. Thankfully, the bell sounded and they rose for tea.

The ladies moved to the other end of the room and milled about in front of the long trestle table. Edges of lace tablecloth hung low against the wooden legs. Annie planned on staying for only a short time, just long enough to show she would not be bullied by Mrs Marsden. She fingered a neat, soft rectangle of cucumber sandwich as she stood on her own. She might be there but she didn't have to talk to anyone.

She chose one of the miniature scones next and felt the soft rice paper stuck to its base. Even though Mrs Marsden insisted on a very English tea, the scones were served just like Shanghai dumplings. As she popped the lot into her mouth, Annie nodded encouragingly at a group of ladies nearby attempting to pluck the rice paper off their cakes.

'Mrs Brand, we're just discussing the recent unrest; terrible affair.' Annie hadn't noticed Mrs Marsden move right beside her until it was too late.

'The rioters deserved what they got, my husband assures me,' Mrs Marsden confirmed as she held up her blue and white porcelain cup. There was a murmur of serious agreement amongst the assembled group. There was no getting away from the Flues that easily. She'd given these Club ladies a name when she first felt the full impact of their relentless judgement. It meant she could refer to them without anyone realising. They were the Flues; foreign ladies who lunched, who gossiped, who played bridge.

Annie sipped her tea, hoping to avoid speaking. It was tepid at best. She turned towards the table to ask for a fresh cup and as she did it slipped from her fingers making a quiet thud on the decorated rug. Milky liquid spilled down her dress into a pool at Mrs Marsden's feet. The president's wife clapped her hands in the air and a servant appeared quickly.

'How clumsy, excuse me while I go and freshen up.' Thank goodness her slippery fingers had given her an excuse to get away. Someone ought to tell the Club that too many Flues in the same room were bad for one's balance. Annie rummaged in her bag for something to dab at her skirt as she made her way to the powder room, ignoring the woman who brushed past her in the opposite direction.

'I think you dropped something.' Annie turned to see a red-haired lady holding out a handkerchief which must have fallen from Annie's purse.

'Thank you, I'll lose my head next.'

'I lose things all the time, Mrs Brand.'

'This isn't important,' Annie said, stuffing the linen handkerchief back into her purse. 'But thank you again for helping, Mrs ... I'm afraid we haven't been introduced.'

'Miss Sosnovsky, Natalia, how do you do. I know who you are because, excuse me for saying, you have a reputation for being overly friendly with the locals and I find it amusing to listen to the Club ladies gossip.'

'I don't care what the ladies here think, although you are the first person to find it amusing. I can't agree with the held view that chatting with the staff is wrong. I know it upsets some of the members no end, which is not my intention, though equally it's not reason enough to desist.'

'Of course, I understand. I never intend to upset people either, but it happens.'

Annie was intrigued by this forthright Russian. Her hair was tightly pulled back into a bun, leaving her face angular and strong; she looked almost masculine except her lips were a striking deep red. Annie noticed her long lashes too, that swept out from eyes lined with black kohl.

She remembered something Alec had told her; the dancing partners in the cabarets were mostly girls who fled Russia during the Revolution, reputed to be tsarists. Though, according to Alec, they tell their customers they are princesses expelled from Russia by the Reds. She'd seen some of these poor, bedraggled White Russians begging in the streets. 'Lowers the European prestige to the Chinese considerably,' Alec said. But this lady did not seem to be suffering.

'Are you here for the bridge class? I see they're running lessons each day this week after we play.'

'Most definitely not,' Miss Sosnovsky snorted which made Annie smile. Then she pulled out a slim, silver case from her pocket and lit a cigarette. She blew out a spiral of smoke that floated up and around them. Annie watched her cheeks concave in as she inhaled another draught of the cigarette. At least she did not construct conversation pieces to be socially acceptable like the Flues; there was no small talk of weather here.

'I'm not a huge fan of the game either, but I play nonetheless.' Annie couldn't stifle a cough from all the smoke.

'Why play if you do not enjoy it?'

'The weekly bridge morning is part of the social diary. Shanghai is so small, and our social circle is here. If I'd turned down the initial invitation to join bridge it would have been taken as an insult. My husband and I have no desire to be outcasts.'

'At least an outcast is still within the realms of society. We Russians are stateless citizens.'

There was something compelling about Miss Sosnovsky. The kohl around her eyes made them stand out like dark globes. Annie wondered if she could be a princess in hiding; she was so self-assured. Miss Sosnovsky pulled out another cigarette and tapped it against the case. But her eyes were fixed on Annie as she placed it in a long holder and lit the end.

'I've never been able to smoke like that.' Annie could think of nothing else to say to break the uncomfortable silence.

'It's easy; you just have to practise, which I've been doing for a long time, although not always with such pretty accoutrements. For these things one must have money.' Miss Sosnovsky held out the silver case as she spoke and rubbed away the smudged fingerprints with her sleeve.

'And there's the essential requirement for social acceptance in Shanghai. Aren't we a superficial lot?'

'Money is a necessary evil, as they say. It is what we do with our money that determines our values.'

'The only problem my husband and I have with money is not having enough. So I think, Miss Sosnovsky, you are talking to the wrong audience.' Annie regretted the words the moment she'd said them. Alec would be furious with her.

'And yet, you are members of this Club, whereas I am merely a guest. So you have been successful. Perhaps there is more to you than you think?'

Annie shook hands with Miss Sosnovsky and listened to her laughter as she walked away. She remained in the corridor, watching the bright sunshine from the day outside pattern across the floor, unable to decide if the Russian had been mocking her or not. The lounge door opened and Chow came towards her.

'You've been out here for a while. Mrs Marsden has gone and the bridge ladies with her. The lounge is empty. Would you like a drink? I believe it is cocktail hour now.' He stood with arms held behind him.

'Yes, I could certainly do with a drink and some quiet. Thank you, Chow.'

Annie sat in one of the chesterfield leathers which faced the three oversized windows and the view beyond. A swooping stretch of manicured lawn extended down to a line of hedge that ran the length of the Club fence and obscured the street. The expansive outlook and natural light that flooded the room made the ladies lounge a favoured spot in the Club. But at that moment only Annie sat beneath the ceiling fan that moved in a slow sweep.

Chow returned with her favourite cocktail, a whiskey sour. She never had to remind him.

'How is your ankle today?' he asked.

'Much better,' Annie smiled, hoping he hadn't noticed that she still walked gingerly on that side. She didn't want him to worry. 'I really am so grateful to that young man. It was very kind and courageous of him to help me. His assistance could have been mistaken by the police for something worse.

'Is he all right after Mrs Marsden's horrible words at bridge? I tried to step in on his behalf. She can be such an old trout.'

'Yes, it was an unpleasant rant from Mrs Marsden. Li Qiang is not usually so clumsy. It was my mistake for allowing him to carry the tray. He really isn't ready for that kind of work but he was so enthusiastic and I did not think anything could go wrong. Yet he wears spectacles and failed to tell me that they were damaged during your street altercation so he could not see very well.' Chow shrugged his shoulders. 'He will get over Mrs Marsden's cruelty, but I think his hurt pride will take a little longer.'

'I don't remember seeing him in glasses? Why on earth didn't you mention this to me yesterday, Chow? I could have replaced them.'

'He only informed me that he didn't have them after dropping the teapot. His mistake reflects poorly on me also. I would not have sent him into that room if I had known. Although now he has asked me to help him with this prescription as his monthly wages will not cover the cost for new spectacles. He will be in debt to me for quite some time.'

'Well, you must let me pay for the cost of replacing the spectacles. It is the least I can do. Give me the prescription and I will get a new pair made. Then I will have the chance to thank Li Qiang again when I hand them over to him in person.'

'That is very generous of you, Mrs Brand.'

'I owe him a debt of gratitude and this will pay it off nicely.'

Annie enjoyed the stillness of her bedroom while Alec was away, when the sheets felt cool and plentiful in their emptiness. She reached for the cup of tea left by the house boy and watched a cloud of steam evaporate into the quiet of her room. Annie missed Alec, but his absence gave her precious freedom. The house was peaceful, no husband leaving for work, no breakfast together. Her legs stretched under the cotton sheets and she wriggled her toes with the audacity of it all. There was no need to be the organised wife and maintain a perfect home. As long as she had food to eat and clean sheets on her bed, the rest could simply unravel. When she was in public Annie played the dutiful, long-suffering wife, engaged with Shanghai society while her husband was away on work. She liked that wife: coping so admirably by herself, always ready to share news of Alec from his latest letter, resilient. But in the privacy of her own home, she revelled in this brief period of independence.

Annie dropped the prescription for the spectacles off at the pharmacy on her way to Mrs Marsden's May Ball luncheon. Then she directed her driver to the Marsden's grand French Concession home on Avenue Joffre. It was set back from the road at the end of a circular drive. Annie heard the gravel crunch as her car slowly circled to a halt by the entrance. Timber panelling on white gave the façade its fashionable Normandy style. Annie knew she'd never belong in this world of pretentious trophy homes. She took a deep breath as she stepped out of the car. The entangled smells of the city—meat frying in peanut oil, street drains warming in the sun, fragrant incense smoke—all stopped. Here the air was clean, crisp and smelt of lawn cuttings and fir trees.

The hallway was wide and she followed the maid past doorways that allowed her a glimpse of the Marsden's extravagant life: an empty dog's basket plumped with velvet cushions sat at the foot of a gold-legged Louis XV armchair. On the wall behind, hung a vast silk tapestry depicting a hunting scene.

Lunch was to be an informal gathering in the conservatory, a light-filled octagonal room that overlooked the garden. An intricately patterned pair of curtains draped against each of the eight windows, their fruity print of peaches and leaves a nod to Chinese design. The round luncheon table was bedecked with eight tall vases of pink roses. Beyond the table, three French gilt wood sofas in the style of Louis XVI were arranged in a circle. Chairs and a smaller table waited to one side for the taking of minutes and other important items of business to do with the May Ball, which was only two weeks away. Annie had heard that this was the party all of Shanghai waited for and begged an invitation to attend. It was being held this year in the newly renovated ballroom at the Astor House Hotel, which added to its glamorous reputation.

Annie was the last to arrive. Two small pug dogs ran towards her, barking furiously and stopped her moving any further as they sniffed and scuffled around her feet. She was surprised to see Chow standing back beside a window, in the long-tailed dress suit he wore at the Club. Mrs Marsden shooed the dogs away.

'Mrs Brand, welcome. I hoped you would be able to join us and we were just debating if indeed you'd forgotten, such is the lateness of the hour. But here you are at last. Do come in, dear; don't be alarmed by Zozo and Bear, they're my little babies.'

Annie stepped over the dogs lolling at her feet. The other guests were seated together across the three sofas. She noticed Mrs Cleary and her daughter Beth—the ball would be their last engagement before leaving Shanghai for the summer. The heat was too much for Beth's constitution so the Clearys had already announced they would leave for the hill station soon after. It was going to be a night of farewells. Mrs Colder sat beside the Clearys and smiled in welcome at Annie. Mrs Sargeant was in typical businesslike mode, directing others to make space.

But before Annie could sit Mrs Marsden nodded at Chow, who came forward to stand by the small table, holding a handful of ivory chopsticks wrapped in linen napkins.

'I've had a wonderful idea for the ball. After dinner, why not start the fun of the night with a game? Chow has been helping me.'

Mrs Marsden nodded to Chow again, like a magician to her assistant. He placed the chopsticks on the table, and with a quick look to the door, signalled to a servant who entered with a bowl of slippery, round steamed dumplings. The young girl looked frightened to be in the room with so many foreign women as she shuffled across the floor in oversized western shoes. After placing the bowl on the table, she looked at Chow nervously for approval, before disappearing quickly back to the kitchen. Annie thought she saw Chow motion to the girl with raised eyebrows, as though telling her to stand tall.

'The trick is to eat a dumpling with chopsticks. What do you think—won't it be a lark!'

Annie watched Chow; he wouldn't look at her, in fact he didn't seem focused on anyone in the room. He had every right to be affronted by these western women's lack of respect for his culture. She wished she never agreed to this luncheon.

'We need a volunteer, to test the game out. Who'll be our first?'

Mrs Marsden looked around the group enthusiastically, and Annie clung to the back of the sofa, avoiding her eyes.

Fortunately, Mrs Colder put up her hand and with a laugh took the chopsticks offered to her by Chow. He patiently showed the woman how to hold the implements and even picked up a dumpling to demonstrate. All the ladies clapped at his marvellous dexterity and he bowed charmingly in reply. Mrs Colder was very good-natured about the whole thing. The dumplings were difficult to lift; no foreigners used chopsticks. But it was decided to go ahead with the idea. Annie listened to the chorus of amused congratulations without contributing. She thought the game was silly, and an insult to the Chinese, who ate like that every day. Thankfully the moment seemed to be over, however, as Mrs Marsden quickly moved on to other news.

'May I also remind the group that there will be a dance class held at the Club next Thursday at midday and I expect you all to attend?' There was a groan from around the room.

'Now, now, settle down. I agree that most of the new fads are ridiculous, but we simply can't be seen to be outdated, or the common dance hall will be more popular than a proper ball and I will not have that happen.'

Lunch was announced and Annie made her way to the table. But Mrs Marsden stopped her.

'Now, Annie, I do believe because you were late, you must have a go at the dumplings game too.' Mrs Marsden gave her a sly look that only Annie saw. She knew this was the older woman's way of challenging her. Annie didn't want to cause a problem. Chow looked across at her then, his hands clenched on the table. She smiled at him encouragingly.

'Pass me the chopsticks please, Chow.'

She clicked them about a few times. Then Chow took her hand, opened her fingers gently, and placed them around the chopsticks. His face was blank; to anyone watching them he was doing his job. But Annie saw the annoyance flicker in his eyes and something else too, a directness that made her drop her chopsticks in surprise. Chow picked them up and she heard them click against each other as he showed her how to open, and then shut them. She stole a glance at him once more and the expression was still there, unguarded, like an invitation.

The dumpling slipped through her chopsticks. It was indeed tricky. Feeling foolish, Annie looked around to see that most of the ladies were already seated at the table. Only Mrs Marsden stayed to watch, enjoying her discomfort.

'It's no good,' she said, annoyed.

Mrs Marsden saw a dish being delivered to the table. 'No, no, not yet—can't you see I'm not seated! Take it back to the kitchen, chop chop.'

'Help,' Annie whispered to Chow while Mrs Marsden was distracted. He leant in and covered her hand with his own, helping her to pick up a dumpling and point it at her mouth. She shook her head, a look of embarrassment in her eyes. She couldn't open her mouth, not in front of him, not so close. He still held her hand holding the chopsticks. But then he turned her hand towards him, and quick as a flash, she'd fed him the dumpling. Mrs Marsden turned back to Annie.

'Well done, Annie, not so hard after all.'

Annie saw Chow discreetly swallow. He winked at her as he left the room. It was all over in a matter of minutes. 'Thank you,' she mouthed to him silently.

CHAPTER FIVE

Annie checked that she had the spectacles in her bag before leaving for the Club the following Thursday. The car jerked over a pothole and she slid across the back seat, reaching out for her purse as it rolled away into the leather's curved rim. Beyond the window a blockade was being erected at the intersection of Nanking and Fokien Roads. Two Sikh policemen stood in the centre of the junction, directing traffic. She still marvelled at the unique makeup of the internationally zoned area where she was subject to the jurisdiction of the British Consul and not, as she first supposed, to the law of the country in which she was a guest. She'd bought a sturdy leather case for the spectacles and she gave it a quick shine with her handkerchief as they approached the Club. She was looking forward to giving the glasses to Li Qiang.

From beyond the lounge door she heard the sound of female voices, and pulled her step back into a tiptoe as she hurried along the corridor. She didn't want to get drawn into sitting with the Flues. She slipped past quietly and headed for the kitchens.

No members ventured into the working areas of the Club, but Annie had broken the unspoken rule during her first visit. She'd been passionate about seeing and experiencing everything and Alec had humoured her. She was shocked at the size and scale of the kitchen where staff worked constantly to prepare food or clean cutlery, plates and glassware. It felt like the engine room of the Club. But those staff were forbidden from entering the main building, considered so low-class they could not be seen or heard. Annie realised Chow's decision to let Li Qiang carry the teapot into the ladies' lounge for their tiffin had been a huge risk, and a very kind gesture to the boy.

Chow stood waiting for her, as agreed the previous week.

'This is very unconventional. But if we are quick then no one will know.'

'I just want to meet Li Qiang in his space—less intimidating. Thank you for agreeing to this, you're so good to me.'

Chow stood aside as he held the door for Annie. Very quickly the kitchen fell silent as the staff stared at the foreign lady standing in the doorway. Two women stopped chopping vegetables and wiped their hands on aprons as they bowed. A separate door was wedged open into a dirty alleyway where rubbish piled up upon wooden planks. At least it let a breeze into the otherwise hot and airless room. A waiter entered from a side door with a tray of dirty breakfast plates and immediately shuffled to the sink to hide the mess. Annie heard the hinges of the door swing loosely back and forth in a slowing rhythm after him. A group of men at a round table abruptly stopped their noisy shuffling of mah-jong tiles. She stood silent, unsure where to move or who to address.

'Come in, Mrs Brand.' Chow moved past her into the room.

He gestured towards the table and the men stood up immediately. Annie hovered.

'It is break time and the men are playing mahjong. Do you know the game?'

Annie shook her head. 'Now is your chance to see how it is played.' He directed her attention to the table before walking over to the back door to talk to a man who was loading dirty laundry into a huge basket on wheels attached to the back of a bicycle.

'Li Qiang is running late today it seems. But his sister is due to start work very soon, so I will find out where he is when she arrives. In the meantime, sit and watch the game.'

'Are you sure the men don't mind?'

Chow smiled and gestured to the players to sit as he pulled back a chair for Annie. 'We welcome you.' He sat down beside her. Annie sipped the glass of water which had been put in front of her; she could feel the throb of heat on her skin and raised the cold glass to her cheek. Chow smiled. 'The heat is so much worse in here. It's like one gigantic oven. Imagine spending twelve hours in this kitchen and you have an idea of what these workers put up with.' Chow turned his attention to the game, rubbing his hands together in anticipation. The men shuffled the decorated tiles. They concentrated on the task at hand, ignoring Annie as they pushed against each other and made a noisy mess of the pieces, some of which flipped and fell to the floor. Chow swept the tiles around the table with the others, moving his hands across the pieces quickly, and deftly sliding tiles in a smooth pattern. She was mesmerised by how fast his hands moved and every now and then she'd catch a glimpse of the green shine of the ring flashing on his slender finger. The men stacked rows of tiles in front of them, to create a wall two tiles high. The noise of the clacking pieces joined with the other kitchen sounds to draw her into the game.

Chow picked up a tile from the wall and then threw one into the centre of the table with an annoyed click of his tongue. The other men laughed and Chow slapped the man beside him on the back good-naturedly as he said something. Cigarettes were shared around and Chow sat back in his chair and inhaled with enjoyment. A rich sweet smell of stewing meat filled the air, with cinnamon flavours that made Annie's mouth water. The sound of a heavy blade chopping through stalks began, echoed by a second rhythmical knife thud. Annie looked around the room and noticed how it was busy and full of life despite the suffocating heat. Kitchen utensils hung from a rack over the bench top and cupboards lined the walls. A pile of lush-looking green leaves sat in the sink, ready to be cleaned by a woman already arm-deep in a bucket of water. A man hung a brace of ducks over a drain by the outer door and blood dripped slowly from their crooked beaks.

People came and went freely through the door into the alley outside. A delivery boy dropped a pile of newspapers with a heavy thud onto the kitchen floor. A separate man unloaded sacks of rice from his cart into the storeroom. The tangy smell of tobacco mixed with the freshness of the day's produce. All the time there was the loud banter of conversation. Chow looked up when someone called to him. Li Qiang's sister had arrived. The woman ran quickly to Chow and spoke in urgent, hushed tones. Chow moved her away to a corner and Annie saw his shoulders tense as he leant in. Whatever she was telling him was not good news. The door to the Club hallway banged as someone quickly closed it before joining the growing number of staff who huddled around the woman. Annie listened with concern to the rising volume from the group, and the wailing that had started from the woman at the centre of the disturbance. Chow clapped his hands and shooed everyone back to their stations. He sat the woman down and fetched her a glass of water.

'What's happened?' Annie asked when he eventually broke away and came over to her.

'It's not good news I'm afraid. Li Qiang has gone missing. His sister has not seen him since last night. She's been searching for him and asking around but no one will give her any information.'

'Where would he go?'

'The two of them arrived from their village a few months ago to live with their uncle. They travelled to Shanghai with the help of the river gangs up north. Li Qiang's sister believes it's this gang which has called in her brother to work for them as repayment for their debt. He would not have had a choice and I doubt he will be back.'

'Will you try to track him down?'

'Even if someone knows where he is, people will not help when there's a gang involved. No one is brave enough to stand up to them. This is what his sister has already discovered.'

'I could go to the police and ask them to look for the boy?'

'You would get no assistance there—he is a lowly kitchen hand.'

'So that's it?'

'Yes.'

'There must be something we can do? Let me talk to Admiral Marsden, please?'

'If you alert the president, then his sister will surely be dismissed.'

Chow ushered Annie out of the kitchen. She wanted to stay longer in the hope that there would be some good news about the boy, but he made it clear that was unlikely. 'We must leave Li Qiang to his own path, Mrs Brand, and hope that he treads carefully. The winds of heaven shift suddenly; so does a man's fate.'

Chow left her in the ladies' lounge and returned to his duties. Annie avoided the small gathering by the fireplace and sat alone. But it was impossible to ignore Mrs Hill's loud voice. She was enthusing over a local brand of mustard sold in the Sincere Department Store. It almost passed for Colman's. Annie listened to the excited rise in the older woman's voice.

'I had cook add it to dear Robert's cut sandwich yesterday at tea and he requested a second, which never happens!'

Usually the Flues drove Annie mad with their superficial chitchat, but this morning she was glad of the distraction; she couldn't shake her sense of disquiet at the way Li Qiang's disappearance was accepted as a fait accompli. A worker was trimming the bushes outside and Annie recognised him as one of the men playing mahjong in the kitchen earlier. She couldn't see his expression, so low was the man bending. Did the boy's disappearance worry him or was he a gang supporter? She would never know, so vast was the world between her and that gardener.

Annie took out the leather case that held the brand new spectacles. Li Qiang's friendly, toothless grin flashed into her mind. She felt ashamed for thinking spectacles and a case was the right way to thank him, when really the boy had much bigger problems. She'd behaved just like a typical western fool, throwing money at a native. Chow could tell her to forget about the boy, but she just couldn't. He was only twelve, not much older than her sister the last time she'd seen her. She wouldn't do anything to jeopardise Chow's position or Li Qiang's sister's job, but she could do some unofficial digging.

Annie decided to talk to Li Qiang's sister herself. If the two of them had travelled to Shanghai through the gang networks, then she must have a fair idea of who they were, and at least a contact. She might be too intimidated to approach them, but Annie wasn't. Li Qiang didn't deserve to be abandoned.

Mrs Marsden's voice carried through from the ballroom, where she was already rearranging the furniture for the dance lesson. Annie continued on down the corridor towards the kitchen. Li Qiang's sister would still be there and Annie knew Chow had gone straight from the kitchen earlier to a meeting with Admiral Marsden so she wasn't likely to bump into him. Now was her best chance.

There was a bustle of activity in the late morning of the kitchen, with lunch only an hour away. Annie walked through a flurry of staff, and blinked repeatedly to adjust her eyes to the smokiness from a fire that flamed below a huge saucepan. Even though the alleyway door was open, the heat was even more oppressive than earlier. No one stopped her, as they'd seen her with Chow only an hour ago. In a far corner of the room, behind a benchtop laden with potatoes, she found Li Qiang's sister. Annie hesitated, realising the woman couldn't understand her. She looked about the room for one of the staff she knew spoke some English and beckoned to a young man she recognised.

'I help you?' he asked.

'Yes, please. Would you tell this woman I would like to talk to her about her brother—Li Qiang?' The man hesitated, looking from Annie to the woman and back. 'Go on, it's all right, ask her. Tell her I want to help her brother.'

'She no see him. She very worry,' the man translated.

'Tell her I am worried too. I only want to find her brother and bring him home. Tell her, please.'

A girl pushed past Annie with an armful of pressed white linen napkins. She disappeared through the double doors into the members' area, leaving the caustic smell of lemon juice and starch in the air.

'She say go look see number 23 Xinzha Road.' The waiter translated as the woman spoke.

'Xinzha Road? Is that where her brother is?' But the man could not get any further information from the woman. Annie thanked them and left; at least she had an address.

A noisy group of women spilled out of the ladies' lounge, laughing and talking and their presence reminded Annie of the dance class. She turned her back, hoping her white dress would blend in with the wall and she'd go unnoticed. But the ballroom was too near and the women gathered Annie up in their midst as they moved in an excited pack through to the dance lesson.

Twenty or so women already hovered in the middle of the room, waiting for the class to start. Annie noticed the usual crowd of Flues and, of course, Mrs Marsden directing operations. All the tables and chairs had been removed and the space was big and empty with a parquetry floor that echoed effectively when walked upon. Annie walked slowly so that the group she was with moved ahead and no one noticed her holding back. Annie liked dancing and rarely got the chance but her head was full of questions about Li Qiang and she needed to think. What's more, the idea of taking a class with Mrs Marsden filled her with horror. She watched the old rhino stamp her feet a few times, as if checking the floor could take her weight in those gaudy red heels.

The charleston and the black bottom had been doing the rounds in the dance halls in Shanghai for a while, but amongst the more restrained members of the Club, this new fad was still a mystery. So Mrs Marsden had handpicked a dance instructor—Lucille, the eldest daughter of one of the American community, an enthusiastic eighteen-year-old. She was dressed in her dancing best; a fringed sheath with heels that clacked like tap shoes on the floor. Her knee-high socks were tightly held in place with a garter and around her neck a long set of crystals swayed as she moved.

The music began and Lucille pulled forward Beth Cleary to demonstrate how to dance a couple's black bottom. Annie moved towards the back of the crowd to stay out of view. Lucille and Beth moved around the room in a waltz-like dance while their bodies wiggled and their feet skipped and kicked to left and right. Even with all the jerky movements, the two young women managed to make the dancing look like pure fun.

Chow appeared to one side during the demonstration dance. Annie watched him quietly open each of the long windows that bordered one side of the room without looking to where they all stood. The skittish flow of air cooled her neck.

'Find a partner, now don't be shy.' Mrs Marsden's directive sent the women into an excited whirlpool of disorder that quickly resolved into pairings dotted about the room. Annie stayed where she was, purposely avoiding any likely dance partners. She would escape quietly once the music started. 'Mrs Brand, is that you hiding back there? Where's your partner?' Mrs Marsden's question was polite but Annie heard the self-satisfaction in her tone.

'I'll sit this one out, I really don't mind.'

'I won't hear of it.' Mrs Marsden was beside Annie quickly, a hand on her arm and she saw, with a flood of heat to her face, that she was motioning for Chow to come forward.

'Come on, come on, hurry up, chop, chop,' she called to him. 'You will partner Mrs Brand for this dance. Do your best, we won't expect much.'

Annie couldn't look at Chow. She let him take her hand and rest it on his shoulder, as he moved his arm around her waist. He held her other hand softly, but she had to clasp her fingers over his glove to stop her arm from slipping. At least he wouldn't be able to feel the heat; she was sure the mortification that burned inside her went all the way to her fingertips. Chow's black patent shoes were glossy and clean, lined up neatly opposite her own brown and plain lace-ups. He pressed gently into her back. She kept her eyes on the ground.

For a moment they were still, and then the music started, boisterous and fast and Annie bounced to the left as Chow went right, their knees bending in rhythm. She danced without focus, automatically following the steps which she did, in fact, already know. There was a lot of laughter as women fumbled against each other, or misjudged the rhythm and stopped altogether before restarting. Annie heard none of it. Her head was buzzing. Her hand rested so lightly on Chow's shoulder it ached from the effort of holding it up. But they moved together without stumbling and as the music shifted into the well-known reprieve, Chow pulled Annie round and round in a whirling circle. He held his body firm and straight as his feet kicked one way and then the other in mirror of her own. A faint smell of cologne wafted out from his neck collar. She allowed herself a quick look up; his eyes stared ahead with determined focus and a formal smile was etched on his lips.

Annie felt her heart race with the exertion of the dance but there was no let-up as Chow moved them into the foot shuffle. For a moment they stopped, while their feet shimmied left and right with knees bent. Annie breathed heavily. Beyond Chow's shoulder the room was a blur of moving skirts. Then he pulled her closer as they began to waltz. Perspiration marked his cheekbone; the smooth line of his shoulders filled out his dress coat perfectly. The tails flapped as he moved.

It was noisy and hot, but the longer they danced, the harder it was for Annie to stay reserved. Chow danced so formally, yet he was very good; he didn't break between knee bends and foot kicks, never lost a beat. She found herself enjoying the dance. Annie kicked one way and then the other. Chow did the same and she couldn't help smiling at him with an apologetic shrug. How ridiculous they both looked. With the next move, he swung her round in a free-flowing rush and it was exhilarating. His hold on her waist tightened and she followed his lead, matching each compli-cated step. The repetitive beat of their shoes on the floor-boards seemed to get louder and the closeness of their heavy breathing filled the space between them. The sounds of the other dancers disappeared within the concentration of their own circle. They swung together on the next syncopated beat and she threw out her feet with unrestrained delight. He held her gaze as they whirled madly and grinned back as she laughed at his splendid bravura.

Then people were clapping and Annie realised the others had stopped dancing to watch her and Chow. The music was over. All she could hear was the sound of her own rasping breath as her chest heaved with the exertion of the dance. Chow took a step back and dropped his gaze to the floor.

'Well done, you two, excellent show!' Lucille ran up and hugged Annie in congratulations. Annie's cheeks flushed but she managed to smile and make a silly curtsey. Chow bowed.

Mrs Marsden moved to stand beside Lucille, address-ing Chow.

'What a dark horse, we shall have to watch you.' It was a dismissal.

Then she turned to Annie. 'Are you all right, dear? How impudent of the boy to think he could show off like that,' as though it were not she who had initiated Chow's involve-ment in the dance class. The smile on Annie's lips died.

'It was rather splendid,' she replied evenly. 'Chow dances better than any men I know, we could all learn from him.'

Then she turned her back on Mrs Marsden and spoke to Chow. 'Thank you for stepping in and dancing with me.' He acknowledged the ladies with a slight incline of his head before moving off.

'Isn't this ridiculous!' It was Miss Sosnovsky. Annie hadn't noticed her until now.

'Are we children that we need dancing lessons?' She sniffed in Mrs Marsden's direction. 'How do you put up with her?'

'With very little patience at the moment it seems. I may be disinvited from the ball after today.'

A waiter appeared with glasses of icy cold water and Annie accepted one gratefully. She held the glass against her wrist and didn't mind the damp where droplets of condensation fell into her sleeve.

'I didn't see you in the class, Miss Sosnovsky?'

'I've been lunching with Mr William Piper—he is a new friend. The sound of your dancing music intrigued me so I popped my head in and saw the end of your dance with the maître d'. You two were very good together.' Her raised eyebrows brought a sudden flush to Annie's cheeks again.

'Mrs Marsden insisted Chow accompany me as we were short of partners, nothing more.'

The Russian laughed as she turned to leave and this time, Annie shrugged her shoulders at Miss Sosnovsky's good-natured play. 'Willie has invited me to the gala dinner here tonight, in honour of the policemen who work so hard to protect us, so I shall see you there.'

Natalia wandered off, leaving Annie curious about how the two had met.

A trail of vine curled along the stone wall that separated Annie's garden from the next house. She reached up to smell the sweet perfume. The day had been full of unexpected turns and she was glad to disappear into the quiet oasis for an hour. The late afternoon light was warm and golden. It felt reassuringly familiar as she wandered between the trees which were dwarf fruits of some local variety, but no fruit grew because they had been nipped and pruned into shape. Hopefully the chicken manure she sprinkled at the base of each tree would help. It was one of her little secret rebellions. On the farm at home this sort of manure worked wonders on the choko vine. Maybe with time the trees would push beyond their pruned beauty and bud with flowers, then swell with fruit she could pick.

She accepted the gin the house boy brought and sat on the steps, listening as he hurried off to continue with his chores. The banter from her servants in the kitchen echoed cheerily through the house. She could have offered Li Qiang a job, maybe then he would be serving her drinks now instead of working for the gangs? Annie put her glass down on the step and stared out across the lawn. The street address which Li Qiang's sister had given her was written in her notebook; she would go there tomorrow. But now she had just an hour to get ready for the gala dinner at the Club for the police who were injured in the student riots. She didn't want to go but with Alec away it was her duty to attend in his absence.

Later that evening, Annie sat beside Admiral Marsden in the grand ballroom of the Club. Candlelight shone off the many tiny crystals in the bulbous chandelier above their heads. Round tables set for eight filled the space and servants weaved their way silently amongst the guests, following paths created by the curve of each table. Everyone stood as a line of policemen entered and clapped in the guests of honour. Annie was grateful for their protection, but she knew the balance of power was never against them. Sometimes she wished she believed in their right to rule and in this Club world a little more, so that her thanks could be given with genuine warmth.

It was a compliment to be seated at the head table with the French commissioner of police and his wife, Marie. Annie smiled at Mrs Marsden and nodded her acknowledgement of the honour. Whatever she felt privately about the nature of the dinner, she knew it was best to keep it to herself in present company. But it seemed someone else was distracting the table anyway.

'I really can't understand this rule: such a big deal out of nothing.'

'What are you annoyed about now, Miss Sosnovsky?' asked Mrs Marsden, who seemed to be particularly perplexed by the Russian's presence.

'This rule of not going into the native town. I want to visit the old part of Shanghai, but I am told it is forbidden. It drives me nut.'

'I think you mean nuts,' Annie interjected politely, pleased to have someone with a bit of chutzpah at their table.

'Perhaps lessons in the King's English might help, rather than listening to American jazz slang.' Mrs Marsden cut through a slice of chicken vigorously and nipped the meat off her fork with a satisfied click of her teeth. She leant over conspiratorially to Annie. 'I do not like this Russian upstart. I'll have to speak to Mr Piper about his choice of guest.' Annie nearly choked on her mouthful; surely she'd misheard Mrs Marsden confiding in her as though they were old pals.

'The restrictions have been put in place to protect you,' the commissioner interjected. 'Having said that, I have absolute confidence in my men, and in their ability to maintain the peace.'

'Well said, François.' Will Piper raised his glass.

'Then why can't we visit the old town?' Miss Sosnovsky repeated, looking at Annie.

'This is not the time for such discussions; I'm planning all sorts of things for the May Ball, now that's more the type of fun chitchat we want!' Mrs Marsden quickly turned the conversation to a more acceptable topic and the talk splintered off at that point. A white-gloved arm slid between them and took Annie's plate. She turned in expectation of seeing Chow. At least he knew she didn't agree with all this self-congratulatory nonsense. But it was not him.

She drank slowly, little sips of champagne from the crystal glass and looked up discreetly each time her mouth dipped to the glass, to find Chow in the room. Only a few hours earlier she'd been dancing with him. Her cheeks flushed at the memory. He stood out because he was a good head and shoulders taller than the other servants, and undeniably good-looking. Annie knew he would be easy to spot. He was serving wine at the next table but he caught her eye and nodded; a slow charming movement like a boat sliding down a wave, sliding towards her.

She turned her attention back to her own table and saw Miss Sosnovsky lean over and give Will Piper a kiss on the cheek before turning to face Annie.

'Mrs Brand, how are you this evening?'

'Very well, Miss Sosnovsky, that colour is so striking on you.' Her thick red hair was tied to one side in a large silver bow. She wore a vibrant cobalt-blue silk dress with an elaborate design of peacock feathers around the neckline. It gave her a regal look, as though she had on a fine ruff collar.

Their conversation was interrupted by a toast to the Club. Annie excused herself, and stood quietly in the hallway. She ran her hand along the smooth wooden curve of the grand staircase. She needed just a few moments of solitude away from the suffocating superiority that filled the ballroom. It was all so pretentious. She held onto the balustrade, enjoying the cool sensation under her palm. The carpeted stairs swept around and away to the spacious upper floor landing where carved black wood chairs lined the corridor of guest accommodation. Everyone said the Club had the feel of a private home, but for Annie there was something missing. It had been built by a British trader for his family, all of whom drowned en route to join him. She wasn't surprised to learn he sold the house before any children had stepped across the threshold.

Standing at the base of the grand staircase, Annie remembered the story and shivered. She turned to re-enter the ballroom and saw Miss Sosnovsky slip out through the door.

'Are you in need of some fresh air too? Sometimes I find these functions can be quite suffocating.' Miss Sosnovsky swung round at the sound of her voice. Annie was surprised at how quickly she moved. 'Excuse me, I didn't mean to startle you.'

'Not at all, I'm looking for the powder room.'

'That way,' Annie pointed to a door at the other end of the corridor. 'See you back in there,' she called after her, but there was no reply as the Russian hurried off.

'No shouting in the Club, please.'

It was Chow, in mock sternness, watching her. He held the door and as she passed through he leant forward ever so slightly and spoke softly.

'It is very nice to see you.'

Annie stopped still, his voice a warm whisper in her ear.

She felt his presence behind her as she moved into the room. It cloaked about her like a buffer from the insincere laughter of the ladies and the undeserved praise bestowed upon the military men.

When he told her 'sit down madaaahm', his voice echoed in her head: it was the highly articulated vowels in the learnt English that sounded so mellifluous. She imagined the extra moment the O's and A's sat on his tongue before he let them drop off into voice.

He pulled out her chair and she gave him a smile. She watched his slender fingers move her cutlery ever so slightly to perfection. *Just-so*, she thought. Under the white gloves she imagined his long, smooth hands. He stood, silent and obliging as she sat. Then she heard his voice, close enough to tickle the tiny hairs prickling at her inner ear.

'Madaaahm, would you like some water?'

'Yes, thank you, Chow.'

Mrs Marsden rose, signalling time for the women to leave the men to their cigars and Annie could only watch as Chow walked away.

In the ladies' lounge a young musician in a white tuxedo played the baby grand. He was on his feet in exaggerated enjoyment, his hips twisting in rhythm to the Cole Porter tune. Annie moved past him and stood apart from the ladies politely finding seats. She took a moment to run her hands down her neck and smooth the curls that twisted over her ears. Miss Sosnovsky walked towards her, and Annie adjusted her belt a little tighter, to ride on the slim bone of her hips without slipping, before greeting her.

'Did you enjoy dinner?'

'The food was not to my taste, too bland. But the company was excellent.'

'Is this your first Club dinner?'

'Yes, I pleaded with Willie to bring me along. He was worried I wouldn't fit in. What do you think, did I pass the test?'

'You stood out for all the right reasons. Your hair is stunning.'

'Thank you, Mrs Brand.'

'Please, call me Annie; this place is far too formal.'

'And I am Natalia, although you already know that. It has been a pleasure talking to you Annie. Now if you will excuse me, I must go and find the powder room.'

Natalia wandered off. Annie moved closer to the piano to watch the musician's enthusiastic playing, thinking how elegant Natalia looked in her silk dress, much more stylish than her own outfit. She'd ask her where she bought the dress when she returned. A bemused frown crossed Annie's brow as she remembered bumping into Natalia earlier on her way to the powder room. She couldn't have forgotten its location already? Annie followed Natalia out into the corridor. She was standing with Chow. The two stopped talking when they saw Annie.

'I beg your pardon, I didn't mean to interrupt. '

'Are you checking on me, Annie?' Miss Sosnovsky laughed cheekily.

'Come, let us see if there is any of that French champagne left.' There was no denying Natalia's enthusiasm as she bundled Annie's arm into her own and drew her through the door.

'I was asking Chow to arrange a day trip for me to the Old City. You should come.'

Annie was surprised by the invitation. She really didn't know Miss Sosnovsky, Natalia, very well at all.

'We will go to the willow-pattern teahouse. It is supposed to be very beautiful.'

Annie had wanted to see the famous teahouse.

'Chow has offered to act as guide for the day. It is all set for next week.' Natalia reached into her purse for a cigarette. 'I don't have any girlfriends in Shanghai; women don't seem to warm to me. The day would be more fun if we went together. Please join me?'

Annie felt a tug of pity in her chest, and something from deeper within that pressed on her heart. The last true friend she'd had was her sister. She knew what real loneliness felt like. 'All right, I'll join you.'

The clock in the room chimed ten and they were forced to turn back and join the daily toast to King George. The room was still while all around people stood in silent importance as though each had a personal connection to the absent monarch. Even the staff paused the drinks service. Annie had come all this way from home and still ended up in the equivalent of the CWA.

Natalia moved off to find Will Piper. Annie chose an armchair and took out her diary to make a note of the day trip to the Old City. The cushion sank comfortably beneath her weight. She heard his melodic voice before she saw him. Behind her Chow leant in to offer Mrs Pike a mint julep and the mother of five laughed coyly at his theatrical bow. Annie shook her head at the older woman's silliness, as though a professional like Chow would be flirting. But she found herself assessing Chow through Mrs Pike's eyes. His thick black hair was slicked down, parted to the side and neatly trimmed around his ears and neck in the European style. His jaw-line was square like a picture theatre star, balancing out the handsome symmetry of his face. She had her finger marking the page as she watched him. He held a tray, white cloth over his arm. But it was his face that she was drawn back to: smooth, unblemished skin, broad lips and lines that belied his age around curved eyes; warm and friendly, alive with light. The gossip in the Club said his mother was a foreigner, more than likely Russian, and that accounted for his exquisite composure. The Russian option was taken up with gusto and there was much talk of the latest soup craze whenever Chow served table. Could a woman sound more insincere than Mrs Alice Hill as she enquired if borscht was a local recipe, brows arched, and all heads leant forward in eager anticipation at the poor man's response. How simple did they think he was?

Ten minutes later, Annie stood outside, waiting for her car. Rain had started, hard driving sheets of it, blurring the distance, wetting her clothes even under the arched drive-way. There was still a bustle of activity inside the Club. Annie turned as the young Mr Piper bumped past her. His friends followed, hooting and whooping into the rain. She saw Natalia walk slowly out after the others. A long, thin cigarette hung from its holder in her lips, as though she could let it drop or swallow it. It felt as though she had no interest in any of them.

The air momentarily filled with the sounds of Cole Porter as more revellers exited the lounge, faces flushed and eager to move on to one of the many late night supper clubs. The call went out for a chaperone from amongst the older members so they could begin the real fun of the night, in the few hours left before the new curfew set in. Then they bundled into waiting cars and were gone.

The quiet hung about Annie like someone left behind after the earlier rush of excitement. Then the gravel crunched with the sound of her car approaching. Farther away, a tyre skidded noisily and Annie looked out across the lawns, through the iron gates to where the road swung past.

CHAPTER SIX

The next morning, Annie hailed a rickshaw for the journey to Xinzha Road. She walked briskly to the corner after asking the driver to stop a little distance from the address. She wanted to take her time and see what the building looked like before deciding whether to knock. The street was still in the International Settlement zone but it was an area she was unfamiliar with. A group of Chinese schoolgirls ran past, their long thin plaits whipping back and forth. She listened to the sound of their laughter as they disappeared behind her.

There were different shopfronts along the road and dotted in between were private doorways. Annie ignored the dressmaker selling cloche hats and looked for number 23. It was a plain building. She stood a few doors down, considering what to do. The street trade began to circulate around her. A man set his barrow down filled with sesame cakes and fried dough sticks. The sweet, warm smell wafted across the air. Annie watched him fit a neat cap on his head, tuck a cloth into his rope belt and begin sliding the cakes around on the hotplate with a pair of long chopsticks. He attracted business by shouting out to passers-by in a sing-song voice.

Another man walked past with a portable kitchen strapped to his back—at one end a boiler balanced on top of a wood-burning stove and at the other end there was a small cupboard. He laboured heavily under the weight of his load as he beat the bamboo paddle he carried to signal his presence to customers.

Annie felt emboldened by the street traders and the air of normalcy their presence created. She shielded her eyes from the hot sun as she approached the door and knocked. In the moments before it opened a rush of nerves made her throat tighten and she thought she wouldn't be able to speak. She swallowed hard. A small girl opened the door, then dashed away. An old woman rose from a straight-backed chair beside the door. She pumped her hands into her thighs as she got up, making a tut-tut sound of annoyance at her old bones. Annie could make out very little of the interior because of the brightness in the street, but a corridor ran from the front door to a back room and there was another room off to one side closer to the entrance where she stood. She smiled broadly at the old lady.

'Is Li Qiang here? I'm a friend, I know him from his workplace.'

The old lady stared blankly at Annie. Then she let out a cough and a drizzle of spittle hit the pavement near Annie's shoe. She turned and disappeared down the corridor.

Annie waited. There was a strong smell in the air and a scratchy jazz tune played from somewhere inside. She didn't want to enter without being asked so she stood patiently on the doorstep. Her feet started to ache and tightness settled into the backs of her knees from standing still. The soup-dumpling seller had a customer and Annie turned to watch as he set down his kitchen, taking his place on the stool between his stove and the cupboard which he opened. He pulled out some dumpling skins which he filled with minced pork and herbs. Within minutes he'd offered his customer a steaming bowl of soup dumplings. The smell was fresh and spicy.

From somewhere inside the house Annie heard a shout. Gingerly she stepped into the corridor but no further. 'Hello?' She could hear people talking now and the music had stopped. She called out again.

A young girl raced past. 'Heh!' Annie called as she disappeared out into the street. She walked a few more steps inside. Then she saw Li Qiang hovering in the room at the end of the corridor. She was sure it was him.

'Li Qiang, it's Mrs Brand from the Club. You remember me? We're worried about you. Your sister would like you to come home. Come and say hello.' Annie began to walk towards him. But she stopped abruptly when she saw a burly man grab him by the shirt and drag him forwards.

'This boy you want?' The man shoved Li Qiang roughly towards Annie. He fell at her feet. She could hear his ragged breathing and realised too late what a horrible mistake she'd made. He shook uncontrollably and looked up at Annie from the ground where the man dumped him. The fear in Li Qiang's eyes was clear.

'What you want with him; pretty boy for you?'

Annie was horrified. She stammered a reply. 'Not at all.'

'Then what?' The man leant forward menacingly over Li Qiang. He was like a great mountain of flesh. 'Police?'

'No, not police. Family, sister.' Annie raised her hands.

The man grabbed Li Qiang and pulled him to his feet. He said something and the boy shook his head vigorously. An angry deep voice shouted from the side room, and the thug hit Li Qiang across the head in response, almost like a father would scold a naughty child with a swift cuff. Only Annie heard the violent crack and Li Qiang cowered and whimpered and fell to the floor again.

Annie gasped; what had she done? Someone moved in the side room and Annie heard banging on the floor. From the corner of her eye she saw a man heaving himself up to stand and reach for something. A flash of silver caught her eye.

Li Qiang groaned and the thug kicked him so that he crawled back down the corridor from where he'd come. The space shrank around him in the semi-darkness.

'Go, go!' the man shouted at Annie.

Annie backed away, bumping her arm painfully against the wall. Then she turned and stumbled into the street. Behind her the door banged shut.

When she got home, Annie was stunned and shaken. The stink of pungent smoke hung in her hair and her skin felt chalky. She asked the wash amah to run a bath and lay in the hot water with eyes closed, glad to be in the reassuring sanctuary of her tiled bathroom. The soothing warmth seeped through her skin and only the sound of a solitary drip hitting the water punctuated her breathing. Gradually the tightness in her limbs eased. But she could not stop thinking about Li Qiang.

The hairs on her neck prickled at the memory of him crawling away from her. She shut her eyes tight and slid under the water. She had made his situation worse. She must tell Chow as soon as she could; he'd know what to do.

Later that afternoon, Annie headed to the Club. She found Chow arranging glasses in the dining room and pulled him to one side. He listened intently to what she told him.

'Why did you do this?' Chow spoke quickly and softly. There was an edge to his voice Annie had not heard before.

'It was naive of me, I can see that now, but we have to get him out of that place.'

'Sit down, please.' Chow steered her to a comfortable armchair. His hand on the small of her back was firm and reassuring. Then he sat in the chair next to hers. His solicitous approach worried Annie. She bit her lip and frowned. Chow never sat down in the members' areas.

'Li Qiang's body was delivered to his sister an hour ago.'

'No!' Annie gasped. 'What on earth are you saying? I saw him just this morning.' The room swayed. Her head felt light and she grabbed the arm of the chair for support.

'His body was left at his uncle's doorstep, a bullet in his head. It is a most tragic end to a young life.'

'Oh my god, Chow. This is my fault.'

'We do not know that for sure.'

'Then why was he killed?' Her voice dropped to a whisper.

'He did something wrong to meet such a fast end. These gangs supply opium to the illegal brothels and dens, he may have taken some for his personal use, or he may have betrayed the gang. We will never know.'

'Or he led a foreign woman straight to them?'

'I don't think you would be considered a threat, Mrs Brand. At least they returned his body to his uncle; it is a sign of respect for the family.' Chow looked around as he spoke.

'Do you think his sister is in danger now too?' Annie clasped her hands together. She could not stop shaking.

'There is no reason for that, but I will keep an eye on her myself.' Chow stood and walked to the door. He checked no one was nearby then shut it so that they were alone.

'Would she see me?' Annie heard the clink of crystal as Chow poured two shots of whiskey.

'It is not the time for visitors. She is in mourning.' He gave one glass to Annie and held up his own in salute. They drank in silence. The fiery liquid stung in Annie's throat but it warmed her from the inside and stopped her shaking. She reached around her neck and unhooked the strand of black jet beads. They tinkled like water as they fell into her lap.

'Give her these.' She dropped the necklace into Chow's palm.

Chow nodded as he folded the beads into a coiled circle and put them in his coat pocket.

'I'm afraid I must get back to work. My absence will be noticed. I am sorry to leave you in such a state.'

'Yes, go, don't worry about me.' Annie couldn't find any other words. She stayed in the empty dining room 'til the evening dark crept in and the electric lights flashed on.

Annie was keener than ever to have Alec home. It had been three weeks since she returned to Shanghai and she had made a terrible mess of things; she needed his support. Li Qiang's death had shaken her and she was mortified by her own naivety in barging in so disastrously. She spent so much of her time exploring the Settlement streets and the cosmopolitan centre around the Bund that she'd begun to believe she was more like a local than a foreigner. Li Qiang's death made her realise how far from the truth that was.

When she first arrived in Shanghai, Annie was intoxicated by the city. As she set her house in order and the servants brought her cups of flowered tea she felt in control of her future. When she'd watched an old man on the Bund in a long silk gown walk a bird which perched on a stick he held and flew off at intervals to the length of its string leash, she felt the excitement of new possibilities tugging at the string; and when Alec had taken her to a traditional teahouse and they stood aside to let a party pass, the women swaying as they teetered on tiny embroidered slippers that looked no bigger than a baby's bootie, Annie felt like her husband's equal. Shanghai had done that for her but Annie realised, too late to change Li Qiang's fate, that she had little real understanding of the Chinese culture and its people; she was a foolish foreign woman, and she had no right to meddle.

She pulled her brush firmly through her hair. The tortoiseshell paddle was cool and smooth. Annie tugged at the knots and stared at her reflection. Today was the outing to the Old City. She didn't want to let Natalia down but she was nervous. At least Chow would be accompanying them. Annie determined not to presume to understand anything she saw; rather, she'd ask questions and listen to Chow. With this outing she could begin to gain some true understanding of this city.

The car pulled up at a set of imposing wooden doors built into the stone wall that enclosed the old walled city of Shanghai. They were south of the French Concession in an area of Shanghai under Chinese Government rule. The gates were open and led into Sanpailou Road, the main thoroughfare. It was very early in the morning, when a mist of dew still hung about the paved stonework like tiny insects. Annie and Natalia had met Chow at the Club an hour earlier, from where they'd travelled together by car, crossing into the French Concession and down to the border with Nanshi and the Old City.

The alleyways of Shanghai were often thin, but the streets within the old town were so narrow it was hard for even a wheelbarrow to pass through. The houses were built of slate-coloured soft brick, only about eight feet wide and paved with stone slabs; many residents had a bamboo pole resting from one eave to the opposite. All manner of laundry, from women's pants to foot-binding strips hung from them. Annie looked away with embarrassment, and caught Chow smiling at her. She only just missed stepping into a puddle of stagnant water.

'Are you sure it's all right for us to be here?'

'This is authentic Shanghai; the Yu Garden has been here since the Ming dynasty, and you will be impressed. The Confucian scholar Pan Yunduan built the gardens for his parents to enjoy. The pavilion in the middle of the lake— the willow-pattern teahouse as you like to call it—is not so old, but very popular. Please, follow me.'

Annie felt water drip on her shoulder as they walked. She looked up to where wet clothes hung from a bamboo pole. Chow led them down the road and as they turned a corner she saw the large, ornate structure of the teahouse, squatting like a buddha in the middle of an artificial lake. Delicate eaves swept out in pointed waves from the numerous roofs that dovetailed into each other.

The zigzag bridge was a mass of people, and Annie gasped at the sight of so much human activity in such a confined space. But Chow led them sideways from the bridge, into the bazaar around the lake and the women walked through it slowly, stopping to pick up a wooden toy boat at one stall, watching peanuts being deep-fried at another. The shop-fronts were makeshift affairs with wood and paper roofs that protected the goods from the weather, but also stopped any breeze. The air was close and still.

Natalia linked arms with Annie. Chow walked ahead, turning and beckoning them onwards. It was pleasant to be out of the thick and heat of the bazaar and walking across the wooden zigzag bridge. Natalia stood on one side watching the water flow slowly beneath them. Annie watched a carp fish hit the lake and disappear swiftly beneath the surface, the man who had thrown it in standing nearby.

'He is showing Buddha how kind he is to living things,' Chow explained as he came up to stand beside her, softly pressing his hands together in prayer. They moved slowly across the bridge, turning with the crowd at each corner. When they finally arrived at the teahouse, the foreigners were ushered inside immediately, past the crowds, and taken to the top level where it was quiet and almost empty.

'I will order tea and cake, if you allow me?'

'Thank you, Chow.'

Annie looked down from her window seat. She could see the bazaar and surrounding roads like a maze, swarming with people. The sun glared off the lake's surface, warming the spot where they sat. Natalia had a paper fan which she turned towards Annie and the cool air tousled her hair. Chow didn't rejoin them.

'Where do you suppose he's gone?' Annie asked Natalia.

'He will be down on the ground level with the Chinese.'

'I really feel so isolated up here and I don't like the fact Chow can't sit with us.'

'Well, let's ask Chow to take us somewhere else for lunch—where we can sit together. There must be many places near here.' Natalia snapped her fan shut. The women descended to the crowded ground level where the tables were full of different groups sharing benches to seat as many customers as possible. The noise was deafening, but they quickly spotted Chow at the end of a row and made their way over.

'Would you take us out now, Chow?'

Once they were back on the bridge and walking slowly, Annie spoke.

'This is truly a beautiful building and location. Thank you for showing it to us. But Natalia and I would much rather find a lunch spot where we can all sit together. We don't like the segregation of this place. Is there somewhere we could visit where we won't be treated differently?'

Chow looked at them and frowned.

'You would be shocked by the poor areas around the old town. No foreigners go there.'

'That's the area we would really prefer to visit, not another tourist tearoom. We might as well have stopped on Bubbling Well Road.' Natalia waved her fan about as she spoke.

'What do you think, Chow?' Annie asked.

'What about the Little North Gate district of Nanshi, I believe it's only a couple of miles from here?' Natalia held up a book about Shanghai, the page open at a detailed map. 'It's so close.'

Chow turned away from them both, and Annie wasn't sure what he would say. When he turned back, he opened his arms wide in acquiescence and nodded slowly.

Outside the Old City Chow waved to their driver. Within minutes the car was crawling along a barren road lined with dirty, ramshackle homes built into the ageing stone walls of ancient shikumen houses. It was hard to see where the traditional wooden gates stood. But Chow helped the ladies out of the car and they faced a stone portico. A crowd of children gathered quickly to stare at the foreigners. Many of them held bowls and kept eating as they watched the spectacle. The impoverished shantytown didn't seem to begin at any distinct point. It spilt into the densely clotted alleyway neighbourhood which the party stood before. The dwellings cascaded into each other, sharing broken-down walls and wooden poles for support.

The ladies ducked down as they passed through the arched entrance where the name Zhenye Li was inscribed. Stretching out in front of them was a stone-paved path with smaller alleyways branching off at short intersections. Tightly packed rows of brick and wood houses lined each alley. The skin on Annie's arms prickled. She'd never seen this level of poverty before. Just inside the alley, they circled around a well, topped with a wooden lid. A woman approached and filled her bucket with water that splashed onto the pavement and trickled along the grooves of stone under Annie's feet. Life didn't stop for foreigners here. She saw Natalia had already walked ahead.

Someone tugged at Annie's skirt and she turned to see a man with no legs walking on his hands, only rags covering his thin torso. She stumbled back against a wall. Her hands fumbled as she pushed around in her purse for a coin. On her hemline she felt the beggar's insistent tug, tug. It was only a matter of minutes, but, against all of her moral judgement, she wished him gone. Then Chow shouted and she saw the beggar swing around and shuffle away, but not before Chow had given him a copper. Annie stood quietly to the side, shamed into stillness by her reaction.

'Don't be frightened, he would not have hurt you.' Chow took her arm.

'I'm no different to all the ignorant Club women. I'm ashamed of myself.'

Chow pressed lightly on her sleeve. 'Don't be, Mrs Brand.'

After that, Annie noticed Chow walked closer to her. They turned down one of the smaller alleys. To her left, Annie saw a man standing above someone seated on an upturned crate. His elbow stuck out at an awkward angle while his hand was in the patient's mouth. A multitude of jagged, discoloured human teeth were strung together in a long necklace across the stall to advertise the dentist's expertise. A cage was suspended above the next stall's wooden roof. Chickens noisily flapped within the bamboo frame. Other cages were sprawled in the dirt—pigs, ducks, dogs, cats. Annie knew these were food.

Children played with sticks and lengths of string, while women sat in doorways and stirred steaming pots. Annie looked around, turning full circle so as not to miss any of it. Her own neat home seemed very lonely compared to this open-door commune. Natalia was crouched down, talking to a little boy. He smiled broadly as she handed over a sweet. Then he ran off. Annie wished she'd had the foresight to bring something to hand out too. A pile of baskets balanced haphazardly and Annie stumbled into them as she turned to follow Chow. He caught her shoulders, helping her to balance and raised his brow in question. She nodded, *keep going*.

They continued slowly. Annie's boots were dirty with mud and animal litter and her hemline caught on the rough cobblestones. She wrinkled her nose at the smell of pig mud and rotting food.

'Come closer, I will help you.'

'I'm a fool for wearing these ridiculous walking clothes. Look how they clog with the mud and cling to my legs.'

'These are the right clothes for a proper lady, of course.'

Annie felt his eyes on her and walked forward a little. She'd abandoned the idea of dressing in something modern for fear of standing out, although clearly that was always going to be the case. Natalia had no such qualms, as she strode forward in trousers and a dark blue shirt. Now Annie wished she was wearing more practical clothes.

A gong sounded and up ahead they saw the man who was beating on it walking round in a circle. There was anticipation in his gait as he swept about, encouraging people to come forward.

'Come, let us watch.' Chow gently steered the women towards him. They stood back as a gaggle of local children jostled about for the best spots in the audience circle which had naturally formed around the performer. Annie could see clearly across the heads of the children and others who were watching the street show. Suddenly the man stopped beating the gong. The murmuring amongst the crowd quietened to a curious silence. The man wore a pair of glasses with fine metal frames and he bowed and took up a thin stick. Annie noticed that he moved slowly and dramatically, looking into the faces of individuals in the crowd. Beside him sat a long-legged monkey with small, clouded eyes and leathery black padded hands that were scuffed like worn-out shoes. When the man tapped the monkey with the stick it plucked off his glasses and put them on. The crowd cheered.

'I don't like this, it is cruel to treat the animal like a performer,' Natalia spoke loudly. Annie nodded in agreement but she was curious to see what the monkey would do. When she turned back to reply, Natalia had wandered off and was leaning against a building further down the lane, smoking.

The crowd was laughing again. Annie turned back to see the monkey move to a big box in the middle of the circle. It opened the lid and picked out a black gauze cap which it placed on its head, pushing the elastic band awkwardly under its chin before jumping around to face the outer circle. People jeered and children threw small stones at the animal to make it move. It walked around the audience, and Chow explained to Annie that it was pretending to be a feudal official. Each time the man smacked his stick on the ground behind the monkey, it moved forward and around the circle, chattering furiously in response before turning a series of somersaults. The audience clapped and shouted. Annie noticed some of the adults turn away from the show at that point.

Then the monkey was in front of them, offering up the cap. None of the children had any money, and very few of the adults offered as the monkey scurried around the circle. It came towards Annie and she fingered the copper she had ready in her palm. But the monkey caught hold of her leg and climbed up Annie's body. It happened so quickly she couldn't stop it and cried out in shock which made the other spectators laugh and point. The monkey stank and Annie reared back as it chattered and screeched madly. It held on to her arm painfully and she tried to push it off. Chow grabbed at the monkey as he shouted to the handler who was doing nothing to help. There were tiny insects crawling around its eyes and disappearing into its nose. Then Annie felt something in her pocket.

'Heh, get out of there!' The monkey was digging around feverishly; it was trying to pickpocket her. 'Get this thing off me!'

The animal's handler slipped a collar over the monkey's head and yanked. It rolled over on the ground before hopping up onto his shoulder. The handler seemed unperturbed by his monkey's behaviour.

Chow led Annie to where Natalia waited.

'Are you hurt?' he asked her.

'No, just completely taken by surprise. I didn't expect that to happen!' Annie couldn't help laughing a little hysterically. The monkey was just a small creature but he'd reduced her to jelly.

'I know his kind, exploiting the animal for his own gain.' Natalia kicked a stone on the ground. 'He will not spend any money on the monkey.'

'Let us find somewhere to sit and collect ourselves a moment.' Chow stood to the side and directed the ladies forward. Swallows darted through the air and into the eaves of a house where a woman appeared in the doorway and threw a bucket of water across the hot paving stones. Steam rose in a fast swirl. A group of boys ran past the party pushing a large steel ring with a long iron wire, shoving against each other in their excitement.

The trio rounded a corner into a large community square. Wooden tables and stools filled the space. Men stood beside enormous fired metal woks throwing dumplings into baskets to steam. Women sat on the ground rolling small pockets of dough into flat pancakes they then filled with aromatic meats, before folding and pinching the edges together in an efficient parcel. Standing a short distance apart was a woman in dirty padded gloves behind a coal oven with a ring of bulbous-shaped sweet potatoes on its lid and more roasting inside. The noises from cooking and so many customers blended into a continuous hum. Queues of people waited their turn for a basket of dumplings. Chow stood in line, motioning for Annie and Natalia to sit down at a table.

Annie looked around and was glad of the sense of space now they'd left the tight alleyway behind. A line of sweat tickled her brow. Her throat was dry and her arm stung where the monkey must have scratched her. She hoped Chow would return with something to drink. A group of diners passed close by and Annie smiled encouragingly for them to join her. But the group ignored the gesture and sat at the next table.

In fact, no one joined the foreign women. Annie watched a table of young men frequently turn to stare. Her good humour after the monkey's antics faded at their intrusive attention. She felt unease creeping into her pores. Natalia lit one of her cigarettes and offered the packet to Annie. For a moment it seemed a good idea to accept one, even though Annie had never smoked, just for a distraction and to appear unconcerned by the attention they were receiving. But she shook her head, straining to see Chow through the moving crowds.

'I don't feel comfortable waiting here. The way these people are staring is making me nervous.'

'I will find Chow, Annie.'

Before Annie could reply, Natalia had walked off into the crowds that were growing larger each moment as more people joined the lunchtime swarm. Now she was on her own, Annie sat straight-backed, looking ahead. She wanted to leave. A man coughed loudly at a table across the square and spat into the dirt. She recognised him as the monkey handler and saw the cage at his feet. She took a deep breath, willing her stomach to settle, hoping the flush of anxiety she could feel wasn't clear across her face. A group of women passed by, laughing into their hands. Their small, bound feet shuffled through the dusty ground. She looked about for Natalia and Chow, wondering where they could be. Instead she saw one of the young men at the next table stand and begin dancing a childlike, clownish version of the waltz. He turned his feet out at awkward angles and strutted like a peacock. His head seemed to dip towards Annie, though she thought it must be her nerves making her see things. She took off her broad-rimmed sun hat quickly. It was a very European appendage. The man's performance continued and now tables of diners around Annie clapped in rhythm as the stranger moved about, madly mimicking the European dance. Then he looked straight at Annie without turning; appraising her even as he mocked her. His stare stripped her bare and she turned abruptly away from him, heart beating madly, sweat prickling on her skin. She sat as though frozen, because there, at a table now in her line of sight, was Chow, head bent deep in conversation with a very large man with a pock-marked face, and the monkey man.

'Annie, Annie.' Natalia's voice was close and urgent in her ear. 'We need to go now, follow me. Quickly, get up.'

'But we can't leave without Chow, he's over there.' Annie pointed to the table, but to her astonishment the monkey handler sat alone, bent over a bowl of food. Chow and the other man had disappeared.

'I don't understand? He was just there, I saw him.'

'Come on, Annie, we're not welcome here. Follow me. Chow can find his own way.'

'We can't leave without him.'

'I don't want to stay, do you? And Chow's already gone, so come on, get up!'

Annie felt Natalia's grip on her arm and her friend roughly pulling her along. Two young men rose slowly after them. Panic pressed on Annie's temple as she watched the men but still she pushed Natalia away and craned to find Chow. Surely that had been him talking to the monkey handler? But there was no more time to think. The men were pushing through the crowd towards them. The two women hurried down a laneway. The smell of burning wood from the woks was close as they passed the food stalls. Footsteps sounded fast and clipped behind them. Annie looked back and could only see clouds of cooking smoke above a crowd of strangers. She searched for Chow's face too, but he was nowhere to be seen. Annie stumbled and felt Natalia grab her arm to stop her from falling. Behind them she heard a monkey screech and turned to see the performer and his animal standing silently watching the foreign women retreat.

They turned down another laneway and another in their confusion and haste, half walking, then running. They passed a bookshop, a school building and then the last house in a row and came out into a large square of barren wasteland.

'We're lost, Natalia.' Annie looked about to see if they'd been followed, swinging this way and that to scour the perimeter and back to the alley from where they'd come. Her head throbbed with the exertion of running. A stinging pain pressed against her chest and her breathing came in shallow gulps. She anxiously took in their surroundings. On three sides a stone wall bordered the area and it felt like a forgotten dead end. It was poorly tended, with patchy dried grass amongst the rough dirt. A few children played in one corner but there was no interest in the two foreign women and as they caught their breath no one else appeared. Annie saw discarded old pots and crates, some there so long the grass had trapped them in its roots.

'We must go back again, we've turned the wrong way, follow me.' Natalia tried to take her arm but Annie stood frozen. A dead baby's body rolled in a piece of old sheet lay on the ground. A few tufts of brown grass stuck up through the ripped end of the sheet where the baby's toes peeped out in stiff, little stubs. Flies hung about the small mound.

'Don't look Annie, come on.' Natalia grabbed her arm but Annie didn't move. Her legs felt stuck though when she looked down there was nothing holding her to the ground, only those other smaller feet, visible through the dirt and grass. It seemed, in that moment, as though they'd been transported to an incomprehensible world framed by old stone walls with her and Natalia lost in the failed humanity at its centre.

Annie grabbed at her nose. The stench was unbearable. The children playing nearby laughed and the sound filled her head with horror. She turned full circle in a confused blur looking for the exit; she had to get out. Her feet stumbled through the stones and grassy dirt as she ran. Behind her Natalia called out. She heard her shoes clip against the stone path but she couldn't see anything through the tears that stung her eyes. Someone bumped roughly against her and Annie fell into a wall, wincing with pain. She pushed herself off and kept moving. She had to get as far away from the dead baby as possible. At a corner she turned one way, then the other, unsure where to go. Her chest heaved and she grabbed at her knees, overcome with pain and fear. A baby cried nearby and she shook her head madly. The small, stiff foot was still there in the grass at her feet. Annie ran again, doubled over, heaving and panting and barrelled straight into a pair of legs. Arms reached down and held her as she mumbled apologies and tried to clear her face of hair and tears. It was Chow and at the sight of him she felt her legs give way. He lifted her gently and Annie didn't care that his arms were round her waist, supporting her. She turned her head into his chest and smelt musk and smoke. Chow carried Annie to the waiting car. She felt the smooth rhythm of his gait as they made their way along the path and kept her eyes closed and her head buried against his shoulder.

'Where have you been? You made me mad with worry.' Natalia put an arm around Annie's shoulder as Chow placed her gently on the seat. 'You ran off so quickly I lost sight of you, silly little thing.' Natalia wiped Annie's face with a handkerchief. 'Thank goodness you ran into Chow like that.'

Annie turned away and watched the street recede as the car began to move. She didn't want to be fussed over. A burning had started in her chest.

Chow turned to the women from where he sat beside the driver. 'I apologise. There has been too much anger in the streets. Though I thought it would not reach so deep into my community.'

Annie wound down the window and let the wind blow into her face til her eyes stung.

'Why did you leave us, Chow?'

'When I returned to the table you were gone. I did not know where to look. It is my fault this has happened, please forgive me.'

'It was just so shockingly heartbreaking to see a baby's body abandoned in the wasteland.'

'I am sorry you saw such a thing. The sight must seem terrible to you but very few can afford a burial. Sometimes a charity organisation will collect the bodies and take them to a burial ground for the destitute. Otherwise they stay abandoned wherever there is open ground, as you discovered. It's purely practical, but it doesn't mean there isn't grief in the family for the loss of the child.' Chow spoke kindly but firmly.

'But it shows such little regard for life, for common decency.' Annie felt the blood pump in her head as she spoke. A wave of revulsion washed over her again. 'How can you talk so unemotionally about such an unspeakable thing? I wish I could forget what I've seen.'

'This is my Shanghai, Mrs Brand, the vitality and the poverty, but perhaps you are not ready. Remember, please, that your standards are not ours, do not judge what you don't understand.'

Annie didn't speak again. They drove along the Rue du Consulate and turned into Tibet Road, towards home, through streets Annie recognised. As the pace of her heart slowed, she thought about what Chow had said. It was impossible to condone the practice of abandoning dead bodies, especially those of children. She knew how precious life was, how tragic death, both deserved respect. This must be part of a universal set of values, surely Chow believed the same. She considered him as he sat in the front seat, oblivious to her scrutiny. This was a caring man, a thoughtful man. She mustn't judge him, yet how would she ever forget that sight? What social rules applied in the face of such pitiable humanity? Perhaps none, at least not her own, as Chow had politely told her; she couldn't judge the people in Zhenye Li for simply doing what was necessary to survive, especially when her own people had such little regard for Chinese life. Yet she couldn't help her intense aversion to Chow's pragmatic explanation for the presence of the baby's body. Annie thought about Chow sitting with the monkey handler, and there'd been another man too.

'I thought I saw you sitting with the monkey man, Chow?'

'No, you were mistaken.'

'How strange, there was another man too, a large Chinese fellow?'

'I don't know who you saw Mrs Brand, but it was not me.'

'We were followed, weren't we Natalia, by two men. That's why we got lost, trying to escape them.'

'Really, Annie, I think you've been reading too many adventure novels.' Natalia laughed off the question.

'But you saw them too, I know you did.'

'No, I took you away from the diners because I could see they did not like us being there. Those men were mocking you, Annie.'

'Yes, I know, I felt it too. But I thought we were followed.' Annie was quiet for the remainder of the journey, trying to make sense of what she thought she'd seen and by the time they stopped outside her house, she was no longer sure they'd been followed at all or if, indeed, it had been Chow sitting with the monkey handler.

'Will you both come inside? Some tea might help restore us.' She hoped Chow and Natalia would join her.

'That is most kind, but I will not disturb you any further.' Chow held the door as Annie, then Natalia stepped out of the car. Then Annie heard Natalia's voice.

'Of course you must join us, Chow. We all could use a calming drink and it would be rude to refuse Mrs Brand's invitation.'

Chow nodded and followed Natalia through to the formal lounge.

'You have a charming home. It is very spacious.' Annie looked around the room and tried to see it from Natalia's perspective. Hardwood panels on the walls, the mirrored sideboard with her display of wooden figurines, three-piece upholstered lounge suite, enough space to add a few extra chairs when company came round. It was comfortable, but not grand by Shanghai standards. Yet in the light of what she'd seen that day her home could easily be a mansion.

'Yes, I suppose it is big.'

'How many rooms do you have?'

'I've never counted. Let's see, there's this formal lounge, the dining room, my sunroom out by the garden, three bedrooms, powder rooms of course, and the kitchen: how many does that add up to?'

'A palace.'

The house boy laid out the tea service. Natalia walked around the room, admiring pictures and small objects but Annie found it hard to join in; her house seemed suddenly pretentious, with its gaudy display of Chinese artefacts. She looked at Chow who stood by the wall, his expression unreadable.

The house boy stared at the Chinaman and clucked his tongue a few times. Chow ignored him. Then the house boy said something to Chow and Annie watched them talking in hurried, hushed voices before the boy stood back, bowed to Chow and left the room.

'Is there a problem?' Annie's question was directed at Chow.

'He thought I belonged in the kitchen, with the other servants. I corrected him. Have you ever entertained a Chinaman before?'

Annie motioned for Chow to sit as she poured the tea. Natalia had already dropped into a chair, and was lounging comfortably, one leg hooked over the armrest.

'I don't like entertaining terribly much, and you're right, you are my first local guest. But that's no excuse for my house boy's behaviour.'

'Don't punish him on my account, Mrs Brand.' There was a formal air about Chow which Annie associated with the Club.

'Of course I won't punish him; I'm not Mrs Marsden, you know! But I won't put up with rudeness.'

Chow was walking to the door. Annie hurriedly put down the teapot and followed him out. 'You're going so soon? You haven't even finished your tea.'

'It is time for me to leave.' He was holding out a small wooden Buddha statue. 'I have a gift for you; you rub his stomach for good luck.'

The statue was a standing Buddha, with his arms raised above his head and flat palms turned inwards. Annie had seen them for sale in a few stalls in the bazaar. He had unnaturally long ears that swooped down and out in two curved lobes from his chin line. His eyes were made of ivory and thin strips of ivory teeth filled his open, happy smile. The portly figurine's dominant feature, however, was the smooth, round dome of his belly, which overflowed the open robes carved low beneath its bulge.

'How beautiful. Thank you, Chow.' She rubbed the Buddha's stomach. 'Do you have to leave so soon?'

Chow nodded.

'I'm sorry for my house boy's rudeness.'

'He did nothing wrong. I am a servant, Mrs Brand, your house boy was correct.'

'In my house you are a guest, and while I think of it, please don't call me Mrs Brand; I'm Annie to my friends.' Annie bit her lip. 'It's exactly this prejudice I can't stand.'

'But of course you must have a house boy, a wash amah and other servants too. It's a matter of social standing. The foreign resident needs such things to set them apart.'

'You may be right Chow, but it doesn't mean I agree with the system.'

'The formalities, the social necessities; this system is arranged by your men to manage us. It doesn't matter if you agree or not, you are a part of it and that is all; otherwise we might all be living in Nanshi. Now, I must say my goodbyes.'

'You are so frustrating, Chow, don't go without letting me defend myself.'

'You are not under attack—I apologise if that is how you feel.'

The afternoon sky was clear. Beyond the house gate the street was quiet. 'How I feel is annoyed, and unsettled, and yet I want to keep talking to you. Don't go.'

'Good afternoon, Mrs Brand.' Chow nodded abruptly and then turned and left before Annie could say anything else. There was a squeaking noise from behind. Natalia stood in the doorway, frowning.

'What is going on out here?'

'Chow's gone. We argued over politics.'

Annie heard her front gate close as she and Natalia returned inside. She opened the French doors in the sunroom and stood in the breeze, hoping it would blow away her sense of frustration at Chow's criticism. But when she thought through Chow's comments, Annie had to acknowledge he was right; she did, indeed, enjoy the luxuries that came with her status as a foreigner. A deep strip of sunshine brightened the floor by the back doors and its warmth massaged her shoulders. She felt the tightness ease but disappointment still hung in her limbs. She wished Chow had stayed longer and given her the chance to look after him as her guest. Natalia produced a small flask of vodka and disappeared. Annie heard her rummaging through the kitchen cupboards.

'This will make you feel better.'

She reappeared with two crystal champagne saucers half filled with vodka.

'We do own tumblers; ask the house boy.'

'I'm happy to help myself, and crystal sounds so much prettier, don't you think? I love the shape of these glasses; did you know they say the style is modelled on the breast of Marie Antoinette?'

'Where do you hear such outrageous things?'

'My father.'

'He sounds like a character.'

'He had strong opinions on everything.'

'That explains a lot about you. Are you close to him?' Annie asked the question cautiously. It was the first time that Natalia had mentioned her family and Annie didn't want to intrude too far.

'No, at least not anymore; he is dead.'

'I am very sorry to hear that.'

Natalia leant over and sounded her glass against Annie's with a ping.

'It was his choice. My father put all his passion into the imperial cause, there was none left for his family. He never came home from the Russian war; he died for the royal family, for his country. Never mind who would look after us.'

'Was Moscow your home?' The alcohol clouded her throat as Annie drank, leaving her warm and tingling.

'Oh, I wish we had still been in my godfather's apartment in Moscow, taking lessons with our French governess and eating pirozhki. No, my passionate father made us all move to the far east of Russia where the White Army was stationed. When he died he'd already given most of our money to the war efforts. My mother found it very hard.'

'What happened, Natalia?'

'I took care of my mother and my sister. I was the eldest, so responsibility fell on my shoulders. But it was not easy. In the end we joined the other refugees and took a ferry from Vladivostok to Shanghai.'

'But you said you had no family in Shanghai?'

'That's right. My mother died on the voyage. When we arrived in '22 I still had Akatarina to take care of. I tried to get a job as a governess teaching French, but there were queues of young ladies at every interview, I had no luck. We took a room in a boarding house and I sold any jewellery we had left. The Russian Orthodox Church fed us each night, it was not so bad. Kati got sick a year ago, pneumonia. By that time we were living in a room in another boarding house, not so nice, but we were together.'

'What a terribly sad story.'

'I do not want pity. It has been easier since Kati died; there's no one left to worry about. I tell you so you will stop asking questions. There is sadness everywhere, Annie, life is hard, especially for us women, but I vow never to be powerless again.'

'I admire your strength.'

'Za-zdarovye,' Natalia raised her glass and downed the vodka in one gulp.

They ate sandwich fingers off the gold-leaf dinner service. Natalia chose the best of everything she could find. Annie laughed at her gasps as she discovered another piece of finery hiding in a cabinet, and for that afternoon, her house was like a treat box.

In the bedroom, Natalia ran her hands over the necklaces that hung on Annie's vanity mirror. The beads and gold clinked harmoniously. The sun warmed the room as they spread the jewellery onto the bed and, sitting cross-legged opposite each other, tried pieces on like they were playing dress-up. Annie picked out a jade and black onyx necklace divided by beads of gold in the run. She put it round Natalia's neck. Together they looked at her reflection in the wardrobe mirror. Natalia wrapped the beads around her neck a second time, so that one strand sat snug against her throat and the jade's green paled on her skin.

'It suits you.' Annie touched the black onyx, warmed by Natalia's skin. 'Take it; I'd like you to have it as a gift.'

Natalia shook her head, but her eyes admired her own reflection.

'Please, I insist.'

Annie had the wardrobe door open as she spoke. Her clothes clinked and rippled as she touched them. Quickly, she threw one, and then another onto the bed. The satin brushed her cheek as she reached for a hanger. She could hear Natalia in the background laughing at her silliness. Within minutes the bed was covered in a mess of dresses and skirts, so she smoothed them out to lie like women without bodies. A sleeve fluttered for a moment under the ceiling fan's breath, a skirt quivered. Above the bed, the fan swooped in a slow, mesmeric circle. Annie grabbed Natalia's hand and together they flopped onto the bed, pushing their arms and legs out like stars.

She felt as free as her younger self once was, jumping into bed in her nightshirt at home, her sister noisy beside her. She gave Natalia a green silk gown to try on, and then pulled her own dress over her head, revealing stockinged legs below the lace border of her slip. Annie looked at the woman in the mirror; her dark curls plumped with air making her look a bit rakish. Then she turned to Natalia, dropped her hand to her side, stretched one leg out the other way, bumped her hips in the opposite direction and pouted.

'I'm a Russian princess.'

Natalia bowed formally then took Annie's hand and held it high as they walked through the house. Annie's silk slip rustled around her thighs. She liked the feeling of weight-lessness that the free-flowing material gave her. In the living room she turned on the gramophone and placed the needle onto the lip of the record—a new jazz tune by Fats Waller. The racy beat filled the empty space. Annie and Natalia danced. The song caught on a scratch at each turn of the record, jumping for a second through the notes, but Annie didn't care. She moved through the darkness behind closed eyes, feeling the music like she was part of the sweet sound. Her arms dipped low to the floor and her slip flew out from her hips as she turned a circle.

For the rest of the afternoon Annie's necklace swung on Natalia as she moved. At one point Annie caught her holding it to the side so she could spit tea back into the cup. She raised her eyebrows.

'Cold?'

Natalia wiped her mouth and nodded. It was getting late. Playing dress-up couldn't last. She waited while Natalia changed back into her own clothes, flicking her fingers lightly across the mess of dresses on her bed.

Once Natalia was gone, Annie realised how long they'd spent together; the evening light had drowned the afternoon in its shadows, and she looked out across a garden washed in dark. She shivered and returned to her bedroom where she hung up her dresses. Looking out into the quiet darkness brought back the tingling fear of that morning. She sat heavily on the bed. She'd been lucky Chow had found her in the alley. His unexpected gift stood beside her bed, the Buddha's belly gleaming.

CHAPTER SEVEN

With only one day left before Alec returned, Annie leant across and smoothed the empty space in the bed beside her before jumping up. She hadn't seen him for a month and now their reunion was so close she felt a thrill of nerves run through her. The boat trip had been the beginning of a new intimacy between them and even though she'd been angry with Alec for sending her home early, she'd missed him.

It was dull and humid that morning as she picked flowers in her garden. There was a thick layer of clouds that made the sky seem low and the air dense. She cut the stems long so that the full-headed chrysanthemums would stand tall in the vase in the hallway, part of her welcome home preparations for Alec.

Annie's hair twisted and curled in the humidity as she moved about, plucking dead leaves off the bushes and thinking through how she'd tell Alec about her involvement with

Li Qiang and his death. Alec would be angry and shocked to learn how far she'd gone to find the boy. A flash of horror seared through her at the memory of her visit to Xinzha Road. She cut another chrysanthemum stem and dropped it into her basket. Alec would completely disapprove of what she'd done and they'd end up arguing. Annie didn't want that. She decided she wouldn't tell him about Li Qiang or about the visit to the old town; there was nothing to be gained.

Annie ran her hand across the flowers lined up neatly in her basket. The delicate petals felt as soft as the graze of her sister's eyelash kisses. But some of them were already wilting. So she dipped her hand into the watering can and flicked droplets onto them. The petals were pale pink. She saw her sister's sleepy morning blush in their colour. There were small splashes of bruise now where the water droplets had landed. They would only live for a few days. She thought about Natalia's story and felt a tug of empathy. No wonder she seemed haughty at times. There was enough heartache in her past to turn anyone to ice. Annie admired her passion. She hoped her friendship with Willie Piper might turn into something more lasting. Natalia deserved some good fortune.

The following afternoon, Annie was busy in the garden again, this time preparing a surprise picnic dinner for Alec's first night home. As the hour of his return approached, nerves sparked and flashed inside her. Annie laid the picnic rug by the line of fruit trees, where the grass was soft and green. The garden glistened with freshness, washed clean by last night's rain. She hung lanterns from the branches of a few trees and covered the tartan with the white cotton and lace tablecloth they saved for parties. Cushions from the sofa were piled in one corner.

It seemed so long ago they were together on the boat. Alec told her he was happy and behind his words she knew he loved her. His energy was rough and strong; she was drawn to it when they met. She'd needed a safe harbour, and with Alec she could stop running. He caught her arm as she tripped one day. His hold was too firm to be comfortable but it stopped her falling.

'Let's try doing this together from now on,' he'd said.

Another time he came into the bathroom while she was in the tub and leant over with a towel. 'Try putting this behind your head, bit of extra padding, like a pillow. It was my mother's trick, made those bubble baths last a whole lot longer.'

She took the towel that he had rolled into a snake-like headrest and, lying back against its softness, closed her eyes, unsure how to react. His attention was so practical, yet he was looking at her naked in the bath. She wondered if he might step into the tub with her. But when she opened her eyes he was gone.

She plucked a few leaves from the low branches and ripped them apart as she assessed her handiwork. The garden was still a bit damp but with a rug down they wouldn't even feel it. She sat and waited. Moths fluttered near to the lantern's swinging dome, their transparent wings glowing warmly.

Annie rearranged the cutlery, wrapped in napkins and neatly lined up beside two plates. She lifted the bamboo dome to check that the large platter of Chinese pork and sliced tomatoes and cucumber was still fresh and flyless. She jiggled the bottle of white wine around in the ice in its silver bucket. Two large glasses lay cushioned in the material.

Goosebumps tingled on her arms as she leant back against a tree and closed her eyes.

The sound of someone moving through the house made her sit up and watch the back door expectantly. She decided to wait for him in the garden, in her picnic oasis. Her legs were tucked underneath her bottom so that her dress fell around her like a cloak. She was nervous with excitement and a little anxious for fear he wouldn't enter into the fun of the picnic.

'Out here in the garden,' she called after a few minutes.

'What's all this?'

Alec stood bemused in the frame of the door, looking down at her.

'Welcome home, my love.' She breathed in the smell of him as she wrapped her arms around his neck. 'I thought we'd do something a little different. It's a picnic supper—surprise!'

He held her tightly. 'It's good to be home.' Then he let go to stand back and admire her. 'Loneliness suits you, blossom.'

'Only because I knew you were coming back.'

She watched him looking down at the rug and tablecloth, the plates, the lanterns.

'Where are the chairs?' Alec seemed intrigued.

'No chairs tonight—cushions and the grass for our bottoms.'

'If it makes you happy, then pass me a cushion and make some space!' She helped him off with his jacket and put some cushions behind his back as she moved beside him. He held the heavy glass of white wine and flicked his fingernail against the crystal so that a light, high sound momentarily flew out into the air. 'I love these glasses; we hardly ever use the good stuff.'

He laughed as he said it. Annie passed Alec his cutlery and plate and watched as he tucked the napkin into his shirt collar and tried to balance his wine glass on the rug. She realised he was positioning things to mimic the dinner setting at the dining table, as though there was hard wood underneath their glasses instead of grass.

Annie turned and served him some Chinese pork. Then she picked up a piece for herself, letting her fingers linger in her mouth long enough to suck off the juice. She could see that Alec was watching her with bemusement.

'It tastes better if you use your fingers, Alec.'

He picked up a piece and then another, eating both in quick succession. 'You're right!' Then he laughed, a big open sound. 'I've missed the way you make me relax.'

Annie leant over with a piece of pork in her fingers and Alec hesitated, then took the meat with his teeth, nibbling a tiny bit of her fingertip in the process. They both laughed at the novelty of feeding each other. He nodded his head in a gesture towards the plate and Annie fed him another piece of meat. This time he didn't hesitate. He grabbed her hand before she could move away, holding onto her there, as they looked at each other. His face was close; she saw the familiar crease in his earlobe, the dusting of grey bristles at his jawline. She ran her finger gently along the scar below his left eye where it felt soft and crinkled. Then she kissed him.

'Thank you for an unusual supper.' He pulled her close.

The dusk had turned the lanterns into many small moons suspended through the garden. There were bugs flying into the plate of half-eaten food, but neither of them noticed. The empty wine glasses tipped drunkenly into the grass. Alec shifted on the picnic cloth so that he was leaning against a tree trunk and Annie rested against his chest. It was comforting to be leaning into Alec's familiar body.

That night, she rolled towards him in the bed. His body was warm and hard. Arms reached around and under her nightdress. She felt his lips on her belly, in the curve of her waist, grazing her nipple. She pulled him close, curling her fingers round his neck. The weight of him pressed against her and she breathed in the smell of the river in the salty strands of his hair.

Annie felt Alec shift beside her in the morning. He pushed the curtains open to let light flood the room.

'This is much better than waking up in my poor man's bunk on the water.' He rolled over and draped an arm across her chest. 'What's been happening while I was gone?'

She pushed herself up to sit against the warm, downy pillows. 'The usual bridge and lunches for me; everyone's about, all looking forward to the May Ball tonight. Mrs Marsden's in a flap over last-minute details, but I'm sure it will run like clockwork.' Annie lifted Alec's arm and gently placed it on the sheets between them before throwing her legs over the bedside. 'Time to get up for me, but you lie there if you like, I'll bring some more tea.'

She hovered at the end of the bed; now would be the perfect moment to tell Alec about Li Qiang. Annie didn't want to have secrets. Li Qiang's cheeky smile came into her head, and the way he'd patted her arm so proudly when he first met her and helped her across the Bund. She felt a heavy weight in the pit of her stomach. *It was your fault*, the voice in her head whispered.

'You all right, blossom?' Alec had hauled himself upright and was looking at her with a worried frown.

'Just Mrs Marsden on my mind; there's no way she'd let the ball be derailed by what's been happening. The city could be under attack by an army of Communists and she'd still insist on replicating her hometown King's College tradition.' She continued quickly. 'The trial of those arrested students took place too, you may have heard?'

Alec ran his hands through his messy hair.

'I did hear they'd been convicted; good news travels fast.' He hadn't yet shaken off the soft intimacy of their shared sleep; she could hear it in his voice. 'I've got to head to the office this morning, a day of going through the ship's log with the boss. But I'll be home by six so we can travel to the ball together.'

Annie breathed in deeply. The air in the long ballroom was humid and smoky and tinged with alcohol. It swirled intoxicatingly in her throat and head. The dance floor was a large square of polished parquetry dropped into the middle of the room. Around its perimeter tables had been dragged together to accommodate large parties, while others were left as singles. Against the far wall, the band sat in a sunken rotunda, behind which a rich mosaic of scalloped tiles fanned out like a peacock's tail. It was the latest design—the indigo and greens shimmered and played with the reflection of brass off a musician's trumpet as the man stood to play a solo. Above him the domed ceiling arched to meet the carved stone women who held it up from their marble plinths. High on the walls, mirrors lined the room.

The black bottom was playing and the dance floor was already a maze of moving bodies as Annie and Alec weaved their way through the crowds. Annie took the glass of champagne Alec offered her through the cluster of people standing around them, lifting her arm high above her head so she didn't spill any on her new satin gloves.

The fast music swirled around the crowded space, making people tap their feet in rhythm to the song. Alec accepted a cigar from a friend to his left, leaning in to light the tip and blowing a series of rings high into the space above the crowd. The rings floated for a second through the open air and then dissolved.

Standing on the edge of the dance floor Annie watched the scene. A couple moved their arms in mirrored synchronisation as they twisted their hips and swayed. The woman wore a dress edged with tassels and as she moved it quivered like a living thing. Her partner had discarded his dinner jacket and was grinning broadly as he moved in and out from her. As she circled around, the beads on her headband tinkled. Her brow was gleaming with a film of perspiration. In one moment they were sucked together by the music's rhythm, her back arched against his open palm. Then they pushed away with hands waving, their faces mirroring each other's expression. The couple was like a two-headed serpent, entwining about itself and then disentangling.

Alec called out to Annie and waved at her from a table. The noise was too loud to hear him but she made her way through the partygoers.

'Get hot, get hot!' The lady seated next to Alec called out to a dancer, who responded with a quickened step. 'Isn't this party the cat's meow?'

Annie nodded and laughed as she took her seat. It was Nancy Langham, the daughter of a friend of Alec's. Nancy had her dance card open on the table and was writing a cross with the little attached pencil beside one of the dances she planned on sitting out. Annie leant back in her chair, relieved to be seated next to this young lady who wouldn't give two hoots about following Mrs Marsden's Club etiquette here. Tonight could be all about the fun of the dance.

The cold champagne tickled her throat as she swallowed and nodded to a waiter to fill her glass again. 'Let's dance?' she said to Nancy beside her.

Their toes tapped the floor as the two women began a foxtrot. The tall feather in Annie's headband flapped as she danced and some light tufts of peacock blue floated down across her face. She blew them off the tip of her nose and laughed as Nancy twirled her skirt so the box pleats fanned out in a circle of pale pink and lilac. The music picked up as the band stood together and slid into a charleston. Annie and Nancy shook their heads at each other wildly.

The hands of a woman dancing behind Nancy caught Annie's attention. They were held up high by a stocky Chinese man. He wore western dress with an opulent watch chain strung across his chest. Annie saw his outfit in fits and spurts through the moving dancers. A man bumped Annie from behind and pushed her into Nancy. It was too busy to really spread out anymore. But a momentary space allowed Annie to see the Chinaman's partner. She was clearly not Chinese; her thick red hair was caught with a jewelled clasp to the side of one ear, from which a diamond and ruby drop hung.

It was Natalia. The music swirled as Nancy laughed and danced in front of Annie. She couldn't hear what Nancy was saying; the sight of Natalia dancing with a Chinaman had completely distracted her. She looked around for Willie Piper; sure he must be somewhere close by.

The familiar dark eyes lined with kohl didn't notice Annie as Natalia swung back to face her partner. Annie watched her friend move about the floor with languid ease; she had to admire Natalia's dancing style. Another bump from behind nearly tripped Annie, but she steadied herself. There was no breeze in the congested space and a line of moisture trickled down Annie's back. Natalia ran her hand around the man's ear as she turned, and Annie stopped still, shocked by the intimate gesture. Around her, dancers continued to move and shake, so that Annie was jostled about, but she didn't feel any of it as she stared at Natalia and the Chinaman. Again she looked around for Willie and saw him in the distance with Alec.

Natalia and her partner left the dance floor. Annie followed them, slipping between dancers as she strained to keep them in sight.

'Natalia, Natalia.'

She could see her friend's back tense up at the sound of her voice. But Natalia kept walking. They were just ahead, in a dark corner of the room, where surprisingly there were a number of vacant tables, surrounding one large round table where Natalia and the Chinaman stood with a group. Annie followed until she could tap her friend on the shoulder.

'Natalia, didn't you hear me calling out to you? I thought you'd be with Will Piper?' She looked around the table politely, taking in the fat cigars and silence. Natalia took Annie by the arm and walked her away a little.

'Annie, this is awkward. It would be better if you returned to your own table.'

'What's going on?'

'It's complicated and you wouldn't understand.'

'Why not?' Annie searched Natalia's eyes for an answer.

They were interrupted by the Chinaman, calling to Natalia. Natalia leant in to Annie so that their faces were very close, just long enough for Annie to see the anger in her eyes.

'Go Annie, this is not a polite request.'

Natalia turned away and Annie watched, mortified as she rejoined her party. The Chinaman tapped the table with his silver-topped cane and motioned for Annie to come forward.

'Be careful who you play with, little white devil,' he said to her, waving his cane in the air. She saw a tiny fish carved into the silver top, with rows of symmetrical scales detailed in the body. Annie stiffened, shocked into silence by the Chinaman's familiar tone, as Natalia accepted a glass of champagne from him. Around her neck, Annie's gold and onyx beads swung playfully.

The band had taken a break from playing. Partygoers moved about the tables, filling the silence left by the music with talking and laughter. A cigarette girl offered Annie a tray of Camels as she pushed her way back to Alec. She shook her head. People slipped around her and waiters brushed past as she rejoined her group. 'I want to go home,' she said softly, leaning in against Alec's ear. He reached up from a drunken haze and kissed her.

'What's happened to you?'

'Miss Sosnovsky, Natalia, is here with a Chinaman—over in the far corner.'

Alec strained to see. 'Well, can't trust the Russians.' He laughed uproariously.

'Do you know him?'

'I've heard he's a local businessman; bad news, not some-one I'd be pleased to meet, but the man's got enough money to buy his way into any social event. Standards are dropping.'

William Piper leant into the conversation. 'Darned shame, I say. Natalia's a smashing girl, but if she wants to go native I'll have nothing further to do with her.'

'That's very harsh, Willie.' Annie shot him a fiery look.

William blew a heavy cloud of smoke at Annie, forcing her to wave her arms about to avoid breathing it in. 'I think I'll go home, Alec, if it's all the same to you. I don't quite feel myself.'

'Very well, my dear, take the car; I'll hitch a ride with one of these devils.' Alec turned back to his drinking buddies, punching Willie Piper in the arm.

Outside on the North Bund heavy rain fell. Annie heard the slush of water as a taxi car drove off from the curb; its headlights sent a beam of colour through the downpour. Why had Natalia been so rude to her? She frowned as a few partygoers hurried past, waving to each other as they disap-peared into the night. The fun had gone out of her evening.

The following morning Annie was at Mrs Marsden's house, attending a post-party brunch for the committee members. Only six committee members were present, the evening's revelries having left a few indisposed. So the ladies were seated in the small lounge room in large, comfortable sofas, the pug dogs asleep in their beds in front of the fireplace.

'It's just too bad, as hard as we try to present an evening of superior enjoyment; we are foiled by the utter lack of social standards. Does a British passport count for nothing in this godforsaken city? I saw at least a dozen Chinks on the dance floor alone!'

'The Chinese who can afford to buy tickets have every right to be at the ball, Margaret.' Audrey Pruce's sensible response did not cut off her host's outrage.

Annie stayed silent. She was tired after the ball and she couldn't be bothered to engage with the old trout. She didn't want Natalia's name to come up either. She'd been with one of those Chinamen, after all. Annie could not stop thinking about her encounter with Natalia. She kept coming back to the same question: was Natalia working last night? The same girl Annie had seen at Mrs Marsden's lunch served them tea. She seemed more comfortable this time, smiling at Annie as she offered to take her cup. She had a smooth brown mole that clung to her top lip like a limpet.

'Next year, I think we should consider a guest list rather than tickets, if we are all still here. The city may be overridden by these gangs by then.'

'Let's wait 'til next year to decide. Right now, I'm happy to hang up my ball committee apron and relax. Did anyone else think Florence Walsh's dress was a tad short?'

The conversation drifted through clothes to hairstyles and chaperones. The ball was deemed a success, and no one bothered to mention the number of Chinese guests again.

Annie excused herself and left early. She was meeting Alec at the Public Garden. Despite the increased tensions in the Settlement streets, he insisted they continue their Sunday tradition of an afternoon walk. Alec preferred the Public Garden to the bigger Jessfield Park, because the garden was on the riverfront, at the bend where Soochow Creek met with the Whangpoo. It had been one of their first views of Shanghai.

She linked her arm with Alec's as they walked through the gates near Garden Bridge. There was a steady stream of visitors that afternoon as birds dived through the thick foliage that clung snugly to branches. The gravel walkway was neatly raked so that Annie's heels crunched in the stones. Alec smiled and nodded at other couples they passed. He bowed slightly, and even turned to watch one man's back as he walked away.

'I hear he ran up such a bill at one of the gambling dens last week I'm surprised to see him out in public.'

'You mustn't gossip,' Annie chided him. They followed a path along the river's edge, and she looked out across waters heavy with junks and steamers, overshadowed by the foreign gunboats. But all was calm behind the iron rails of the Public Garden.

Music sounded from a bandstand. The freshly painted rotunda sat in the centre of a grassed circle. Paths splintered off at angles, simulating the quarter hours of a clock face. Annie looked about as they stopped in front of the musicians. A few deckchairs were dotted on the grass and on the other side of the path Annie saw the compact garden of peach trees, so popular in the spring months for their delicate pink bundles. But the early summer heat had hastened their bloom and now the portly trees were a lush green mass of leaves. Annie loved the sweet smell of the spring blossoms. Two police constables passed by with pistols holstered at their waists. They were an incongruous sight amongst the peach trees and Annie wondered why they needed to patrol the park on such a glorious day.

Alec took Annie's arm and they followed the path to the left through the peach tree garden. They were cut off from the general circle of the park as they meandered through the slim path between the trees. A few birds hopped about in the shaded earth.

A loud crack sounded sharply. Annie looked about, expecting to see something whistle through the air. Then she heard a second shot and grabbed hold of Alec. He didn't react; there was a sudden grim focus in his stillness which frightened her more than the noise. He pushed her towards some trees.

'Stay here,' he entreated quietly and urgently as he disappeared in the direction of the shots.

A branch grazed her arm as Annie stumbled back. Alec was gone quickly. She looked out from within the maze of leaves. The path was empty but she held her breath and listened. The sound of her watch ticked loudly in the silence; there were no more gunshots, and no shouting calls for help either. The freshly turned earth smelt musty. The birds that had flown off angrily at the disturbance now began returning, dropping quickly back to the earth in a skilled flutter. Annie pulled her coat more tightly around her waist and a branch caught in her hair as she moved, forcing her to turn and untwine the finicky mess. She moved back to the path, looking along the dirt trail but no one approached. From a distance, the sound of band music started again with a rousing crescendo. She brushed down her coat and flicked a dead leaf off into the dirt.

In a second the birds were gone. They'd heard the man's careful, slow tread, as he came up behind Annie. His arms pressed painfully into her ribs as he dragged her into the bushes. There was no chance to run. Her feet scrabbled in the dirt, sending stones and twigs flying but he put his weight into the hold he had on her and she was pinned. Her nostrils flared with panic as a hand covered her mouth.

'We know who you are.' His voice breathed hot in her ear. Annie struggled and he tightened his grip even harder. She kicked out and tried to roll her body to dislodge his hold. A searing pain tore through her side. His hand pushed into her lips roughly. Annie bit down hard. Warm, rubbery skin pressed against her tongue. He jerked his arm and she released, tasting metallic blood in the saliva that pooled beneath her tongue. Then she screamed for help. He let her go and she fell hard. Bushes rustled and branches cracked and she knew he was fleeing through them. She lay, rasping and heaving and unable to call out again. The fall had winded her.

'Annie, where are you?' Alec's panicked voice grew louder and louder until he was there, lifting her gently into his lap where he cradled her. 'Are you hurt? Annie, Annie?'

Only a painful cough sounded. She began to cry and the sting of salt on her lips made her wince.

'There you go, I've got you. It's shock, that's all.' He pulled out a crisp white handkerchief and dabbed gently, at the same time feeling up and down her body for any wounds. 'Try speaking again, take your time. What happened?'

Annie took a deep breath. She'd begun to shake. 'Someone attacked me.' Alec's arms tightened around her. 'No, that hurts, let go.' She spoke in a whisper.

'Let's get you up and away from here.' Alec supported Annie to stand, leaning against him. They walked slowly out of the thicket of trees and Annie let Alec lead her. She was shocked and shaking. Ahead the two policemen from earlier stood huddled together. Alec called to them and they hurried over.

'Someone attacked my wife.'

One of the policemen ran back in the direction they had come. The other stayed with Annie and Alec. 'It may have been a kidnapping attempt.' Alec led Annie to a park bench where he sat her down and moved away to continue talking to the constable. They were in an open grassy section of the park. She rubbed her hands together for warmth despite the summer heat and tucked her chin into the scarf Alec had wrapped snugly around her neck. The shakes had stopped but her body ached with bruising that she could already feel pressing against the skin beneath her clothes. Alec hurried back.

'How are you feeling?'

'A little better I think.'

'We need to get you seen to by a doctor. Did your assailant harm you?' Alec spoke gently but Annie could see the question in his eyes.

'No, nothing like that, Alec. I just want to go home and lie down.'

'All right,' but Alec paused. He'd seen the other policeman returning.

'Anything?' he asked quickly.

'No sign of him, sir.' Then the constable turned to Annie. 'Could you give us a description of the man who attacked you, madam?' He took out a notebook and pencil.

'I didn't see him I'm afraid. He came up behind me and ran off before I had a chance.' Annie coughed again, the dryness in her throat caught on her words.

'We'll do our best, but without a description there's not much to go on. These two might offer a clue.' Annie looked beyond to where he was pointing and saw two bodies lying side-by-side on the grass, covered with white sheets. She gasped.

'What happened?'

'They turned on the constables for no reason at all, or so we thought, but now it makes sense.' It was Alec who answered Annie's question.

'It's probable they were a distraction so the kidnapper could get to you, Mrs Brand,' the policeman took over explaining. 'Foreigners are a lucrative business and we've seen a worrying increase in the number of kidnappings this last year.'

The two policemen began loading the bodies into a cart. An arm flopped out and Annie's hand flew to her mouth in horror. One of the men pushed it back in before covering the load efficiently.

'Will you be right, sir?' The policemen asked Alec.

'Yes, thank you, officers.'

Annie watched them heave the cart upright and stagger off down a path cut through the parkland, away from the main thoroughfare. She closed her eyes, grabbing Alec's hand tightly.

'What if the man was not a kidnapper, what if he was sent by the Green Gang?'

'Now you're being irrational.'

'I'm frightened, Alec. I need to tell you why.'

'Hush, hush. The police do a good job, Annie. They'll find your attacker.' Alec wrapped her in his arms and she buried her head into his chest.

'"We know who you are," that's what he said,' Annie's muffled words trailed off.

'What are you talking about?'

Annie sat up and faced Alec so she could answer him properly. 'A young kitchen hand from the Club went missing and I stupidly thought I could help him, only he'd joined the Green Gang and the same day I confronted him about it and asked him to come home, he was killed. I'm sorry I didn't tell you sooner but what if the men were from the Green Gang?"

'I doubt the Green Gang would consider you a threat, blossom.'

'What have I got myself into?' Annie shivered uncontrollably and Alec put an arm around her shoulder.

'I don't want you thinking about it anymore. Let's go home, shall we? If it makes you feel better, I'll speak to Roger tomorrow. We'll both be at the station on Nanking Road and I can talk to him about it then.'

CHAPTER EIGHT

A shaft of sunlight cut through the curtains and lit the bedroom. Annie never slept deeply so the brightness woke her easily. The previous night, sleep had been even more elusive. Her body ached from the attack. When sleep came she dreamt of shadowy figures running away from her, blurred grey visions that never eventuated into anything recognisable. She opened her eyes to find Alec was not beside her. A moment of panic quickly turned to relief when he appeared with a tray.

'It's my turn to look after you.' He put the tray down between them and leant over to kiss Annie's forehead. 'How are you feeling?'

'I'm sore all over. A bath might help?' Annie sipped her tea as Alec disappeared into the bathroom followed by the sound of running water.

'Have you heard anything from the police?' she called to him.

'Nothing, but don't forget I'm meeting Marsden this afternoon. I'll go into the office, then head over to Nanking Road. I should be at the Club by five to meet you for a drink?'

'Sounds lovely. Can I use the car today? I'll feel safer.' Annie had decided there would be no more walks through areas she didn't know. This was a city without order and if the rules were breaking down, it was time to start taking care.

'Yes, of course.' Alec gave her another kiss on the forehead before leaving her to her bath.

Annie took the car to the Club after a quiet lunch at home. She would be late for bridge but after her attack yesterday she could only do things slowly. As they turned into Fuzhou Road, she noticed a bamboo cage hanging from a telegraph pole. Inside were two rotting heads, Chinese criminals, cut through at the neck and left to fester in the fly-swarming heat. The men's eyes were open and staring at nothing, opaque and bulbous. Annie swallowed but her mouth quickly filled with saliva again. Her stomach churned. She opened the window as they turned down Sichuan Road and leant into the rush of air. A newspaper stall flashed past with a headline: 'Student Sentencing Galvanizes Anti-Foreign Movement.' It was gone before she could read any further, and she turned away. The car paused at a set of traffic lights and a street hawker shook his fist at a regular customer who stopped at his rival's stall to save the effort of crossing the road. He spat into the dirt, cursing loudly at everyone around him. Men here shouted less but louder: the heat made them quick to anger, the humidity made them slow to respond. Annie shrunk back from the sight. This was more than the usual edginess of summer heat; there was fresh tension in the streets.

Annie pulled on her day-gloves and tightened the clasp of her bracelet as they pulled up at the Club. If she was lucky she might have missed bridge altogether and there were only a few hours before Alec said he'd meet her for a drink. She could catch up on her reading.

Mrs Marsden approached Annie as soon as she saw her enter the lounge.

'My dear girl, what a horrifying ordeal you've been through. You are so brave to come out and join us, even after bridge.'

'Thank you, Mrs Marsden. I'm not feeling too bad today.'

'Well, your health is my main concern.' She raised her eyebrows at Annie and leant in as if expecting a secret confession.

'I've nothing to hide. My attacker ran off before he could really hurt me.'

'That is a relief. The police will no doubt find the culprit and that'll be the end to it.'

A servant approached Mrs Marsden and spoke to her quietly. She followed the man out of the room, returning not long after. A mottled flush coloured her neck. She clapped her hands again and drew the ladies together around her.

'I don't want anyone to panic, but there's a riot of some sort passing by the Club. I'm told it's nothing for us to fear, however, my husband says we must stay in the lounge 'til they've gone. I suppose we are getting quite good at this lark!' She laughed theatrically before seeking out a chair. Annie watched her sit heavily and struggle to pull out a handkerchief from her pocket. She patted her lips rapidly.

'What's it about, do you know?' Annie sat beside Mrs Marsden.

'Roger says they're heading to the police station where the student prisoners are waiting to be transferred. I'm not to alarm the women but he said they are armed with all sorts of homemade weapons, quite nasty.'

'Is it the station on Nanking Road?'

'Yes, but it's a long way from the Club. They'll get short shrift from the police once they get there.'

'I thought Admiral Marsden was at the station?'

'My dear, I've just spoken to him in the corridor.'

'But Alec is meeting him there …'

'Not any more. Roger is staying right here 'til this threat has passed.'

Annie's book fell to the floor with a thud. Someone had to warn Alec. She must find Admiral Marsden. He was standing in the foyer, with a group of men, deep in conversation. As Annie approached she saw the concern on their faces.

'Admiral Marsden, may I speak with you?' He broke away from the group.

'You shouldn't be here, Mrs Brand. Didn't my wife tell you to stay in the lounge? This is no time for socialising.'

'She did, but I'm here because I know my husband is at this moment waiting for you in the Nanking Road police station.'

'Oh lord, yes, I'd quite forgotten my appointment with Captain Brand in all the hoo-hah.'

'Has someone been sent to warn him?'

'No one can get out now. There's a mass of angry Chinamen beyond the gates and it'd be murder to send one of my men into it.'

'But what about the men at the station, are they safe?'

'Safe enough if they keep their heads screwed on, nothing to be done now anyway.'

As they spoke a swell of drum-like noise drowned out the Admiral's voice. Annie looked towards the Club doors which were being hurriedly pushed shut by two servants.

'How can you be so blasé?'

'It's a police station; with guns and trained constabulary. If needs be, Alec'll get his hands dirty.' Admiral Marsden tugged at his jacket as he buttoned it about him. 'I'm sure the Captain would not appreciate his wife pleading on his behalf in such an indecorous fashion.'

'I can't see anyone else showing the slightest degree of concern for my husband so I'd say my indecorous pleading is the best he's got.' She turned away in anger. Chow was standing beside her, with an empty drinks tray tucked under his arm. He motioned for her to follow him and she found herself standing in the cloak room.

'He is wrong, you know. This is more serious than the police are willing to admit.' Chow spoke quietly.

'Alec is at the station, Chow. What can we do?'

'I'm afraid this time Admiral Marsden is correct. It's too dangerous now to go out.'

'But they have no idea what is coming.'

'It would be madness to go. You must stay here and trust the police will keep him safe.'

But Annie had no intention of hiding in the ladies' lounge like a coward. She walked away, hoping Chow would assume she was returning to the lounge to wait. Then she peeled off to the kitchen and slipped out the staff exit to the alleyway which led into the lane behind the Club.

Two waiters sat on upturned crates, smoking. They stared at Annie as she approached. She was glad to have come across them as they could help her get away. She asked them to find a rickshaw quickly.

It was surprisingly quiet while she waited. No police guarded these gates; she'd be able to slip through easily.

The men returned, followed by a rickshaw. Annie gave them each a copper and stepped into the seat.

'Nanking Road,' she told the driver.

'Mrs Brand, what are you doing?' It was Chow, running towards her shouting.

'Stop, stop.' He pulled on the driver's pole forcing him to stop.

'It's too dangerous for you to go, please, be reasonable.'

'I won't leave Alec. I'm going to bring him back. There's every chance I'll beat the protestors to the station and we'll be in the Club having a drink in half an hour.' She forced herself to sound convincing.

Chow turned away briefly and mumbled something under his breath. His shoulders rose and fell in quick succession. Then he took a step towards her.

'Move over, I cannot let you go alone.'

The rickshaw was old, but its owner had not been in business long, his young legs and the rickshaw's wheels worked quickly together to pull the carriage over the potholes and dints in the road. They swung left together as the rickshaw swerved around a pile of rubble too big for the old wheels to ride over but it moved apace and before long they were only two streets from the police station, travelling north on Nanking Road. Annie noticed some of the shops were closed: a sign of nervousness amongst their owners but she could not yet see any of the protestors. Chow directed the driver to take a side road, and Annie understood he hoped to avoid the demonstration altogether. She heard thunder in the distance but the sky was clear.

'Chow, do you hear that?'

'Yes.' He peered around the canopy of their seat, as the oversized wheels wobbled along rhythmically. The rickshaw pulled up abruptly. Annie lurched forward and saw, in a hurried moment of awkward clambering, the large gathering in the street. Their passage was blocked. The rumbling sound wasn't thunder. It was the communal throb of the noisy crowd. Chow leant forward and slapped the driver on the back to get him to turn around. But the young man spat into the dirt, dropped the poles and ran off. They were faced with a wall of slowly moving protestors. Chow was still there, beside Annie; he could have run off like the driver and melted into the crowd, but he stayed. She grasped his arm and he took her hand and held it firmly.

'I will continue to the station alone, this crowd will not harm me. But you must hurry and go now, before they are upon us.' Annie felt his heat on her skin. She knew the sensible response was to get out of the mob's path as Chow suggested, but she couldn't move. A sickening sensation bubbled in her stomach as she watched a lone, bold man rush towards them. His mouth stretched wide as he shouted.

Annie grabbed at Chow as the rickshaw rocked. The man grasped onto the edge, trying to jump up. His hand was right there, so close it looked like a ghastly amputation. Then Chow hit him fiercely across the head, again and again.

'Annie,' Chow's voice was urgent. His hands on her waist were strong and it hurt as he lifted her up to standing.

'Listen to me. You must go back and turn left; there are guards at the gates only yards down that road. I will get to the station. I will find Captain Brand, I promise you.' He had to shout to be heard above the din. Then he pushed her roughly. 'Can you run?' he shouted, impatiently.

The pressure of his hands bruised her shoulders. But it shocked her into wakefulness. The noise of the crowd had grown louder, sucking all the air from the street.

'Watch me,' she replied and as she leapt from the rickshaw Annie shouted frantically again, 'just watch me.' Then she ran, though her chest hurt and her panting sounded like someone else was beside her. She lost a shoe, but she kept running, as fast as she could, away from the angry mob, away from Chow in the rickshaw, away from the horror of this moment, and all the other moments of pain and loss.

Chow's voice reached her: a cry of defiance, echoed by the mob's roar. She had to look back. She saw him grab at the rickshaw to get some traction from the rocking. The crowd pushed and swayed. His head moved about frantically as he tried to watch them all. But there were too many. His arms flayed and scrabbled through the air as he was thrown from the vehicle.

Then hot, sweaty hands pulled at her. She had watched Chow for only a moment but it was long enough for one of the protestors to catch up to her. An overpowering smell cloyed in her nostrils amongst so much body heat and sweat. The man pulled her skirt and it ripped easily. She grabbed at his arm, pushed it hard away. A wooden pole stabbed into her stomach and she gasped and doubled over with pain.

Everything swayed. The face in front of her leered; teeth and lips drawn wide in a distorted, grotesque smile. Then he fell against her, mouth open on her chest and she felt the single bullet's thud of impact, intimately close. Warm, bloody wetness seeped through her blouse and she knew he was dead.

The mob's chanting was muffled; the sound of the gunshot deafened everything to a dulled echo that throbbed in her head. Where had the shot come from? She was on the ground; her blouse clung to her skin with the sticky warmth. The man's heavy body felt limp. One rough push sent him slipping from her. She looked down at her dead attacker, staring for a moment into the unclosed eyes of someone's son, overwhelmed with nausea and her own gushing relief at still being alive. Then the sound of shouts flooded through to her brain, and she was up again and running. She ran fast, her dress flying, stockings and legs exposed, heart thumping as each foot hit the ground. The air rushed past her but there was not a moment to breathe it in. Ahead, she saw guards and barbed-wire gates. She knew safety lay behind them. The guards held up rifles, pointed towards her. She covered her head with her hands, still running, and shouted at them not to shoot. But as she got closer she realised that it was the men chasing her who the guards were aiming for. She heard their feet stamping the ground and felt panic pushing through her laboured breathing. She ran past the guards, couldn't stop running, unaware of the gates groaning with the weight of heavy metal as they shut behind her. Someone tried to grab her; she heard a Scottish accent calling her to stop and come back. But she couldn't stop. She had to keep running.

It was the silence of her own home that finally calmed Annie. She slid down the wall of her living room, panting and coughing up bile as she collapsed. There was soft carpet under her feet, a wall to hold onto, framed pictures reassuring her from their familiar mountings. Her breathing slowed. She shivered with cold from the sweat and the tears that came in a torrent of exhausted shock.

'Alec, Alec, are you here?' Annie ran frantically from the living room to the kitchen and through to their bedroom. There was no answer. Her feet barely sounded as they flew across the floorboards. The house boy appeared but said nothing as she pushed past him through the French doors into the garden, turning full circle in a mad frenzy.

'Alec,' she screamed into the emptiness.

CHAPTER NINE

August 1925

Sometime through the night, Annie woke. It was past the hour when the moon still shed light on the silent garden, past dark, in the blackest time of night. She wandered to the kitchen and walked around the familiar room, moving her body through the darkness. There was no sound save her breathing. Her fingers ran the smooth edge of the kitchen table as she circled it. She caught the sob in her mouth, but her need to cry was too strong and she bent over with the pain of it.

It had been two months since the Nanking Road incident and Annie had not left her house or allowed in any visitors, although there'd been a steady stream of flowers and food parcels delivered to her house. She turned away the Club ladies, Mrs Marsden, even Natalia. Chow had come each week but she wasn't ready to face him.

It was in the newspapers and everyone was talking about it; the May 30th incident. The protestors moved past her and Chow to the police station where the students were being detained for transport to the gaol, demanding justice be done and the students released. The British inspector ordered his men to fire; there was no time to send for reinforcements and he feared his station was in danger. Within an hour, men lay dead near the station gate, while many more died later. The police claimed they had no choice but to open fire in response to the attack, but the incident was quickly branded a British imperialist crime. More students were joined by merchants and workers in a strike that left the city floundering. The governor saw the hand of the Bolsheviks behind it all and claimed the new nationalism was merely the old anti-imperialism relabelled. He vowed to show the Chinese that they were not intimidated, and the foreign community produced its own militia composed exclusively of non-Chinese: the Shanghai Volunteers Corps.

Annie no longer cared about any of it. She shut herself away from the world altogether. Alec was dead, killed by a bullet that no one could confirm was fired by a rioting local and not one of their own police.

She roamed through her house. Her body ached with memories. When the day got too hot, Annie retreated to her bedroom. She slept 'til dusk shrouded the blood that stained the streets in darkness and fear could be disguised by Shanghai's night-time distractions. The dance halls and gambling dens reopened and the city throbbed with life 'til curfew time.

Annie untied the cord of her dressing gown and sighed as she looked around for a house dress to wear. She shivered in only her slip and knickers and turned away from her reflection in the dresser mirror; it was her fault Alec was dead. He'd gone to the station because of her meddling. She felt her insides churn. She couldn't think about the riot without being overcome with shuddering grief. So she blocked it out.

The city was in turmoil. The smell of the river intensified each morning and with it the stench of fear. Men were employed to sweep the shoreline along the Bund with nets, catching dead rats and debris, in an attempt to ease the smell: forever under the watchful eyes of the Volunteer Corps. Street patrols were increased too, calling on the services of any young, fit foreign resident men willing to protect their own. The gaol houses filled and their occupants were regularly shipped to workhouses or discreetly disposed of in order to make room for the next wave. Clean water was monitored closely, in case the heat left a fetid film across its surface that brought malarial fever and dysentery to the foreigners. Time still took each day to its conclusion, the police to raid more tearooms and mahjong halls, a shop to close its shutters, the tide to turn and settle into the shallows. But inside Annie's house, time and everything connected to it stopped.

She lay in her garden, with the smell of hot earth in her nostrils. The sun burnt into her hands, it was almost too hot to stand. But Annie stayed there, feeling herself melt into the grass where she'd sat with Alec. Her mind went back to their last picnic in the garden. His tenderness towards her had started then, like an unexpected green shoot on one of her trees, fresh and hopeful, ready to grow. But the possibility of sharing intimate truths and fears with him was gone forever. She rolled over and pressed her face into the grass, suffocating the thoughts that tormented her daily, only lifting her head when the need to gasp a breath was overwhelming.

The house boy appeared on the steps. 'Mister Chow, come look see.' He'd been to the house every week since Alec's death. Annie didn't know what to say to him. She stood wearily and shook her head. Seeing Chow would mean dealing with what had happened and she couldn't do it, not yet, maybe never. The house boy disappeared.

There was a commotion inside. Voices shouted loudly and banging carried down the corridor. Annie looked up to see Chow hurrying towards her, the house boy chasing him.

She stood quite still, overwhelmed by the sight of her friend. 'Leave us,' she told the house boy. Tears slid quietly down her face. A bird ruffled its feathers in the branch above her head and flew away. Annie shook silently and hung her head. The sight of Chow had brought it all back; the panic, the fear, her shocked disbelief and the utterly overwhelming sadness. Then she felt his hand softly lift her chin, forcing her to look at him.

'I failed you.' He spoke simply. 'I failed Captain Brand.'

Chow held her silently. Annie pressed her eyes tightly shut and the red pain of loss filled her vision as she shook and cried uncontrollably. His body was taut and still. Even when she'd calmed down and offered him her handkerchief to wipe the wet marks off his jacket, Chow remained still and calm.

'I'm sorry you had to see me fall apart.' Annie spoke unevenly through heaving gasps as she tried to quell the final untempered emotion from her speech. Chow handed back her refolded handkerchief.

'I know you came to see me and I'm sorry I couldn't …' Annie's voice trailed off.

'You do not have to explain. We are here now.' A shadow fell across them as he moved to stand beside Annie, his presence close and comforting. She led them back into the house. Tea was waiting in the sunroom and so they sat for half an hour in companionable quiet. From a bag Chow produced a round of thin red paper which he laid on the table between them.

'I have some ceremony to show you. It is customary for such a time as this. We must cover any gods you have in the house with this paper. Even though it is already too late, this is the right thing to do.'

'I don't think I've got anything like a god?' Annie looked confused.

'You have the statue of Buddha I gave to you. He must not be exposed to death.'

'I see.' Annie led Chow to her bedroom where the statue stood. After placing paper over the Buddha's head, Chow walked to the living room. They stood before the fireplace where a photograph of Alec in his naval uniform stood on the mantelpiece.

'May I?' he asked as he reached into his bag.

'Yes, do what you wish.' Annie watched as Chow lit a stick of incense and placed it in a holder to one side of the photograph, bowing and chanting as he did. The stick hissed momentarily. She took a step back to allow him the space to continue and perched on the edge of an armchair. He lit a white candle and placed it on the other side of the photograph. Alec's portrait glowed in the flame's light. Chow placed a piece of joss paper into the flame and it flared up before curling into a dusty black scrap. He burnt prayer money next and Annie knew this was to help Alec pay his way in the afterlife. The house boy came into the room at the smell and silently joined Chow in front of the fireplace where they both knelt. Chow held a hollowed block of wood called mu yu, a 'wooden fish' and as they chanted the Buddhist scriptures he beat the rhythm on the wood. The knocking sound absorbed Annie. After a while she joined them, whispering the Lord's Prayer while slivers of tears slipped down her cheek. The house boy went to a small gong which he had placed to the left of the front door and the rich full sound resonated around the room.

'He says the taipan spirit does not know how to leave the house, so he is helping.' Chow whispered to Annie before joining the house boy who had opened the door as he continued to sound the gong. Warm air blew through Annie's hair. A car horn sounded and some leaves danced across the porch. The pale afternoon light stood out against the dark wooden doorframe. Annie closed her eyes.

'Earth to earth, ashes to ashes, dust to dust.' She repeated the words the minister had spoken as they buried Alec, only it felt like letting him go this time. Her skirt flew out and her hair flapped into her eyes as the breeze blew straight into her.

'Tomorrow we will light a string of firecrackers to drive the bad luck out of the house, if you feel able' Chow stood beside her.

'Yes, tomorrow.' Annie closed the door.

'I think we'll have a drink—whiskey, if you'll join me, Chow?'

'I would be honoured.'

Annie waited until Chow had his glass. She filled a third glass and gave it to the house boy. 'Let us all drink together.' When they'd finished, she sat tucked into the armchair like a cat. The house boy gathered the empty glasses onto a tray and disappeared to the kitchen.

'I didn't think I'd ever be able to contemplate that day, but you've helped me do it. I don't know what happens now, though. What is my future to be, where will I go?'

'Why must you go anywhere if you are content to stay here?'

'I'm a widow, with no support. I don't think I get to decide.'

'Then who does? I don't understand this logic. You are in mourning; it is not the time to think about the future.'

'Yes, you're right. The problem is I don't ever want to think about my future. I want to stay here, in my safe little house with my books.' Annie reached for her volume of Yeats. She stroked the gold-embossed cover.

'You must keep living, that is all.'

'Will you visit me again?'

'Yes, I will, each day if you allow me.'

Chow kept his promise, arriving at a different time each day but always there. Annie could tell from his energy if his visit was timed before he began work at the Club or if he arrived at the end of a long day. He was considerate, bringing her small things like the latest copy of an American women's magazine, or a parcel of small egg custard tarts sprinkled with nutmeg and still warm. He brought news too, none of it good. A formal state of emergency was declared and Annie's Club friends barricaded themselves at home, many employing private bodyguards as fear for their own safety mounted. There was little time for social niceties. The bridge games and tea dances, the cocktail hours and evening promenades in the Public Garden—all the usual gatherings were cancelled as Shanghai's foreign community focused on self-preservation.

'I was such a fool to believe I could save one boy from the Green Gang's perfidious hold. Judging by the news reports, they're getting bolder every day, arming the discontented and well and truly fuelling this unrest.'

'You had good intentions but this city is riven with dark and deceitful entanglements. Why should you know how to battle this when even your top men do not?'

One day Chow arrived with a bird in a cage, concealed under a cloth. He set the cage down on a table in the sun-room and pulled off the cover. The moment light hit the cage there was the sound of song. Annie saw a small, perfectly shaped bird— red beak, yellow feathers, small and skittish, it flew from perch to floor to cage bar. She ran her hand over the elaborate box design. The wood was smooth and soft, bent into the curve of a roof and arched high into a miniature cathedral-like dome. The bird jumped to the other side; wherever her hand touched, the creature retreated in quick response.

'She is so delicate.'

'You can train it to leave the cage and sit on your shoulder. But we must be careful she does not throw herself against a closed window.'

Annie reached in to the cage and placed a small pot of water on the floor. She tried not to bang her hand against the bars but it was impossible and the bird flew against her skin; she felt its tiny beak. The peck was insignificant but it felt as though the bird had marked her and for a ridiculous moment as it hopped along the swing, that it was making room for Annie. She placed the cage where the bird could hear the garden sounds, and feel the breeze through the doors. It flew around frantically. The space was too small; its little body seemed to move more quickly than ever as it found the boundaries of its home and back again.

'It feels cruel to keep her caged.'

'This is all she has ever known. I am sure you have seen the birds in the market. This one will have a good life with you and now you have a companion. Bird song is a happy sound.'

'Thank you, what a beautiful thing to do for me. I will take good care of her. Now, tell me news of the Club. What are the ladies up to?'

Chow settled himself opposite Annie on the cane chair. He accepted the cold glass of sarsaparilla which the house boy brought without being asked. Annie smiled at the familiarity which had evolved between the two. She shook her head when he offered her a glass and sat back into the sofa, eager to hear Chow's news.

'It is still very quiet. The fear stops many from going out, different to your own.' He nodded respectfully in acknowledgement of Annie's self-imposed house arrest. The way he made it seem normal allowed Annie to relax. She knew she couldn't stay at home forever, but Chow's daily visit enabled her to put off thinking about it.

'It must be strange not to have them all milling about at the Club. How do you spend your time?'

'Well, as of tomorrow, I may be busy again. Admiral Marsden is fed up with his Club being empty so he is inviting people to a special evening of cocktails and dancing to reinvigorate the community, as he puts it. He is inviting some members of the Chinese community also, as a show of collaboration and unity. I wonder if you may feel able to attend?'

'I don't know, Chow; it sounds like a grand affair. When is it?'

'It is next week.'

'That's very soon. I can feel my heart begin to race just thinking about it.'

'Mrs Brand, do you think that perhaps it is time you rejoined your society? I am sure Captain Brand would not want you to hide away at home forever. If you will allow me to escort you out for a walk, you will find the streets in the Settlement are well protected. I have walked to your house each day to make sure. Will you let me do this for you?'

'You've been walking here each day to check my street. Chow, I had no idea. You are so kind to me.'

'It is my duty, and my pleasure.'

'You've become such a dear friend; I asked you once before to call me Annie. Please call me by my name.'

'Well then, Annie, what do you say; shall we venture out together?'

'Very well.' She smiled. 'But I can't guarantee I will go far.'

The next afternoon Annie waited nervously for Chow. She was ready early, in her long coat and wide-brimmed hat. She opened the front door at the sound of footsteps clipping past her house, but closed it again when there was no sign of Chow. The house boy ran out, thinking he'd been lax in his job, but walked slowly back to the kitchen when he saw it was only his mistress in her skittishness.

When Chow did arrive, Annie linked her arm through his and grasped his hand with her other arm. Despite the heat, she was cold. She turned back as the gate creaked shut and for a moment stood still. Her house had settled into the warm flood of afternoon sun, the trees were still in the breezeless air, it was all very normal. She felt Chow's gentle press.

'Shall we go?'

They wandered along Carter Street and took the turn that led them away from Nanking Road. Chow chose their route without asking. He talked about the weather, and pointed to where a cat lay sunning itself. Annie pressed closer to him when a group pushed past but they were gone in a moment and Chow kept walking and her heartbeat slowed. He hesitated at the next corner and Annie saw that just ahead of them a small crowd was gathered outside a shop.

'What is it?' She couldn't keep the panic out of her voice.

'Just people waiting to buy hot water from the tiger stove shop. That is all, nothing to alarm us. But we can turn around if you are not comfortable?'

The tiger stove was a large wooden barrel on top of an oversized wok, and there were four smaller boilers right in front of the big one. A fire of coal dust and wood chips smouldered beneath the cement tabletop. The queue moved forward and customers jostled to place their container onto the long wooden table in front of the small boilers where a man ladled boiling water into each one. Annie felt her body stiffen despite the fact no one paid them any attention. Voices rose and fell in the general melee of conversation.

'We can keep going,' she sounded overly bright but she repeated herself. 'Let's keep walking, Chow.' The words were a challenge to her own nerves. She wanted to be able to walk in the streets again without feeling this fog of fear. Chow nodded and they began to move past the queue. She felt his arm move protectively across where she held onto him. The heat from the stove blanketed them both. Then Annie accidentally bumped an old woman who shuffled slowly along the line. Her metal pot banged onto the footpath noisily, and the water hissed and splashed. Annie froze. She could hear the grandmother's incomprehensible ranting but a grey haze blurred her sight. The heat off the fire pressed into her skin. The woman was shouting and the noise was unbearable. It brought a Sikh constable running to them from his position on the road. He grabbed the old woman, twisting her arm painfully so that she was forced to fall to the ground. He was adamant she apologise. Annie's head filled with blood and a flash of shame ran through her.

'How dare you treat her like that? Help the old lady up immediately.' The authority in her voice came fast and strong. 'I will report you to your superior if you do not assist this woman right now.'

The policeman did as he was told before marching back to his position directing traffic without so much as a nod to Annie. In his hand he carried the metal pot. Chow ran after him and Annie didn't call him back. Instead she turned and offered her handkerchief to the poor woman. She had no right to be mistreated, she was someone's mother, but respect had clearly disappeared in the streets these days and moments like this one seemed to escalate too easily. Annie stood back since the woman was ignoring her offer of a handkerchief. She heard the egg crack on her back before she felt the wet yolk sliding down her leg. It smelt foul; she guessed the egg was rancid. She waited for another smack of shell against her skin, but felt nothing. Then she heard the old woman shooing away some children who must have been the culprits. Chow hurried to her side with a fierce look of protection on his face, but Annie didn't feel threatened. The old lady hugged the pot Chow had returned to her and the two women looked at each other in silence.

'Come, I will take you home.' Chow spoke gently, taking hold of Annie's arm but she shrugged her shoulders. The afternoon had not turned dark and troublesome and the queuing customers were not interested in the foreign lady and her companion; there was nothing to fear.

'Children's games—if only I had an egg to return fire.' As she smiled her shoulders dropped and Annie realised her fear had gone. She looked about as they walked home and breathed in the welcome smell of sweet jasmine that trailed a stone wall. She plucked a sprig; it was good to be out again.

'Will you be at the Club on the night of the cocktail party?'

'Of course.' Chow led her through the gate.

'Then I will be there too.'

CHAPTER TEN

Annie spent longer getting ready for the cocktail party the following Friday, pairing her cream dress with just the right shade of sapphire earrings. She smudged her lips with a deeper red than was her usual and stood back to admire the warmth the colour gave to the rest of her face. Her bird twittered a final song as the evening closed in around them and a rattling noise sounded from the bird's cage; Annie knew it meant the house boy was covering it with a cloth. She considered her reflection; a photo snapped before the girl was ready. Those red lips warmed her eyes but couldn't cloak her pain.

'Be quiet,' she whispered to the bird that was already silent. 'Be quiet.' She grabbed a cotton handkerchief and roughly wiped the red from her lips. Then she stepped out of the dress and threw it to the floor. There was the naked face she recognised. She chose a black velvet dress instead and wore it unadorned by jewellery or makeup.

Even though strict curfews still applied, the Marsden's subdued party at the Club was anticipated with excitement. It would be a show of strength to the rabble-rousers. There were fairy lights strung along the high perimeter wall, and through the trees that lined the curved driveway from the outer gates to the Club's entrance. The lights disguised the barbed wire. Annie held a damp handkerchief to her forehead. A breeze played amongst the trees, making it appear to the guests as though the fairy lights were dancing to the music that wafted out from wide-open doors. A chorus of voices sang out a tune loudly and Annie took one last, deep breath before moving inside.

In the ladies' lounge, she sipped on champagne and looked around the familiar room, busy with women finding friends while others stood together and swayed to the sounds of their piano-mad musician. There was an older Chinese lady standing in a group by the window, dressed in western style, and a few more Chinese women dotted amongst the Flues. None of them had an inkling of the tremors that shook Annie. This had been Alec's favourite place and she felt off-balance without him beside her. She held her glass with two hands to stop the shaking. It felt like she'd drunk three champagnes in quick succession.

The lounge was alive with people talking and drinking. Mrs Marsden was in a bright pink dress, amongst a group being entertained by a Chinese businessman. He said something which made Mrs Marsden hide her face behind a fan coquettishly. Annie looked more closely and saw it was the same man she had seen at the May Ball, dancing with Natalia. Mrs Marsden was putting on a very good show of enjoying his company, Annie thought. The man bowed and moved on to a group of gentlemen, where he accepted a cigar. Soft rings of smoke spiralled into the air.

Admiral Marsden walked towards her and she didn't offer her cheek in welcome.

'Mrs Brand, I am extremely glad to see you up and about. The last time we met was …' his voice trailed off. 'Yes well, er, we won't dwell on that.'

'The last time you saw me was at Alec's funeral, Admiral Marsden, correct.' Annie drank her champagne quickly in the awkward silence that hung between them. She didn't care that he saw how her hand shook. Admiral Marsden cleared his throat but didn't speak. He lifted his glass to his lips but it was empty.

'Go and get a real drink, Admiral.' It was Natalia. The Admiral walked away quickly and Natalia chuckled. 'Good riddance to him.' Then she turned to Annie and gave her a stern look. 'Why have I not seen you in these long weeks? I wanted to look after you. Why did you refuse my visits? I feel very hurt.'

Annie held out her glass to be refilled by a hovering waiter. She closed her eyes a moment and focused on the music. Natalia poked her in the stomach.

'Ouch!'

'Well, you are ignoring me.'

'No I'm not; it's just that this is still difficult for me. All this,' she flung her arms wide and champagne sloshed from the corner of her glass. 'Alec is gone and you'd never know from all this fun. I'm the only one who cares.'

'You are wrong. We all feel very sad, it was terrible—'

Annie interrupted Natalia. 'No, I correct myself.' She pointed her finger in the air for effect. 'There is one other who cares: Chow. Did you know he's been visiting me every day?'

'No, I did not. Is this such a good idea, my friend?'

'Oh, don't you start getting all judgemental as well. He's the reason I'm here tonight. Without his support I'd probably still be in my bed.'

'In that case, I suppose we must all thank him.'

'Quite right!' Annie took a fresh glass of champagne from a passing tray and leant into Natalia as she corrected her balance. 'Have you seen the Chinese man over there? Isn't that the fellow you were with at the May Ball?'

Natalia turned her gaze to where Annie was pointing and if she felt embarrassed she didn't show it. 'He is someone I do business with occasionally. I prefer not to advertise the arrangement.'

Annie frowned. 'An arrangement?'

'Don't ask me anymore questions and I won't have to tell you.' Natalia made a slicing movement with her hand. 'Do you like my stole—it is fox. Willie gave it to me. He's such a darling. I'm very sad about how things have gone sour between us.'

'If you like him very much I could have a word with him?'

'It's easy to like a man who is so generous.'

In the tall mirror above the fireplace Annie caught sight of their reflection; the overdressed Russian and the pale brunette. She took another drink and scanned the room for Chow. Coat-tails disappeared through the adjoining door into the men's smoking lounge. Another moment and she watched the back of a waiter walk the length of the corridor in case it might be Chow. But there were too many servants, too many identical dinner jackets, and in amongst it all there was a strange quiet which Annie noticed for the first time. In the noise of her friends' conversations, while the music played and gentlemen argued, Annie felt the silence of the other people moving amongst them; taking orders, refilling glasses, emptying ashtrays.

The Chinese man looked straight at Annie and she couldn't help the shiver that ran down her spine. He was wearing a different suit tonight, but he held the silver-topped cane she'd seen him with at the ball and he tapped it on the ground as his gaze hovered on her. Something about him made Annie stare. A memory of Li Qiang being dragged to the doorway flashed into Annie's mind. Then a fuller picture emerged; she remembered the man in the side room shouting orders to the thug holding Li Qiang, the flash of silver. He had used a cane with a silver top too. Annie's chest began to pound very fast. She turned back to Natalia.

'That Chinaman, how well do you know him?'

'He is an acquaintance, nothing more. Willie will understand, I'm sure you can convince him.'

'That's not why I'm asking. He's got an unusual silver cane. I think I've seen it before, at the house where I went to find Li Qiang.'

'Who is this Li Qiang?'

'A waiter at the Club and a friend of mine and of Chow.' Annie spoke quickly. 'He joined a gang and was killed. I think your friend might have had something to do with his death.'

'And so the Club is now allowing murderers to its cocktail parties? I am worried about you; perhaps this evening is too much, too soon? Let me take you home?' Natalia took hold of Annie's elbow and began walking towards the door.

'No, I'm fine, really I am. I just need some air.' Annie pulled away.

'Very well then, come and find me when you're ready.' Her friend walked straight over to where William Piper stood with a group of at least ten men, the Commissioner of Police amongst them. Natalia quickly joined the conversation, listening intently to whatever the men were discussing.

Annie went out into the corridor, looking for Chow. He was standing at the main door, formally welcoming each guest, even these latecomers. For a moment she stood and watched him. He turned in surprise at her tap on his shoulder.

'I must speak with you, it's urgent.'

Chow turned away from the door, first talking quickly to a member of staff to ensure that someone took his place. Then he led her to the cloakroom and sent the attendee to look for a coat. They were alone, for a few moments.

'How are you faring this evening? Is something wrong?'

'Yes, I think so, I'm not sure.' She blinked as the room tilted. Chow moved to the opening of the doorway so they were in public view.

'You are not well; it is time to go home.' He began panelling through the coats, looking for Annie's.

'I'm fine. But I must talk to you.' She took hold of Chow's arm, but let go immediately when she saw him stiffen and the muscles in his neck tense.

'Please, Mrs Brand,' his whispered breath curved over her cheekbone. She raised her hand to touch the spot, and he grabbed at her wrist, continuing in a sterner tone. 'You should not be so familiar with me in the Club. Here, we are two different worlds.' Annie's veins began to pulse with the pressure of his hold. Neither of them spoke. But in that moment she felt as though all of her was held within his grasp. Then Chow let her go, and at the very instant his arm dropped to his side she knew it was not what she wanted.

Annie stepped back, confused and shocked. Where did these feelings come from? Her arm still throbbed where Chow had held her; she felt a warmth flood through her whole body.

'Boy, I say you there, fetch my coat. Chop, chop.'

A man's voice broke the intimacy of the moment. Chow looked quickly at Annie, and then dropped his eyes to the ground as he disappeared into the cloakroom.

'Annie, I didn't see you standing there. Don't hide behind the counter, leave the coats to the coolies.' Annie walked away, holding to the wall a moment before entering the lounge. She didn't want to be there when Chow returned with Edward Mantree's coat.

Annie hovered by the door as she formed a smile on her lips and, reaching for a glass of champagne, joined Natalia. Her body swayed slightly as she listened to Willie Piper's story. A waiter offered a tray of champagne and Annie took a fresh glass. She scanned the room for the Chinese man but couldn't see him amongst the guests.

The champagne fizzed and popped in her glass. She needed another drink.

Her eyes searched the room, from the gentlemen leaning against the marble fireplace, to the ladies by the baby grand, swaying their hips to 'Crazy Blues'. She spotted a waiter and raised her hand to get his attention, but someone else stopped the man.

'Call him over would you, Willie, I'm dying of thirst here.'

He snapped his fingers and whistled. It was garish but effective and for once Annie didn't care. As long as there was more champagne she could cope. She lifted a glass for herself and one for Natalia. The champagne sent a welcome flush of heat to her head as Natalia turned her round in a pirouette. She stumbled and her head began to spin again. The waiter hovered a moment as though to help but she was too drunk to notice. It was only as Natalia walked her to the window for some fresh air that she saw it was Chow who stood aside to let them pass, tall and proud, one hand balancing the tray of crystal perfectly as he watched her.

She couldn't sleep that night. The sheets caught around her legs and under her back, knotting her into a mummified plank. She rolled herself out of the bed onto the floor. For a moment she lay there, legs pressed into the cold wood, wondering how long she could continue in this ghost of a life.

In the kitchen she put some milk on the stove to heat and sat at the table waiting. The silence of the house was broken only by the flash and spit of the gas flames on the stovetop. Since last night when she'd recognised the Chinaman, the image of Li Qiang being dragged to fall at her feet wouldn't leave her. If only she'd told Chow, but thinking about Chow made her feel even more jumbled. The milk murmured in the pot as it began a slow boil. Annie hoped it would help her to sleep. Warm milk had always been a comfort. It was part of the winter night's ritual she'd shared with Judy when she'd let her little sister take the hot drink to bed and they'd snuggle together under the covers telling stories. Moving about the kitchen, picking a teaspoon from the drawer, turning off the stovetop, pouring the milk straight from the saucepan into her cup, all this made Annie feel better. The teaspoon hung in the air as she remembered the pained look in Chow's eyes in the cloakroom. He had been there every day and he was there last night, worrying about her even when she'd behaved appallingly.

It was well past breakfast when Annie eventually awoke the next morning. Her bedroom was a torrential mess; last night's dress thrown over the wardrobe's open door; her shoes haphazardly balanced against each other on the floor where she'd tipped out of them; the sheets pushed back and down in a heap.

The house boy knocked nervously before entering.

'Missy, Chow come look see.'

Annie sat up quickly. What was Chow doing visiting her at this time? She hurriedly bathed and dressed. Chow was sitting in the sunroom, his glass of sarsaparilla finished by the time Annie appeared. He stood quickly and bowed.

'Please excuse my uninvited intrusion. I came to see how you are? I think you were not well last night?' Annie saw the veins on his arms pulse. She gestured to him to sit.

'That's one way of putting it. My behaviour was unacceptable, I'm so sorry. I was overwhelmed by memories and it was the first drink I'd had in ages. Can you forgive me?'

'There is no need to ask.' He handed her a pair of gloves. 'May I return these?'

She took her gloves; the silk felt cool and soft. 'They've already been cleaned.'

'I would not return dirty items to you.'

Annie sat and as she did Chow came to stand beside her. His hand was on the back of her chair, she felt his body right there. As he leant in to pour her a glass of sarsaparilla, the ring on his finger clinked against the bottle. The sound made her catch her breath.

'You have been so kind to me during these last few weeks.' As she spoke she played with the gloves, lining up the fingers and smoothing the slippery silk. 'There is something I wanted to tell you last night before we were interrupted.'

'You had many glasses of champagne and it did not agree with you.'

'No, there was something else ...' Annie paused. 'Last night at the Club, I'm sure I saw a man who was in the house where I found Li Qiang. He was the boss, barking orders at the thug who was holding the boy.'

Chow played with the ring on his finger before speaking, revealing a glimpse of tattoo ink as it spun. 'This is a serious accusation.'

Annie called for the house boy to clear their glasses. Then she turned back to Chow.

'It was him, I'm sure of it.'

'Then I will relay your information to Admiral Marsden and we will let the police take over from here.'

'Thank god you believe me, Chow! You've no idea what a relief it is to finally do something right by Li Qiang, at least for his family.'

Chow picked up the book of Yeats she had left on the table and opened the cover. Even with his jacket still on, she could see the pull of his muscles.

'I have seen you many times with this book. Do you wish for cloths of heaven?'

The question took her by surprise, but it was like a slip of silk in a line of poetry to bind them. She felt her breathing slow and a weight of certainty settled in her belly.

'I didn't know you liked poetry?'

'There is much we do not know about each other.' Chow spoke softly as he placed the book into her hands. 'Of course, that is as it should be.' He was so close, Annie held her breath. Then his finger grazed her palm. It was only a moment really, but she felt alive.

'You must let me thank you for all you've done since Alec passed away.'

'There is no need; I am here because I want to help you, not through any obligation.' His words were polite but there was something in his gaze that made her insides flurry like snowflakes in a gathering storm.

'I was considering going for a drive today.' She hesitated for just a second. 'Would you join me?'

'Where would you like to go, Annie?'

'Why don't you decide, Chow, this is your city.' Chow stood and ambled over to where the bird sat on its swing in the bamboo cage. He bent and whistled encouragingly through the bars, digging his hands into his pockets as he thought. Then he swung back to Annie and for a brief moment she was conscious of an inexplicable excitement.

'Well then, we'd better get started.' His eyes glinted with pleasure.

She watched him follow her out to the car, tall and slim, legs swinging purposefully as he shrugged his jacket on and dug his hands into the pockets again. It was as though she was seeing the man for the first time; strong, confident, charming.

The car wound its way through strange streets on the outskirts of the International Settlement. It reminded Annie of the area around the old town where Chow had taken her and Natalia. 'We will soon be past these streets and out into the green of the riverside. I am taking you to a very special place for me, somewhere I have enjoyed visiting since I was a young man and first arrived in Shanghai. You will like it, I am confident.'

He smiled and wound down the window. There was a freedom in the movement which Annie hadn't seen before. Chow had taken off his jacket and his fitted linen shirt draped smoothly across his chest. He lit a cigarette, offering it to Annie. She shook her head and watched him smoke it instead. Outside the scenery shifted from dirty stone alleys to open grassland and Annie peered out of the window and breathed in deeply.

They stopped at a deserted spot beside the river. The water spread like a vast living canvas before them. It was impossible to tell how fast the river moved; its glassy surface belied no current. Here there was no smog from factories, no sampans tied to the shoreline. Annie marvelled at the privacy of this locale.

'How did you find such a secluded part of the river?'

'This is a place very few ever find—you must know the right people to be brought here.'

Beyond them the thicket of reeds whispered as a breeze rustled in the banks of the river. Annie breathed in the luxury of open space and took off her shoes. Her fine silk stockings caught the sunlight and glinted as she laid them out beside her. The sky was clear and high. She felt weightless below it, freed of expectations.

Chow sat beside her and pointed towards the river, where it disappeared in the distance ahead. 'My home is far away, a village many miles from here.'

'Do you miss it?'

'I cannot afford to, it's my duty to work in Shanghai and send money to my family.' Chow paused and turned to face Annie. 'There are other reasons why I stay in Shanghai.'

Annie ran her hands through the grass. The sensation was soft and tingled. She felt Chow watching her and she left her hand there, in the grass beside him, where her body waited.

'Is the water cold?'

His eyes creased as he laughed. 'Oh yes, the water is cold and invigorating, good for the soul. Would you like me to test it for you?' He stood and began to take off his shirt.

'Enough, enough,' Annie begged teasingly as she looked away. But when she turned back, Chow was already striding towards the reeds. He stopped and turned; lines of muscle moving thickly across his back as he stretched out his hand in invitation to join him. She shook her head, laughing with the shock of seeing his half-naked torso. Annie knew what she was feeling was forbidden. A heat flushed deep within her body. She couldn't stop watching him.

In the water, Chow dived under and swam out from the shallow verge. His rolling arms broke the surface in rhythmic splashes.

'Swim back to me.'

But Annie didn't really want him to stop. She sat up and leant forward to see how far out he'd gone. A twinge of concern made her strain her neck; deep water always made her nervous. But Chow was in no trouble. The joyous freedom of his swimming was intoxicating. He rolled onto his back as she watched, and waved at her. He dived and dipped, showing off his style and Annie clapped and laughed. She wondered if he knew what he was doing, did either of them.

Later, he joined her on the hillside above the riverline.

'I believe I will remember this day for all time.' She rolled onto her side to face him. 'Thank you for bringing me here.'

'It was your suggestion, remember? I should be thanking you.' Chow shook his hair about as he spoke and drops of water splashed on Annie's shoulder and cheek. She felt a glorious liberation with each cold dash; as though all the rules she was brought up to follow were swept away. She laughed for the pure joy of the moment, raising her arms in mock protection from the shower of water.

Chow stretched back into the grass and closed his eyes. Annie traced the line of him, down through his neck and shoulder blades to the delicate muscle contours outlined across his torso. She wanted to touch his skin. Water droplets were suspended in his eyelashes. She could just see his fingertips pressed into his thick, dark hair. His wet trousers clung to his thighs, already drying at the ends so that the colour changed to a dark shade of water at the waistband.

Then Chow propped himself up on one elbow, hanging over her. His eyes were smiling, little lines creasing up around each one like the sun's rays warming to her. Only a slim line of grass separated them but Annie thought about how much lay between them. Then he moved her hair, pulled a curl through his fingers and tucked it into another one, clearing her face. She followed his hands with her eyes as he reached for her and she felt the rise and fall of his breath in the slight movement of his wrists as he gently traced each line on her open palm.

'Beautiful girl,' he said and kissed her. She arched her neck so she felt the kiss in her body. And she hung, suspended in that space with him where only the feeling of the moment mattered.

CHAPTER ELEVEN

With Chow, Annie didn't have to protect herself from memories; the only storyline they needed was each other; the past was never questioned, nor the future talked about. He slipped into her life easily, as though there had always been a place waiting for him beside her.

Annie soaped her arms and lay back in the warm water of her tub, waiting for Chow's daily visit. They had fallen into an easy routine. Chow came to her house at whatever time he was able, with a nod to the house boy who let him in and then disappeared. Annie listened to the melodic drip of the tap. She rubbed the condensation off the brass with her toe and the water splashed over the edge as she slipped back down to rest her head on the rim. How far away she felt from the wife who'd sat in this bath nervously contemplating her husband's presence. Alec was gone and she missed him every day but now, waiting for Chow to arrive, happiness stirred in Annie.

There was a knock and she hurriedly slipped on a dressing gown before letting Chow in. He'd come straight from work. The formality of his dress coat made her picture him serving the Flues in the Club. She pulled him towards her and tugged on his sleeves, shaking the coat off. Then she stood back, admiring him. There was a dry patch on her bottom lip that her finger caught on as she brushed across it. Chow held out his arms, his head cocked to one side. She unclasped the small ivory cufflinks on each of his wrists, kissing the soft underside of skin as she freed them. Then she slowly undid each button on his crisp white shirt. He stood before her, half naked, a mixture of surprise and pleasure playing on his lips. Annie met his gaze. The silk dressing gown clung to her body.

'If you catch me, you can wear this,' she taunted him, holding her arms out wide so that the deep blue floated away from her. Then she turned and ran down the corridor, the material flying behind her like a kite. She squealed at the sound of his feet on the floorboards. He caught her quickly, wrapping his arms around her so that all she could smell was him and the freshly cleaned silk.

Annie's thighs pushed against Chow's. They lay on her bed, the curtains drawn so that a shaded afternoon light surrounded them. He reached inside her dressing gown and she felt the heat of his hands on her stomach. His finger lightly trailed up from her bellybutton and circled her nipple. The liquid pleasure of his touch was overwhelming. She arched her back and the dressing gown slid to the floor. He kissed her small breasts roughly and she groaned and pushed against him. Then his warm breath was on her cheek as he traced the line of her face and neck, bringing his forefinger to rest in the little pool of skin where her collar bone dipped; she felt her pulse through his finger. Annie squirmed and slid her hand around the nape of Chow's neck, pulling him closer until there was nothing between them except the taste of each other.

Later, they sat together while eggs bubbled in a pot on the kitchen stove. He perched on a stool in the black-blue dressing gown that folded over his legs to the floor like seeping ink. She fed him a ball of deep yellow yolk and he held onto her wrist a moment.

'My beautiful bird,' he whispered, kissing her.

She noticed dried blood caught under his nails.

'You've hurt yourself?'

'No, silly thing, it's just red paint. I thought I'd cleaned it all away.'

'What have you been painting?'

'We are short of staff at the Club with so many afraid to come to work, so I am getting my hands dirty as they say.'

The house boy coughed discreetly behind them and Annie stood quickly.

'Yes, what is it?'

'Lady visit come see.'

'A visitor? I wasn't expecting anyone. Tell her wait, we'll have tea in the lounge.' Annie hurriedly disappeared to change. Chow threw off the dressing gown and rolled it into a ball before retrieving his shirt and pants from the corridor where they'd fallen. He hovered by the lounge room door, out of sight.

Annie dressed quickly, wondering who was waiting for her. The state of emergency meant there were very few foreigners out and about, and Annie was surprised one of them would take the trouble to call on her at home. She cursed softly as she mismatched the buttons on her shirt and had to start again. She certainly hadn't entertained for quite some time. She tucked her curls tightly behind each ear and assessed her reflection in the mirror. It would have to do.

Before entering the lounge, she stopped, pressing her finger to her lips in silence as Chow moved towards her. She peeped into the room. Mrs Ilma Pitt stood in front of her escritoire, admiring the wooden figurines. Annie's chest dropped with a relieved laugh as she quickly went to greet the older lady.

'Mrs Pitt, what an unexpected and wonderful surprise. How good to see you.' Annie clasped Ilma's hands in her own.

'Mrs Brand, my dear.' Ilma's sympathetic expression told Annie she knew about Alec.

'You don't need to say anything.'

'What a waste of a young life. I only wish I had been here to comfort you.'

'Well, you are here now. Tell me, why are you in Shanghai?' There was a cough at the door and Annie saw Chow, waiting expectantly.

'Please, come in. Mrs Pitt, this is Chow, my friend and the maître d' at the Maritime Club in Shanghai. He was visiting me when you arrived.' Chow shook Mrs Pitt's hand before taking a seat on the edge of the sofa. 'Some tea will be here shortly,' Annie continued quickly. She turned her attention back to the older lady. 'Do tell me what brings you to Shanghai, Mrs Pitt?'

'Like you, my dear Annie, I have lost a loved one. Fred passed away a month ago.'

'I am so very sorry to hear that. I know how close the two of you were.'

'Indeed, my body is still whole but I am not. So I find myself in Shanghai, as there is no longer a home for me in Ichang. The Club has a new manager who needed accommodation so I had to leave. Unfortunately, Fred and I made no retirement plans beyond the Club.'

'What will you do now?'

'I dread the thought of returning to England, so I must sort out something here.'

'If you need somewhere to stay you are very welcome in my home. There is more space than one widow needs.'

'I have taken a room at the Maritime Club for a month, as of today, and I can't think further than that for now, but thank you.'

The tea arrived and gave the three a reprieve from conversation. Annie looked from Chow to Mrs Pitt and wondered what the old lady made of him.

'Are you from Shanghai, Mr Chow?' Mrs Pitt asked politely.

'No, I am from a village in the north. But I have lived in Shanghai for some time.' He stood. 'Ladies, if you will excuse me, it is time I left. Thank you for the tea.' Annie walked Chow to the door. She felt Mrs Pitt's gaze upon them.

'It's been a pleasure seeing you, goodbye.' She curled her fingers through Chow's hand a moment, resting her palm in the warmth of his before watching him go.

Annie sat beside Ilma on the sofa and took both her hands once more. 'How are you, really?'

'Surviving, my dear, although I never wanted to out-live Fred. I scattered his ashes across the river before leaving Ichang and it feels as though I left myself behind with him.'

Annie thought about her own experience. Alec's funeral had been a subdued Shanghai affair held in Holy Trinity Cathedral. She had sat between various Flues and listened to Admiral Marsden give the eulogy. The day was a blur; she remembered the hard wooden pew pressing into her back and the hollow sound the handful of earth made when it hit the wooden boards of Alec's coffin. It reminded her of scattering seeds in the house garden at home, such a long time ago.

'You will find your way through this, just as I have.'

Ilma patted Annie's hand. 'Yes, I will. One must accept death, however much one rails against the grief. So, I will try not to be maudlin.' She got up and closed the door into the hallway before sitting down again beside Annie.

'Tell me, what is going on in your life?' Ilma's question sounded innocent but her raised eyebrows implied otherwise.

For a moment, Annie froze. She hadn't told a soul about Chow. But she edged forward on her seat and rubbed her damp palms roughly against her skirt. She closed her eyes and Chow's face came before her with a wash of certainty.

'I've fallen in love with a Chinaman, with Chow in fact.' She took a deep breath and opened her eyes. 'There, I've said it.'

'I might have been surprised had I not met Chow just now, and seen the two of you together, but never judgemental; you would remember that about me, I hope? There's an electricity that pulses between the two of you, even as you walked him to the door, I felt it.'

'So you're not shocked? I can't quite believe it. I haven't told a soul, you see. I truly expected you to be appalled, yet I couldn't keep the secret from you.' Annie sat back and let her head fall against the soft cushions. There was something luxurious about having confessed.

'He's given you life again and passion. Perhaps I need a lover too?' Ilma laughed until the sound became a croak in her throat. 'Age does not favour the idea I fear.' Then she leant forward and grasped Annie's hands. Her mouth pressed into a firm line. 'Unfortunately, my opinion is not the one you need to worry about. Do you plan on going public with this affair? My dear, have you thought seriously about what this will mean for your future?'

The future; it struck Annie like a blow across the face. Chow would be part of her future; she didn't doubt for one second that he'd agree with her and, Annie realised with clarity and relief, she wasn't worried about living with Chow in Shanghai. It was her home now because this was where Chow belonged, so she would too.

'I'll be quite relieved to stop pretending that I agree with all the patronising ignorance of the Club ladies. I won't have to stay silent any longer when they insult the Chinese. I can cook and clean and shop—I did all that before coming to China. I actually might enjoy feeling tired at the end of the day rather than just too bored to stay up.' She turned to Ilma with a shrug of her shoulders.

'Don't make fun, it's not that simple, and you know it. Before you start living this idyllic life you first have to survive the scandal and the judgement of all your peers. You'll be banished from every social circle in China, life will never be the same, and it will be a very difficult and poor life at that.'

'I'm not afraid, Ilma. Didn't you once say that knowing where home is makes you stronger and that with your husband at your side, you could suffer any criticism? Well, I've found my home here with Chow and I can face anything the future throws at me with him by my side. He's my Fred.' How easily she'd spoken the truth, yet it had taken so long to find it.

'This will be the biggest challenge you are ever likely to face.'

Ilma was right. Annie hoped she was strong enough to withstand the gossip and the hatred they would elicit, from her Club world and Chow's world. She knew so little about his family. But she would ask him to tell her about his childhood; it was time to share her own story too.

'Your support means the world to me, Ilma. If Shanghai won't accept us, then we will just have to find somewhere else to live. You did.'

'I may be eccentric, but I'm English, and so was Fred. There is no comparison to you and this Chinese man. My dear, the only foreign women I've heard of being with natives are in the brothels.'

'I've made so many mistakes before now; but I won't give up on this chance with Chow. He's a good man.'

'I believe you, but I will be the only one who does. Are you sure you are ready to give up on the life you know?'

'What life, Ilma? I'm a widow with no children and no home. I don't belong anywhere anymore.'

'Very well, my dear, I will help you if I can but I do hope you know what you are doing.' Ilma stood up and stretched her arms back. 'My old body is stiff; I can't sit still for long anymore. Would you pass me the pot of tiger balm in my purse? I find if I rub it into my wrists it helps the aches.'

Annie opened Ilma's bag and pushed aside handkerchiefs and packages looking for the pot of cream. The purse was a disorganised mess and she tried not to take any notice of the papers as she rummaged around, searching for the tiger balm.

'Finally, here it is.' Annie's hands caught hold of cold glass and she pulled out the pot. As she did a leaflet fluttered to the ground too. She saw the familiar colours of the Moral Welfare League.

'Do you mind if I take a look at this?' She held it out for Ilma to see.

'Not at all, I've been a member of the League for years but not in Shanghai so I'm looking forward to attending this month's meeting. They've finally managed to get rid of most of the opium hongs and brothels inside the International Settlement. It's very impressive.' Ilma chuckled as she rubbed her palm over her wrist, massaging in the tiger balm. The cream was so strong Annie's eyes began to sting. Annie opened the pamphlet. She already knew most of what was written inside—of Shanghai's dangerous gangs and debauchery; the bars and brothels which serviced the floating population of seamen, never their own men of course. But it reminded Annie that Chow hadn't told her how his conversation with the police went. She thought by now they would have at least taken the Chinaman in for questioning and Chow would certainly have told her if they had. But he hadn't mentioned it since that day.

'I'm hoping the League will help me with the programme in Ichang and encourage the local men who are now in Shanghai to go home to their villages. It's just getting worse and worse—the numbers leaving for Shanghai to join the Green Gang is terrible. I befriended a boy who got me a copy of the tattoo which the local river gang uses. He thought he was humouring an old woman's painting hobby,' Ilma chuckled again. 'But I'm taking it to the meeting. Hopefully it will make it easier to find the Ichang men and with the help of our programme, encourage them to go home.'

Annie took the small square of paper which Ilma held out. The tattoo symbol was innocuous as an image; she imagined it would be a dragon or some other intimidating animal. But it was beautiful, the small fish turning as though in the water, with each scale symmetrically placed.

She'd seen the image before, on the silver cane of the Chinaman. She distinctly remembered it because he'd been so rude and garish, brandishing his cane in her face that evening at the Club.

'Are you sure this is a Green Gang tattoo?'

'Yes, I told you the local river gang in Ichang sends our young men to the Green Gang in Shanghai and this is the branding they all receive before they leave.'

'Can I hold onto it for a few days? It could be very important.' Annie knew she had to get this information to the police. It proved beyond doubt that the Chinaman was in the Green Gang, from Ichang of all places. When this new development was coupled with the information she'd already given to the police which put the Chinaman in the house with Li Qiang the day he died, then it seemed to Annie there was a good chance he would be charged with murder.

'Is it that important, Annie?'

'I promise to get the picture back to you, Ilma, but right now I really need to get this to the police. It may be an important clue in the murder of a young boy I knew.'

Ilma nodded. 'The meeting isn't until next week so just get it to me by then; I've come a long way with this bit of paper not to lose it at the last minute!'

Annie hurried out of the room and called for the house boy as she scribbled a note and quickly slipped it into an envelope along with the leaflet. She told the house boy to take it directly to the Commissioner of Police and gave him two coppers. When she'd seen the boy off in a rickshaw, Annie returned to where Ilma sat waiting in the lounge room.

'I'm sorry I took so long but I could not hold on to that knowledge a moment more. It may not make any difference, but I feel at least I've done the right thing, finally.'

Ilma left soon after. She seemed shorter than the last time they'd met, Annie thought, as she helped her friend on with her coat. The smell of tiger balm was still strong.

'I haven't told another living soul about Chow yet. Please keep my news private, Ilma, until Chow and I have decided together what to do.' Annie kissed her friend goodbye and stayed by the door watching the car recede. Her stomach rumbled and she realised she hadn't eaten anything since the eggs with Chow earlier. Annie poured herself a large glass of sherry and wandered through to the sunroom. In its cage, her bird jumped noisily around. She opened the latch and it flitted back against the bars; foolish thing. She felt an overwhelming desire to free it.

'Come on, out you go, find your way.' She gently gathered the bird into her hand, stroking its head with her fingers.

Annie laid her palm flat and the bird darted quickly up to the ceiling before landing on the back of a chair. It cocked its head from side to side. Its feathers quivered with nervous energy and its breast throbbed visibly. The French doors were open and Annie moved quickly to close them but before she could the bird shot through and was gone. She watched from her back doors, but it was dark now and she couldn't see amongst the trees and open space in her garden. The bird had disappeared.

An hour later, the house boy found Annie still sitting in the sunroom, with the empty birdcage beside her. He gave her a note from the Commissioner. Annie read quickly; it was unexpected. The Commissioner had no knowledge of her claims against the Chinaman. Indeed, he said it would be highly presumptuous of a servant to even think he could approach the Commissioner of Police, let alone with an accusation against a well-known local businessman. But the Commissioner reassured Annie that now he had this information he would speak to the Chinaman. He admitted that the chances of an investigation were slim though, unless Li Qiang's sister was brave enough to name her Green Gang contact and in his experience this never happened. Annie was confused. She read the note a second time but the Commissioner's words were clear; he had no idea what she was talking about. Chow had not done as he said he would.

At least the police now knew about the Chinaman, Annie thought as she gathered a rug around her knees and folded her legs up into the seat. The house boy brought her supper and she ate in the quiet of her sunroom. But her mind spun; why hadn't Chow spoken to the police? She would ask him when he visited the next day.

A knock at the door roused Annie late that night. She lay, still and alert, at first thinking she had misheard and it was just her house creaking. But when the knock repeated more loudly and insistently she could not ignore it. She turned on the hall light and walked softly to the front door, holding her breath.

'Annie, Annie, let me in.'

The sound of Chow's voice was a shock. She pulled open the door and caught him as he fell towards her. He had been badly beaten.

'Dear boy,' she whispered. 'What happened?'

But before he could answer she led him through to the kitchen and gently sat him down to clean the blood and cuts. Chow pushed her hands away, embarrassed to have her tending to him, but he wasn't strong enough to persist and gave up.

'My god, who did this to you?' She cried as she wiped away the blood and dirt. He took her hand and stopped her still.

'I am all right, it is not so bad. Look at me, I am all right.'

For a long while neither of them spoke. Annie cleaned Chow's wounds methodically, squeezing the cloth tightly after each application as the bowl filled with pinkish water.

He told her quietly, slowly, how a group had set on him as he left the Club, calling him a flea on the foreign dog's back. He tried to fight them off but they were strong and outnumbered him. Some of the blood she wiped away was not his own. She heard his indrawn breath.

'I'm sorry if this hurts. Come with me.' She held Chow's hand and led him through her bedroom and into her bathroom, locking the door behind them. They sat in silence on the tiled floor, listening to the water fill the tub. Then she undressed him, hesitating only a moment as she pushed his trousers down to his ankles. He stepped naked into the bath. She washed his face, his back, his hair. Then she undressed and got in. The sound of water echoed around the tiled room. They sat half submerged at opposite ends of the tub, eyes closed, listening to the other's silence.

'Chow,' she paused, trying to find the right words. 'What are we doing?'

'Listening to the night, my bird, and being together.'

'What do you want from me?'

'I want to make you laugh, beautiful girl, silly question. I want to make you happy.' He reached across and found her hand in the water. 'I want you to be safe also, Annie. I am worried that being with me is not safe for you.' She heard the shift in his tone.

'You have saved me from danger more than once, Chow. When I am with you I feel completely protected.'

'Why don't you go to the hills for the remainder of the summer? It is becoming dangerous for us to be together.'

'Were you beaten up because of me?'

Chow looked at his hands as he spoke. 'This is not your fault. You must trust me, Annie, it would be better if you left Shanghai for a while.'

'Why?'

'I cannot give you a reason, do not ask me, just listen, and know that I only say this because I care about you.'

She nodded but her eyes searched Chow's for the answer he would not give. She wanted to know, too, why he hadn't gone to the police when she'd asked him. Yet even in her unease, Annie realised this was not the time for more questions. She shifted in the now cold bath as goosebumps prickled her skin, but it was Chow's secrecy which made her shiver. After the bath when she'd bandaged his wounds, they lay together on her bed, their nakedness covered with a sheet. She smelt the soap powder, tangled with him in his cleanliness. He pressed firmly against her. It sent a sliver of something like treacle through her very core, making her groan out loud. She clapped her hand to her mouth, surprised at herself. He wasn't kissing her. He rubbed and pushed and moved his finger into her wetness and she began to writhe with pleasure.

'Do you love me Chow?'

'I am here, aren't I, my bird?'

His hand stroked her face. She held it there against her cheek, kissing the palm as she tightened her grip on his wrist.

Chow left in the early hours of the morning when the empty streets could not judge them. Annie slipped back to bed and didn't wake until the house boy stood over her and spoke loudly, having given up on knocking and leaving tea beside her bed. He had another note from the Commissioner. It had arrived that morning but Annie had slept for much longer than usual. She scolded him for not waking her earlier. The poor boy disappeared with a disgruntled cluck of his tongue. Annie propped herself against the pillows as she read. They had taken the Chinaman in for questioning. Annie sat back and closed her eyes. Li Qiang's death had not been forgotten. She hadn't saved him but at least she'd helped to find his killer. It was up to the police now to put the pieces together.

With the note was the returned image of the fish tattoo. She could give it back to Ilma. Annie rolled over and didn't bother to wipe away the tears. An enormous sadness welled up in her for Alec and for the young boy; for all the waste.

CHAPTER TWELVE

Annie took the car to the Club. She couldn't wait until Chow finished work and came to her house to ask him why he hadn't passed on her information to the police? The brute would already have been taken in for questioning, if Chow had done as he said he would; she needed him to explain why he hadn't. A niggling disquiet still rang in her ears after their conversation in her bath the previous night. She'd seen him beaten and spooked and this was a different man to the Chow she knew.

Annie also intended on telling Natalia but that was not such a straightforward exercise; she didn't even know where her friend lived, let alone how she knew the Chinaman or what hold he had over her? So she quickly wrote a note for Natalia and left it with the desk staff. In the note Annie explained that the Chinaman was under investigation and it would be a good idea for Natalia to stay away from him. She was yet to see Chow.

As she turned back to the ladies' lounge room and some tea, Annie caught sight of herself in the mirror. She brushed her curls down firmly with the palms of her hands. It was her own fault she knew so little about Natalia, but she would change that. Annie looked about for Chow but could not see him.

Mrs Marsden was in the lounge. 'Mrs Brand, have you heard the news?' She grabbed at Annie's arm and dragged her to sit. 'Do you remember that oafish Chinaman at the May Ball? You'll never guess what the police have uncovered!' Annie waited patiently, sensing she already knew what Mrs Marsden was about to say. 'It turns out he was an underground criminal, no less! The police raided his offices early this morning and they found Communist pamphlets and the paraphernalia required to produce them. He was even paying for students to go to the Soviet Union for training, so audacious! Apparently the man's tattoo gave him away; a Green Gang insignia, can you believe it?' Mrs Marsden waved her hands in front of her face, and a mottled flush of unconstrained satisfaction flared across her chest. She leant closer to Annie. 'The Commissioner told me in strictest confidence that the man believed the Communists were a power to be reckoned with and thought he was getting in early and securing his own future. What a fool! It appears his Bolshie contact evaded capture, but at least they got the Chinaman.'

This was much more than Annie had known. She gladly took the sherry Mrs Marsden offered, going over the information in her head. So the Chinaman was not only a killer, he was a Communist? She took another long drink as she looked around again for Chow. The cold liquid sparked in her throat. Mrs Marsden called for more drinks, but Annie excused herself and headed home; Chow was probably at her house already, impatient to share this latest news. She should have waited for him there.

But the rest of the day passed without any visitors. Annie watered her trees and picked flowers. She sat a while hoping to see her bird in one of the fruit trees but knew it was a pointless exercise. She ate a sandwich for lunch and lay with her Yeats through the afternoon, dozing when she wasn't flicking through the poems. Eventually she went for a walk, frustrated with waiting. The house boy would find her if Chow arrived while she was out, he knew her route. As she followed Carter Road to the corner Annie remembered one such walk when she'd only been in Shanghai for a few months. So much had changed since then. She'd bought a light bulb in Frenchtown only to get home and discover she couldn't use it because the French had a different volt electricity grid; a uniquely Shanghailander's conundrum. Indeed, it had only taken Annie ten minutes to walk from the shop to her home.

It started to rain as she turned for home. Streaks of water formed patterns in the roads. Strangers moved through the rainy shadows; it was busy in the streets despite the wet conditions. From within the grey, she saw a familiar shape momentarily come into focus; the shoulders, the slight imbalance of weight leaning to the left—she pushed away her hair, straining to see, sure it was her father. She wanted to call out to him in the rain and wet and see him raise his face to her and spread his arms wide, as if to say, 'I forgive you, my daughter.' But the man didn't acknowledge her waving hand and the stranger kept walking into the distance.

Still, her father's face stayed with her, the familiar disappointment in his eyes. Even in Shanghai, where she'd run to, so far from home, her father's judgement followed her.

Annie rubbed down her wet hair and changed into dry clothes when she got home. The house boy scolded her for staying out in the downpour but she was glad for the wash of cold, fresh rain. Chow didn't turn up all that evening and Annie finally went to bed disappointed.

The next day she took the car to the Club. It was unusual for Chow to miss a visit and Annie was worried. She waited until the late afternoon when she hoped it would be quiet, as it was past the time of day when ladies' activities took place, so fewer Flues to bump into; Annie knew she would struggle with making small talk. There were still many police around, on every corner and outside every foreign commercial building but they were standing idly, unthreatened by the milling pedestrian crowds. She wound down the window and listened to the bubbling noise of traffic and chaos in the street. She slipped each hand into a glove as they approached the Club gates.

There were two women sitting together talking quietly and they looked up when Annie entered the ladies' lounge and acknowledged her with a nod. She moved past them to a chair by one of the long windows that overlooked the gardens and sat alone, looking out at the view. Despite the turmoil and fighting of the previous months, within the Club grounds it was as if there had only ever been trimmed lawns, clean space and quiet industry. A man raked leaves, and the image reminded Annie of so many other days when she'd sat in the Club lounge looking out at the life beyond these walls and wondered if she would ever really understand the Chinese. But with Chow as her guide, she had a chance to be on the other side of that wall and the thought filled her with excitement.

She rang the bell and waited, expecting to see Chow appear. But a waiter she didn't recognise arrived quickly and took her order for tea. She asked to see the head waiter and he disappeared. She knew she wouldn't be able to talk openly to Chow in the Club, but he'd accept her invitation to tea at home. She poured herself some water from the sideboard and waited, as the glass frosted over with icy cold and she felt condensation wet her fingers.

The same man returned with her tea, followed by a stranger dressed in the coat and tails that Chow would normally wear.

'Good afternoon, madam. I understand you asked to see the head waiter, may I help you?'

'No, thank you. I will wait until Chow arrives.'

'Excuse me, may I introduce myself? I am the new head waiter.'

'I don't understand, where is Chow?'

'The previous head waiter is indisposed. I am very happy to assist you in any way that I may.'

'That won't be necessary, thank you.'

'Very good, madam.'

Annie drank her tea in silence. The perfumed aroma reminded her of bumping into Chow in the Happy Joy Tearoom where he discovered this blend. She couldn't remember him ever having a day off from work; he was so dedicated to the Club. But maybe the beating two days ago had left him more badly injured than he'd led her to believe. Did he have anyone to take care of him? She had no idea and realised how little she knew of Chow's life. The sound of a peacock calling out in the garden broke through Annie's thoughts. She watched the gardener put his rake away and shoo the bird out of the flowerbeds. Then he sat in a corner propped on his haunches and closed his eyes, as though resting.

From beyond the door Annie heard the familiar sound of Mrs Marsden's voice. Even though she planned her afternoon visit to the Club to avoid such a meeting, Annie was pleased to hear her. As the President's wife, and one of the biggest gossips in Shanghai, she would know about any staff changes.

'Mrs Marsden, how are you?'

Annie stood and waited for Mrs Marsden to join her.

'Good afternoon. Twice in two days, we are meeting a lot!'

Annie didn't know what to say but Mrs Marsden barrelled on and for once Annie was glad.

'I'm here arranging next week's bridge meeting. You'll be there I assume. Let's hope poor Flora has picked up her game.' Mrs Marsden groaned dramatically.

'Who are you dealing with while Chow is unwell? I met a different chap claiming to be the head waiter. I've never seen him before.'

'Oh, he's all right, understands English and knows how to make tea. Chow's not ill my dear, haven't you heard?'

'No.'

'Chow's disappeared. He simply didn't turn up for work yesterday. No one's seen him or heard from him since but we suspect he's involved with the gangs and did a runner. The police are doing a terrific job of rounding up these illegals.

My Roger has put the cat amongst the pigeons, that's for sure. Typical Chinks, can't trust any of them.'

'Are you sure? I can't believe that of Chow.'

'My dear, if anyone is going to be in the know it's me!'

'What if something happened to Chow—has anyone tried to contact him?'

'What's the point? He clearly doesn't want to be found, and left us very much in the lurch.'

Annie was stunned. She didn't know what to say and looked at the older lady bleakly. A dusting of powdered makeup was visible in the light hairs on her upper lip and around the corners of her mouth where deep-etched lines snaked out like tentacles. Mrs Marsden was still talking and Annie nodded without really listening. She'd been so certain of seeing Chow that now she felt unsure how to proceed.

'Why are people suspicious of Chow? What has he ever done?'

'Don't interrupt dear, it's bad manners.'

Annie felt a wave of frustration at the older woman's patronising tone. Mrs Marsden wagged her finger at Annie.

'You will come to tea tomorrow, won't you? The Clancy girls will be there and, as I say, I've got some ideas for an end of season soiree I want to discuss.'

'I'm just so surprised by Chow's disappearance; I can't believe he would be caught up in anything illegal. What exactly are people saying?'

'They are saying that it is no coincidence he went off somewhere the very day a Green Gang hideout was raided. He must be connected; there's no other logical explanation.'

'Apart from any number of reasons like a sick family member, or his own ill health, or worse, some terrible accident has befallen him. Really Mrs Marsden, must we always be so perfunctory when it comes to the Chinese. They do have families and lives just like us, there may be a very simple and understandable explanation.'

'There's nothing understandable about his behaviour at all. It's scandalous and he's not worth the bother when there's another capable replacement standing by. Now, tea tomorrow, I'll expect you at eleven.'

Annie stayed in the lounge after Mrs Marsden left. She needed time to think. Chow had certainly been in a bad state when he came to her the day before yesterday, and of course the Flues would jump to the most salacious conclusion. She put her head in her hands and rubbed her eyes, hoping for some clarity. The lounge was empty now and all she could hear were her own audible sighs as she tried to make sense of the situation. She thought of Chow's intelligent comments about the country's politics and knew his opinions were more radical than conservative but it didn't follow he'd join the Green Gang to fulfil them. Possibly his views put him more in line with the Communist beliefs and even though most of her fellow expatriates would brand such thinking as treasonous, Annie didn't care and she knew Chow was careful who he shared his opinions with. He had saved her from a riot and put his own life at risk to save Alec. These were the actions of a responsible and upstanding member of the community. She knew it to be true. She remembered when Chow had tucked a curl behind her ear and there was only affection in his eyes, not hatred for her foreign blood. But whatever way she looked at it, Annie kept coming back to the same dead-end conclusion: she had no way of contacting Chow, no address for him, not even a full name. She only had three pieces of information about the man: he was the maître d'hôtel, his name was Chow and he was her lover.

Annie thought about the time when Chow had calmed her down after the altercation in the street with the old woman. She thought about lying beside him with eyes closed and fingers touching. If he was sick, then she should be nursing him.

The familiar corridor echoed with the sound of Annie's shoes. She pushed through the kitchen doors briskly and stood, hoping to recognise one of the men who had played mahjong with Chow, or the young man who had translated for her when she spoke to Li Qiang's sister. These people worked with Chow every day, surely one of them could tell her where he lived?

It was not as busy as the last time Annie had visited the kitchens. The subdued activity reflected how few guests were in the Club. There was no blast of heat or constant noise, two women were cooking at the stove, and a man cleaned cutlery. Another entered while Annie stood in the doorway, moving past her with an empty tray. He spoke to the woman at the stove who turned and began ladling soup into a bowl. Annie walked up to them both.

'I am looking for Chow?' No one answered so she turned to where the man was putting cutlery into a drawer. 'Chow, the head waiter?' She spoke his name slowly, hoping someone would recognise the word. One of the men pointed to a sheet pinned to the wall where she saw Chow's name with a line through it and another name written beneath, his replacement. But this did not help her.

'Help, please, Chow?' As she spoke the new head waiter appeared.

'May I help you, madam?' She sensed his annoyance at her presence.

'Thank you. I am looking for Chow. I was hoping one of the servants who worked with him could tell me where he lived?' The man frowned at Annie.

'May I escort you back to the ladies' lounge; the kitchen is no place for members.' He held his arm out towards the door and stood to the side. The other staff had stopped what they were doing and were watching. But Annie had no intention of leaving.

'I will not go until I can speak to someone who knows Chow.' She raised her voice to include the other staff in the kitchen as she spoke, looking around so that they could see her genuine concern. Water from the pot on the stove splashed onto the fire with a hiss and the woman turned back to take it off the heat.

'He might be sick and need help,' Annie entreated, looking first to the young men and then back to the head waiter who still stood to the side, waiting for her to lead the way back to the ladies' lounge. He inclined his head politely but didn't speak. Someone shouted loudly from the doorway into the alley as a delivery boy dropped a large box of vegetables to the ground. One of the women began inspecting its contents. There was no point in staying. Annie shook her head at the head waiter as she left but he simply nodded stiffly and followed her out.

She wanted to be gone from the Club. She flagged a rickshaw down in the street and told the driver to move on quickly. Annie paid little attention to where she was going, she needed to think. She'd been so critical of the Flues ignorant approach to the Chinese but here she sat with only superficial knowledge of a man she wanted to entrust with her happiness. A young woman moved agilely across their path, balancing a bucket on each end of a pole over her shoulders with a sleeping baby strapped to her chest. They turned a corner and the woman was gone. Annie recognised the street; it was busy with food hawkers and pedestrians. It was Xinzha Road, and there was the house where Annie had found Li Qiang. She leant forward and shouted to the driver to stop. He hauled on the rickshaw's poles and Annie fell backwards. She sat still, watching people pushing through each other along the street and listening to the noisy cries of the traders. When she stepped down, the driver called out and Annie realised she hadn't paid him; she'd been wondering what had made her stop here. She looked at the building on the other side of the road. It was cordoned off with a barricade and she remembered Mrs Marsden mentioning that the police had raided the Chinaman's office. Maybe she just needed to stand where she'd last seen the boy one more time. She paid the rickshaw driver and steadied herself with a deep breath; if there was any chance Chow was connected to the gangs it was worth asking around here.

She smoothed the curls on her neck. Her pulse quickened. She needed a moment to collect herself.

She waited for a break in the traffic. A group of children were playing a game with stones on the street in front of the building. They sat in the dirt, oblivious to the noise and the mess around them. A man emerged from number 23. He ducked under the barricade and turned into the alley nearby. Annie moved along the footpath. There was something familiar about the way he held himself. A large car rumbled past, blocking her view for a moment. She tapped her foot on the curb impatiently as bicycles and rickshaws made it impossible to cross. Then her chance came and she moved forward with a group of other pedestrians. She hurried to the opposite curb, jostled about by the crowd, and saw that the man had stopped in the alley. Her curiosity turned instantly to shock when she realised she knew who it was—Chow. She could see his face now, though he was preoccupied and had no reason to look across to where she waited. Chow walked further down the alley where houses bent into one another in a long and endless-looking line. Annie stopped for a few minutes, unsure how to proceed. Loose stones fell around her from where the entrance portico had crumbled with age. She remembered their visit to Zhenye Li Alley and how Chow had helped her, and was reminded again of why she was there. She would not jump to any conclusions without first finding out what Chow was doing in the Green Gang house. She raised her hand to wave and call out to him, but stopped mid-action. He was taking something from another man, who clearly didn't want the object to be visible on the street. They were hunched together and Annie moved slowly forward, leaning into the wall to get a better view. She shooed away a few of the children who approached her with outstretched hands. But the street and alley were so busy it didn't disturb the two men who were focused intently on their transaction. She watched as Chow reached out and quickly slipped a gun into the loose sleeve of his robe. For a moment the metal caught the glint of sun. The man nodded to Chow, held his shoulder a moment and then turned back to the street. Chow looked around then, and Annie felt herself fall against the wall in her haste not to be seen. The stone pressed into her legs and she felt a chill on her skin from the shadows. There were goosebumps on her arms, and her eyes smarted from the shock but still she watched. Chow was smoking now, and she wondered if indeed she had seen a gun at all. He was so calm and unperturbed and it happened so fast. He was only a few yards away, yet there was an invisible barrier between them, and it felt in that moment more foreign a world to her than ever before.

She crossed the road again to where rickshaws waited for business in a side street. She would come back later to speak to Chow; she couldn't do it now, not like this, not spying on him.

CHAPTER THIRTEEN

Once again, Annie braced herself for Mrs Marsden's loud welcome as she pressed the door bell, wishing she hadn't agreed to the morning tea. There were so many questions whirling in her head that she felt distracted and dismayed. It would be hard to appear relaxed and join in the conversation with the other ladies, but Annie was there because it was all she could do. The tea invitation gave the rest of her day some structure, which she needed amidst so much confusion. Annie sat robotically with the other ladies, while Mrs Marsden fussed over the tea arrangements. She laughed and nodded at the appropriate moments but her mind was awash with images of Chow; secreting a gun in his sleeve, weaving towards her through a Club party with a silver tray held high. Her commonsense struggled with the disjunction of the man she knew and the man she'd seen yesterday.

The table was laid with finger sandwiches and tea cakes, small scones and strawberry jam, savoury tartlets and pick-led onions. She viewed the amount of food with resignation. There was enough to feed three times the number gathered around the table. The ladies took their seats and old Mrs Colder passed Annie the scones. She didn't feel hungry at all but took one out of politeness. Annie reached for a plate of sandwiches to pass back to Mrs Colder but before she could, her hostess had whisked it away. Mrs Marsden called over the girl who'd brought the sandwiches to the table and gave her the plate to take back to the kitchen. Annie lis-tened with astonishment as she admonished the poor girl; there was not enough filling and Mrs Marsden was embar-rassed to offer her friends such sub-standard examples of an old-fashioned English egg sandwich. Annie knew she should have held her tongue and let Mrs Marsden dictate the rules in her own house, but something snapped in her. She could not bear to hear the old trout shout at the local girl a moment longer.

'It's only a sandwich for goodness sake, Mrs Marsden, stop haranguing the poor girl.'

Mrs Marsden gave Annie a fierce but quick stare as she continued to berate her servant. Annie could see the young thing was nearly in tears, as her hands holding the rejected plate of sandwiches began to shake.

'Let the girl go, Mrs Marsden. We can all do without egg today, don't you agree?' Annie looked around at her fel-low guests for support but no one spoke up in agreement or would even look at her. 'There is enough food here to feed us all three times over. Would you just please be quiet and let the poor girl do her job.'

'Mrs Brand, may I remind you that this is my house and you are my guest.'

Annie watched Mrs Marsden speak; her lips pursed and twitched furiously as she struggled to control herself. It was typical behaviour for the matriarch, used to dominating a room. But Annie suddenly felt very tired.

'I don't care, really I don't. You're acting like a bully, talking to the girl like she's sub-human, invisible even. It's uncalled for and I simply can't stand by and listen to you any longer. Excuse me; Nancy, Joyce, Mrs Colder.'

Annie nodded stiffly to the ladies as she rose and left the room. Her head was pounding. She wasn't sure where she was going, but she couldn't stay a moment longer. Seeing Chow had utterly shaken her.

Annie sat down in the kitchen. It was much bigger than hers, with a round table in the centre surrounded by six chairs. The staff had been busy preparing the evening meal—a pot bubbled on the stovetop and someone was chopping carrots on the side bench—but a hush descended on the room as she entered and the servants stopped their chores and stared at the stranger, unsure what to do in the presence of a foreign lady. The young servant who Annie had defended returned from the dining room and quickly spotted her at the table. She shooed the other staff out through the back door, closing it after them so the two were alone. Annie was grateful for the privacy and admired the girl's sensitivity. She noticed the mole on her upper lip as she came towards her.

'Are you all right?'

Annie didn't see the sack she was holding until it was too late. She felt it roughly pushed over her head, and the hessian scratched down her cheek as it was tugged. The dark enveloped her with a claustrophobic closeness that made Annie cry out in fear but the sound was muffled by the material. Her nose pressed against roughness, she breathed in deep and fast, feeling her chest contract quickly with each gasp. Her hands scrabbled at the hood as it was tightened around her neck. But someone grabbed her arms and tied them firmly behind her back. She was disoriented and afraid. A voice spoke low in her ear.

'Be quiet and walk.'

Annie stood unsteadily, stumbling into a warm body that pushed her upright and roughly grabbed her by the shoulders. She was led away, a door shut as she walked, gravel crunched beneath her feet, a car engine growled low as she was tipped headfirst into a seat.

'Where are you taking me?'

Her voice came out muffled and coarse from within the blindfold, but there was no answer.

The car stopped after some time and it was impossible for Annie to tell their direction or even how long she was in the car. She looked around, responding to the sound of a door opening even though she couldn't see a thing. A blur of frightening white light filled her vision as she stepped from the car. She sucked air in through the hessian material, fighting the sensation of suffocating. Her head throbbed as panic razed back and forth through her.

Then they were inside and the quiet darkness calmed Annie a little. She was seated and someone untied the rope. She gasped with pain as she gingerly pulled her arms back around.

'Take off the blindfold. She is hurt.' Annie's body froze, she listened intently. Chow spoke again. 'Annie, are you all right?'

Even though the room was shaded and the single high window was covered, Annie flinched as the hood was removed. Before she could do anything, Chow had dropped to his knees in front of her.

'My bird, I am so sorry to treat you this way, please forgive me.'

He clasped her hands and stroked them as he spoke. Annie thought his fingers looked like disconnected little lizards running across her hands. The air was light and filled her lungs easily now so that she felt dizzy with the pressure of breathing in too quickly. She noticed he wasn't wearing the jade ring and saw in its absence the tattoo she'd only glimpsed previously. It was the Ichang fish. Her body swayed.

'Annie?'

Chow's dark eyes were filled with a familiar look of concern. It was confusing and Annie blinked laboriously and stared at him. Everything seemed discombobulated.

'Get her a drink.'

The young servant from Mrs Marsden's handed Annie a glass of water. She took a sip and gave it to Chow. He dipped a cloth in the glass and pressed it gently to her neck and throat, resting the cool towel behind each ear. She thought of the time she had cleaned his wounds just like that. The cold water against her skin made Annie shiver and a clarity returned to her head.

She looked around; they were in a small room at the back of a building. They must have come in through the one door, which was shut now. The room was bare and felt unlived in. Even the few chairs seemed lost. Chow held her hands with concern.

'What is going on, Chow? What have you done?' She heard the panic in her voice as she pulled her hands away from his. 'You can't kidnap me like this, it's madness. What on earth were you thinking?'

'I know, Annie, let me explain. You are not in danger here. It was the only way I could see you. It may seem like madness to you but this is how I must live now.'

'I don't understand?' She looked at the young girl, who was standing by the door. There was no one else in the room. 'Who is she?'

'That is my sister, Chin Feng.'

The girl smiled shyly at Annie and stepped forward.

'Thank you for defending me, I am sorry to have scared you but my brother is a good man. You can trust him.'

'Chow, what is going on?'

Annie was frightened now. A pounding started in her ears. She looked from Chow to his sister and back to the man she thought she knew. She felt as though she was dreaming.

'We do not have long before we must return you to Mrs Marsden's, so I apologise for the hasty delivery. They think you are unwell and resting in the guest bedroom. Do not worry, no one will know of your absence, if we are careful.'

'All right, Chow, then you better start explaining damn fast.'

'You see, Annie, I am in the Green Gang.'

'You're a gangster? I don't believe it.'

'I'm so sorry for deceiving you, but I had no choice. The gang sent me to work for the Communists. The red paint under my nails was not from painting the Club walls but from writing which is required for the Communist propaganda posters. We gain support through these.'

'You're a spy too? You lied to me all this time. I don't know you, dear god, I don't know you.'

'My job is to pass on information that I gather from overhearing conversations at the Club between the chief of police, the admiral of the fleet, the influential bankers, any foreigner of note. Sometimes I come across documents indiscreetly left lying around by half-drunk members—it has been very easy.'

Annie was scared and her eyes flickered across Chow's face and away to the far wall where the door was closed, then back to his mouth, smiling at her.

'Annie, it is still me. Look at me.'

Chow took her by the shoulders and forced Annie to return his stare. His hold on her was tight and she felt his fingers digging into her skin. Her throat was dry and scratchy. She licked her lips and looked away again, to the stained walls streaked with water marks, but the fierceness of his gaze compelled her to return his look and she stared at him, fearful of what she might see and unnerved by her vulnerability. Yet he was being honest; she saw it in the raw tenderness of his gaze. In those eyes radiating gentleness was the man she knew. Her shoulders dropped and he loosened his hold.

'Why risk so much, Chow?'

'When the gang helped to bring my sister to Shanghai from our village in the north I became obliged to assist. But I do so willingly, for the future of my country.'

'Are you an opium dealer, an assassin?'

'I do not believe violence will bring about the change that we fight for. But I became a killer when I shot the man who attacked you in the street riot. I could not let anyone hurt you, Annie.'

'I thought it was a policeman who fired that shot.' Chow shook his head. 'So, I'm more valuable alive than dead, as part of your strategy to get information?'

Chow laughed and Annie felt anger flare inside her. 'You are not that important. I killed the man to save your life, because I love you.

'I should have stopped seeing you, which would have been safer, but I could not. The gang put someone on to work with me a long time ago, someone political and acceptable in Settlement society. I wanted to be released from the gang, Annie; after I met you I saw a different future for myself, for us, maybe a better one. I know now how foolish that was. When I asked for my freedom they threatened Chin Feng and beat me.

'You must stop prying into the gangs, Annie. I saw you at Xinzha Road yesterday. Next time it will be someone else and they will not let you go.'

'I was looking for you. I thought you were sick and that's why you weren't at the Club. I wanted to help you.'

'It was too dangerous to stay in my job. There was a chance someone might talk after the Xinzha Road raid; the police interrogation methods are very compelling. It has broken me to leave the Club, but I am careful and clever. As long as I continue to work for the gang they will not harm Chin Feng and the world does not stand still, change will come and then I will see my fate and act.'

'You never told the police about the Chinaman, did you?'

'I could not risk being undone. Now you must return to Mrs Marsden's. My sister will travel with you.'

'I don't want to go yet, Chow, I have more questions. This is all so unbelievable, I need time to think.'

'No, it is impossible. You've already been gone too long.'

'Please, don't disappear again.'

She reached for his hands, and held them briefly, curling her fingers around his so that they twisted together and she held tight.

'My name is Chiao Chin Pao, I was only ever Chow at the Club. You are part of my life now; you should know my real name.'

The car ride back to Mrs Marsden's was very quick. Annie didn't have time to think about the enormity of what she'd heard. She saw the streets in a blur as she went over all that Chow had told her. She couldn't stop her hands shaking.

Chow's sister slipped Annie through the laundry entrance and up the servant stairs to the guest room where she was glad to lie back and pretend sickness. *You are part of my life now.* Chow's words looped relentlessly in her mind. This was what she'd wanted to hear from him but the truth of his life was a shock. She didn't even know what to call him. There was a knock on the door and Chin Feng opened it quietly as Mrs Marsden pushed her way through.

'Are you feeling any better, Mrs Brand?'

'Yes, thank you, though I think it would be best if I go home. I am sorry for my outburst earlier.'

'Never mind, dear, some of the local viruses turn us all into beasts; I've forgotten about it already. Let me call your car and we'll get you home to rest. I don't like to think of you alone in that house.'

'I'm fine, really.'

'Very well, but you must let me know how you are tomorrow.'

Annie let Mrs Marsden fuss; her supposed illness distracted her host from the real reason she looked so pale. Even when she was alone in the car, all Annie could do was sit in shocked silence, contemplating the truth of Chow's story.

She sat up in bed that afternoon, rubbing her wrists which still ached from the tight binding. Her book of Yeats lay open on her lap. In the past, when she needed comfort, Annie turned to it. On the ship to Hong Kong, it helped her grow accustomed to losing her history, her family and to a future without her father. In the days following her wedding to Alec, Yeats fed her poetic notions of romance, and even dull afternoons at the Club were more bearable when she opened the well-worn cover. Now she hoped it would give her a sense of resilience and the constancy to get through the next weeks.

A page turned and she stopped it with her thumb. 'Aedh Wishes for the Cloths of Heaven'. This was the poem Chow knew. When he recited the first line to her all those weeks ago, it had bound her inextricably to him. She read it again, seated in the garden that evening with a drink—their worlds were not so far apart. He was not a stranger, even if there were things about him she was only just discovering. There was so much of herself that Annie hadn't told Chow either; how could she blame him for keeping secrets, when she'd been avoiding her past ever since she stepped off that boat in Hong Kong.

She began pacing the grass and pressing the soil around a tree down firmly with her shoe. The house boy approached with a note. It was from Ilma, reminding Annie to join her at Mrs Marsden's the next day for the monthly Moral Welfare League meeting. She expected Annie to bring the picture of the Ichang fish tattoo with her.

Annie stamped her feet into the soil with vigour. She'd completely forgotten about the meeting. But she'd promised to return the image of the fish tattoo. At least it meant she could get a message to Chow through his sister while she was at Mrs Marsden's. Nerves pinched in her stomach. There were so many unanswered questions she needed to ask Chow.

The next morning Annie found herself returning again to Avenue Joffre and the Marsden's mock Tudor mansion. Mrs Marsden frowned when she saw Annie enter her parlour. She disappeared soon after to finish getting ready and left Annie alone and wondering where were the other League ladies? The parlour was a small and friendly space, where Mrs Marsden's unfinished needlework took up the table. The two little pugs yapped at Annie's ankles before rolling over noisily and chewing each other instead. Annie watched the door for Chow's sister. Mrs Marsden reappeared and Annie listened patiently to her description of the latest work of the Moral Welfare League. She was tempted to suggest that it was because the Moral Welfare League had forced most of the brothels and opium dens outside the International Settlement that the criminal networks were flourishing. The gangs offered protection to the now illegal businesses as well as supplying the opium. But she knew how much that would distress Mrs Marsden, founding member of the League, and even though she was an old rhino, her passion for the cause was genuine.

'I'm sorry I am so early, I think Ilma may have given me the wrong time,' Annie looked around hopelessly at the empty room.

'Never mind, the household is running slowly today, I'm afraid, but the lemonade should be here shortly.' Annie tried to focus on the conversation as Mrs Marsden continued. 'I thought we'd had enough drama yesterday with your episode, Annie, but I fear you'll find my household is fraught with problems. It's exhausting.'

'I hope I haven't inconvenienced you too much.'

'I don't like to share mishaps to do with the servants, it seems so common, but I am miffed, I must say. One of my best girls has gone missing. It's sent the others into a proper flap in the kitchen over who'll take on her duties. I like to think I run a fair household, and my staff has no complaints. Now I've got to ask the others to do extra work while I find a replacement.'

'Which girl was it?'

Annie tried to keep the apprehension out of her voice. She had a terrible feeling she knew what Mrs Marsden was going to say and that it wasn't a coincidence this had happened the day after she saw Chow and met his sister.

'Quiet young thing from the country, so much promise, although she had a horrible mole on her lip that was an utter eyesore for the guests. I suppose we all have to compromise these days.'

Annie nodded. 'Will you try to find her?'

'Only if there's jewellery or money missing. I put her in the Mingxing Boarding House for servants in Fukang Li Alley, on Xinzha Road. To think she could be so ungrateful after all my generosity! Don't expect she'll wait around to be discovered, though she was such a friendly thing, I feel I knew more about her than most of the servants. There you go though, can't pick who will be reliable these days.'

Annie didn't stay for the League meeting. She gave Mrs Marsden the envelope with the image in it for Ilma and made her excuses, all the while distracted and unfocused. Her mind was already at the boarding house.

Annie told her driver to leave her on Xinzha Road; it was a beautiful afternoon and she would take a rickshaw home. She didn't want her driver knowing where she went. She recognised the road; she was not far from number 23 where she'd seen Chow.

As Annie walked she listened to the click of her shoes on the stones, attempting to pace her racing heartbeat with the rhythm of her gait. A group of men sat around an upturned box, drinking tea and talking. The alleyway was part of a densely clotted neighbourhood of shikumen houses. She walked briskly, trying to appear confident. Voices from the open windows above made her turn her head towards the sky. Laundry hung from long struts of wood attached to windows; it was like a welcoming fanfare.

But further down the alley there were no old men playing board games, or children running about. This part of the lane felt abandoned and even the sun was eclipsed by the condensed buildings that seemed to collapse in on one another and obscure the light. Annie stopped by a doorway where a sign hung vertically on a swinging pole: the Mingxing Boarding House.

The front gate was open and what would have been a small outdoor terrace was now crowded with washing, chairs and upturned baskets. A crease of light spilled out from the doorway, stretching across the stones to the lip of the gate. It felt later in the day than it was and she looked back towards the main road where traffic moved. But there was a sense of wakefulness in the open door.

A thin staircase ran against one wall. The front room downstairs had been converted into two separate dwellings. Annie couldn't see down the dimly lit corridor to the back of the building. She stood a moment, considering whether to knock on one of the doors, but light spilling from an open doorway upstairs caught her eye. It was very quiet for a boarding house and as she climbed the stairs she saw a damp patch had painted a corner of the ceiling in ugly browns and greens.

Her feet felt their way slowly across the wooden boards. She stood cautiously on the doorstep. There must be forgotten food inside, a musty smell hung in the air.

'Hello,' she called out nervously.

There was no reply. A dog growled and barked and she took a step back towards the staircase. The house creaked in response, as though the tired stairs and walls were trying to tell her something. Annie listened but there were no further dog noises. She looked through the door cautiously, and could just see laundry hung on the back of a chair and strung across a wardrobe. It gave the space a homely feel. The dog must be in another room.

She moved further into the room. There were two single wooden beds, a small square window strung across with homemade curtains, and a kitchen corner set up with a rudimentary-looking stove over a dead flame. No one seemed to be home.

The bed closest to the door was covered in a richly woven bedspread, embroidered with lengths of ivy and small motifs. She ran her hand over the material, uneven and soft as she looked around the room. The other bed was close to the window, and Annie could see something had pushed the covers off and into the thin recess between the bed and the far wall. She walked over to have a look.

A man's body was crumpled on the floor. The sheet had caught around his torso and legs, half wrapping him in a mummified bundle. Soft messy pulp oozed from a bullet wound where his head was ripped open. Thick black hair stuck in a mass to one side of the smashed skull. Annie fell backwards against the bed in shock. Her hands scrabbled frantically across the sheets. She pushed and kicked her legs away as though fighting off the horrific sight. The solid bed head pressed firmly against her back and she stopped still. She held her breath and listened. Her knuckles were white where she clutched the bed. She focused on any sound that might mean the killer was nearby—the creak of a floorboard, a rustling of mice. Her heartbeat deafened any sound in the room, though there was no noise except her own whimpers of fear. She was alone.

A ripping pain in her stomach pushed the air from her throat as she vomited. There was so much blood, pulling her into the richness of its colour. Her shoe slid in the stickiness as she gingerly leant forward to check the body. She hesitated as her hands shook. A choking, blinding heat razed through her, roaring in her head, suffocating her thoughts.

She dropped to her knees beside the body, smoothed out his crooked, still warm hand, rolled her fist over and over in the softness of his palm. It was always his hands. Chow was dead.

Around her the room blurred as Annie leant down and took hold of him. She lifted his head to see his eyes but her hands slipped hopelessly with the unexpected weight of his lifelessness. One of her fingers dragged his slack lip down as she grabbed at him, but she was oblivious to the incongruity of what she was doing. She sat down solidly to get a better hold of him. Wetness soaked her stockings where the blood seeped in. She pushed him heavily to get him to sit up but his body slumped. She caught him as he toppled. Even limp as he was, the feel of his body leaning in close was instantly familiar. He fell back against the window. She wanted him to sit up, it was essential. The heavy pounding in her head made Annie shake.

For a moment she rested back on her haunches, looking at Chow through a disoriented haze of grief. Gently, tenderly, she wiped the blood from his face and from in his hair. A clump came away in her hand. It was muscle and skull, wet and warmly congealed. His hair was twined in the thickest bit of it. About her the room watched quietly. She pushed Chow's skull back into the bloody gaping hole, patched it with her fingers, patted it down and watched him hopefully.

His body slid loosely sideways again. A fresh line of blood dragged down the wall. His skin was warm as she stroked his cheek and held his chin. She didn't taste the acidic, richness of his blood as she licked her handkerchief and wiped, over and over, like a mother to a child, like she used to clean little Judy's cheeks after a sugar bun. But the open bullet wound continued to weep liquid down his forehead. She breathed in one long, thirsty moment of hope, looking towards the empty doorway. Then she crawled in beside Chow, oblivious to the blood and smell, hooked his arm around her body, wrapped her leg over his, and closed her eyes. He still felt warm and soft. She buried close into the forgiving darkness, unable to do anything other than cling to him and moan.

'Annie?' A hand was on her shoulder. Annie was cold, she didn't know how long she'd been in the room but her body shook uncontrollably and her limbs were screaming with the pain of immobility. She huddled closer to Chow.

Arms reached down to help her. She let them take her weight.

'Get up, it's time to go.'

She was relieved it was Natalia. Annie couldn't think past Chow's dead body to why Natalia was there helping her. It was enough to have her friend find her. But when they got to the staircase Annie remembered Chow's jade ring and she couldn't leave without it. Natalia was holding her firmly, but Annie twisted free and ran back to the room, stopping abruptly at the sight of the Alsatian dog standing over the body, sniffing curiously. The animal must have slipped in to the room as they left. It looked up at her and growled low and deep. Annie didn't move; her legs had petrified. For a long moment she wondered why she'd come back into the room, trying to find some logic in the thick haze of fear and shock and grief. But she couldn't form any full thought in her mind, every snippet flew out of her head the moment she tried to think. Then she heard herself scream. The dog was snuffling around Chow's body, licking up the mess of blood and brains.

Natalia dragged her roughly from the room and down the stairs. Annie stumbled and fell, ripping her stockings on the nails in the floorboards and bruising her palms. Natalia picked her up and pushed her out into the lane. She gasped and retched uncontrollably. Then she was pushed into a car and they drove away from the alley, away from the boarding house, away from Chow.

CHAPTER FOURTEEN

Annie must have fainted. When she woke she was no longer in the car. She lay on a bed in a small, poorly lit room that smelt of a dusky, sweet vapour. Her stockings were ripped where she'd fallen down the stairs and there was dried blood smeared across her clothes, across her hands, everywhere. She gasped with horror at the sight, as though seeing it for the first time.

Annie's eyes took a moment to adjust to the darkness of her surroundings. Rough matting covered the dirt floor and something rustled beneath it. There were small holes where an animal had chewed through the material. A murmur of activity from the other room made her sit up and listen; she heard a jazz tune playing. As her eyes adjusted she saw she was not alone. Someone was in the corner, though the girl was quiet. Her head slumped forward and her shoulders bunched together slackly where her arms were tied behind her. Annie didn't dare move. The girl was unconscious, or worse. An air of defeat festered in the silence and curled about the legs of Annie's bed like a creeping mist. Under her dress, her skin itched. She wanted to take it off and scratch away the dried blood and dirt. Instead, she concentrated on the single, high window above the bed, painted firmly shut. It was the same window she'd seen in the room where Chin Feng had taken her to Chow. She was back in that room.

Voices grew louder, male and female. Her eyes flicked to the door and back to the girl. A new jazz rhythm started up and the thump of her heart matched its syncopated frenzy. The door opened and instantly lit the room in a harsh, unshaded light. Annie flinched and then saw quickly that it was Chow's sister in the chair. An empty washbasin and chamber pot were in the corner, and a single chair seemed set aside for visitors. Otherwise the room was bare except for some garish material which hung on either side of the window in two straight strips.

Her attention was drawn back to the door as three Chinese men entered. They were dressed in traditional clothes, and could have come from the markets to deliver some produce. But they stood ominously silent and waiting. One had a scar across his cheek that crossed his eye in a nasty mess of poorly healed, bulbous skin. At his waist was a knife tied in a sheath that was open at the base so the sharp-tipped razor edge was visible. One of the others carelessly blew a mouthful of smoke into the room and Annie's nose filled with the smell of incense mixed with a heady fragrance that cloyed at her throat. His fine metal glasses fogged over for a moment and she was reminded of the monkey handler in the Nanshi alleyway. But she was too distracted and frightened to continue the thought.

Then the men straightened visibly as footsteps sounded. Annie sat up and her head spun. She held her hands tightly together to stop them shaking and to ward off the icy cold that had begun to creep into her fingers.

Natalia entered the room. The men stood back as she waved them aside. Annie sunk into the mattress with relief. Her arms dropped loosely, her eyes ached with a tiredness she only then allowed herself to feel, but she managed a smile. The semi-dark was kind to Natalia's face, softening the tired circles Annie noticed. Natalia walked over to the bed and her feet hit the old floorboards with purpose.

In the moments of silence that followed Annie was aware of the noise of voices beyond the door. She soon smelt the pungent odour of opium smoke. In the room it mingled with the damp earth. Natalia had turned away from Annie and was lighting a cigarette. She laughed harshly as she turned back, one finger wrapped around the slim sheath of tobacco as she pressed it to her lips. She was wearing Chow's jade ring. It glared at Annie from its new owner's finger.

'You've been very foolish and arrogant.'

Annie felt the room sway a little as she watched Natalia walk around, waving her cigarette like a baton. 'How much do you really know about me?'

This did not sound like the friend who brought vodka to drink instead of tea. Natalia was dressed like a man, in baggy trousers and a loose-fitting shirt with a long tie draped round her neck. Her thick mane of brilliant red hair hung loose too, like an expensive cloak around her shoulders. It made her masculine dress style stand out even more. Why did she have Chow's ring?

Annie's shoulders slumped and she lay back against the bed.

'I don't know you, do I?' she whispered.

'Very good, quick learner; so this may not be as painful for you as I thought.'

Natalia dragged the chair close to the bed, and swung into it, leaning back with her legs stretched forward. She drew on the cigarette and inclined her head slightly so that one of the men quickly brought her an ashtray. Then she leant forward aggressively, clapped her hands together and rubbed them vigorously.

'First of all, my apologies for the death of your lover.'

Annie drew in a loud breath at the mention of Chow. Her chest exploded with a fierce heat that made her breathing quicken and her head swim. Natalia was playing with his ring on her finger, watching Annie's reaction.

'Such a foolish, foreign girl; playing with fire, as they say. You must realise it was you who got Chin Pao killed. I helped, but only a little—the police were very grateful for the tip-off, they'd been looking for the Communist connection to the gang and then they found Chiao Chin Pao, in the grotty little room, packing up his belongings to run away, or so they thought.'

'I don't understand? Why would you betray him, why?'

Annie didn't realise she'd shouted until she felt the cold pain on her cheek as Natalia slapped her.

'Shut up. You might have convinced the police to spare his life if you'd arrived at the boarding house a little bit earlier. But you didn't, and now Chin Pao is dead. You don't save people do you, Annie? You would rather have adventures to escape your boring life. Chiao Chin Pao, or should I say your man Chow, was an adventure to you, a bit exotic, like me, your Russian friend. You thought I might even be a princess.' Natalia laughed again. 'You used us all as distractions. But there is no more running away now, Annie.'

A dull weight pressed on Annie's lungs, making it hard to breathe; there was a horrible truth in what Natalia said. She never considered the affair from Chow's perspective until that moment. It opened up so many questions she didn't want to ask but she couldn't help wondering: had she been blinded by her own selfish desire?

'Chiao Chin Pao told you too much, him and his stupid little sister. They risked exposing our work with the Green Gang when he took you into his confidence. But he couldn't help himself, so in love, when really this is where his loyalty should have been, with his only allies.'

Natalia stood and opened her arms expansively, as though there were more than the three men and two women in the room.

'Chin Pao was grateful for the Green Gang's help when he needed them to get his sister to Shanghai, but he was a fool to think he could walk away. He was too useful—how do you think he got the job at the Club in the first place? Not because of his dancing skills, that is for certain. That ugly, pock-marked Chinaman you saw me with at the ball, he helped Chow get the job, and Chow joined his *bang hui* and met with him every month. His sister got a nice little job with Mrs Marsden too, no complaints when it suited them. I had the unsavoury task of working with the Chinaman to build up the Bolshevik base in Shanghai. Until you exposed him, and all because of the death of an insignificant kitchen hand.'

Chow had known the Chinaman. Annie suddenly realised with absolute certainty that it was him she'd seen sitting together with the pock-marked man and the monkey handler in Zhenye Li Alley.

'I saw Chow with him briefly in Zhenye Li, that day we visited the willow-pattern tearoom, didn't I? That's why Chow disappeared.'

'Well done.' Natalia lit another cigarette and the tip flared red hot. 'The Communist Party book store is in the Little North Gate district of Nanshi. I needed to pass on some information and you, my dear, were such a useful distraction that day.'

Annie looked again at the man wearing glasses standing by the door and realised it was indeed the monkey handler. His expression was vacant but she felt an instant, choking panic at the desperate hopelessness of her position. Natalia was still talking.

'I endured so many boring teas with you and the other ladies at the Club. But I just kept thinking about the Party taking over, when we would end the imperialist, foreign rule with its corrupted social values. No more brainwashing the people, just like my misguided father. And it was working excellently, until you came along. Now we have a dead brother and sister to dispose of.'

Natalia jerked her head at Chow's sister, slumped in the chair, not moving. She grabbed a set of notebooks and threw them at Annie.

'Look, look, all these books filled with information, now at risk because of you.'

Annie flinched as one of the books caught the corner of her eye, cutting the skin. All those moments when she'd seen Natalia and Chow together at the Club, they all took on a new meaning.

'Even you, Captain Brand's wife, helped our cause without ever realising it. The jewellery, that expensive necklace you gave me, it all sells for good money, dollars we can use to buy allegiance, send men back to the Soviet Union for education, produce our pamphlets and teach. Did it make you feel charitable to give me your cast-offs?

'You people only care about the value of gold and silver and the search for profits. Foreign women are so easy to fool but your men are even more gullible. Mr William Piper, the English banker with expensive gifts—I detested being his love interest, but it gave me access to the inner circle of decision-makers. No one questioned a woman listening in to their conversations. Well, they will fear me when the Bolsheviks take power. Poor Willie Piper, he had no idea what I was doing, but at least he got something in return for his money.'

Natalia stood up then and leant over, placing one foot on the bed as she shook her chest at Annie aggressively. Her breasts pressed against the silk shirt. Annie could see skin and red-tinged nipples through the material. For a horrible moment she felt her body sliding towards Natalia, as the bed's mattress gave way under the weight of Natalia's leaning frame. She didn't dare move, caught between mortification and terror. Natalia lit another cigarette as she looked Annie up and down, appraising her. There was a tight crease in her arms where they crossed in judgement as her dark eyes bore down on Annie's modest figure.

'You're not so pretty anyway, not my type.'

Annie watched the Russian press the cigarette butt into a saucer dramatically, bright red nails smudging out the last wisp of smoke. It was like a performance, part of an act she'd done many times before. Then Natalia moved even closer. Annie looked straight ahead, her stomach felt weak and loose and she stared at the far wall rather than into Natalia's eyes, bleak and soulless without the kohl to define them.

'I don't want your pity.' Annie's voice was a whisper.

'It doesn't matter now; we will move on, clean up this mess and start again. It was lucky Chin Pao told us about this safe house, although I think after today we will find a new base. But there will be no new beginnings for you. I will make it easy though, not painful, opiate drugs are quite nice really, and foreigners overdose in these illegal dens every day.'

Natalia stood back observing Annie for a moment. She lit another match and Annie watched as her lips took the thin cigarette and a line of smoke drifted up from the smouldering tip. Then she flicked the match away and walked out of the room.

The three men left with Natalia, one loping in front of her and two behind. None of them looked back.

Annie heard the key turn in the lock and the room closed in around her. She dug her nails into the skin on her palms, her shoulders hunched and tight, listening and waiting. A thread of blood collected at the white curve of her nail. Feet shuffled on dirty flagstones beyond the door, she heard wheezing sucks on a pipe and unintelligible voices. Annie imagined the men huddled together, discussing her fate.

Above the door a spider's web floated in an air current. Annie looked towards the window but it was sealed shut. She couldn't see where the faint breeze originated. The spider worked nimbly on a broken thread that dangled with the weight of a struggling fly. Another current of air sent the web shivering anew and Annie's muscles throbbed as she watched.

Something rustled under the matting and Annie looked around. It moved again, oblivious to her presence. She watched the light flit back and forth in the thin line beneath the door, steadying herself against the bed when the signs of movement stopped abruptly. Tasks had been allocated in the next room, one of the men had been given the job of killing her; she could feel it.

Sharp pain shot down her legs as she stood; her body had tensed up over the last hour and every muscle felt cramped. But she needed to check Chin Feng and she didn't know how long she had before Natalia's men returned. The girl was dead but she was Chow's sister and she deserved Annie's attention. No, she was Chin Pao's sister. A wave of hopeless lethargy as thick as tar sunk into her bones; she never really knew the man. The effort of walking across the room suddenly felt overwhelming.

She breathed quietly through the pinching tightness of each muscle as she moved. Voices from the next room made her catch her breath and stand painfully still, listening for louder sounds of someone approaching, but still she heard only soft, indistinct murmurs. The smell of opium intensified.

Annie gently pushed the young girl's head to rest against the back of the chair. She was limp but her skin was still warm. She couldn't have been dead for long. There were bruises on her neck, down her throat, visible beneath the buttoned turn of her ripped cotton shirt. Annie recognised the smell of stale, damp blood, mingled with sweat and the ammonia sting of urine. It made her gag and turn away. She sucked in air to flush the stench. Chow's sister had the same square jaw and thin lips as him. A matted strand of hair stuck to her cheek. Annie dropped to her knees and untied her. Then she reached her arm out to rest in Chin Feng's lap, linking her own warm palm with the remembered gentleness of this young girl. It felt damp in the fold of her skirt and Annie felt the wiry roughness of bare pubic hair beneath the material. Dried blood streaked down her leg.

Annie wished for a different end for Chin Feng, one that only eventuated after many more years of living than this wretched girl had been allowed. She cursed Chow for not making the safer choice to leave his sister in their village. Chin Feng might have been her sister too, in a future where she and Chow were together. But there would be no future now and she would never feel the sense of being part of a family again.

Annie looked at the light flickering beneath the door. A chair scraped and she heard voices. It must be the men, weighing out the opium to administer the lethal dose. She wanted it to be the one with the scar across his cheek so she had something to concentrate on while he went to work. She wanted him to kill her quickly and not to assault her first, like they'd done to Chin Feng. Her head throbbed and her body shook with a coldness that cut through to her bones. Hoping for anything at this point was fruitless; she had no control over the next minutes or hours of her life—however long this process would take. Choking panic pressed on Annie's throat at the thought of the vast abyss of nothingness ahead.

A car horn sounded and Annie jerked her neck in shock at such a familiar noise so close, yet unreachable. She thought of the ship's fog horn sounding its position on the Yangtze, and the car's insistent horn was like a marker too, of daylight and normalcy in the world beyond the window. That was where she belonged. This small, grey room could not be her final view. She gently placed Chin Feng's hands back into her lap before standing. Moving was slow and painful. But she clambered onto the bed and reached for the window, stretching her arms as she scrabbled to grab hold of the ledge. The bed creaked and she stopped, then tried again, repeating each attempt with the dogged futility of the spider repairing his web. Her arms ached, and her breath came short and fast. She balanced the chair on the bed, felt it wobble as she stood gingerly and for a moment her fingertips touched the sticky, dusty ledge before the chair dislodged and she fell hard to the floor. A sharp pain spiked in her wrist but she didn't move.

The opium smoke seeping under the door made her groggy and she had a sense of falling, like a weighted feather, plummeting in an uncontrollable swirl of heaviness. This was the end; she could finally give up, stop running, just stay on this floor and let her body and mind slip away. Did Judy decide to stop swimming; did she make a choice to die in the river? Her sister would have fought to live.

Annie grabbed at the rough matting beneath her. She raised her face to the window, the muscles in her neck stretched as she tilted her chin up and warmth coursed through her, releasing the tightness along with all those years of guilt. Annie closed her eyes and saw Judy's smiling face. She gently stroked her sister's cheek and felt the warm glow of life on her skin. She felt calm, waiting for her opiate. The air was thick with the smell of it and she breathed in deeply.

'Help me.'

The voice was barely audible, and could have been the rustle of mice under the mats. But Annie heard it, a second time, a cough or croak, it sounded cruelly painful. She looked at Chin Feng's body and saw her foot move. Annie grabbed hold of the girl's hands and leant in close, listening to the sound of her shallow, soft breathing.

'Chin Feng, can you hear me?' Annie whispered for fear of alerting the men. She cut her breath short and held it in her throat, straining to hear.

'Help me.'

Someone moved next door and Annie grabbed Chin Feng's face roughly and held it still. She put a finger to her lips and felt it shaking. She motioned for Chin Feng to be silent and swung around to watch the door. Blood rushed into the white spots on Chin Feng's cheeks where her fingers left their marks and bruises coloured immediately.

'We have to get out.'

Annie clamped her hand over the girl's mouth and held her head close against her stomach. 'Shut up or they'll come back.' She whispered the words into Chin Feng's hair. There was movement next door; light flickered again beneath

the door. Annie watched it, frozen and mesmerised by the
changing hues, but no one entered. Chin Feng's chest rose
and fell against Annie's body. She pressed her fingers into
Annie's arm. There was no strength in her grasp, but Annie
saw the intention in her eyes.

'We escape. I know this place, we use it.'

Chin Feng shuffled her feet across the matting. Annie
pointed down in question and Chin Feng nodded. She
lifted the threadbare carpet and saw a round, dulled metal
handle submerged in the dirt. It was rusted and concealed
by years of disuse. But when Annie rubbed away the earth
she saw a trapdoor. There was rustling and she realised that
the animals she'd heard earlier were beneath the trapdoor,
not the matting.

Annie looked to the door beyond which their captors sat,
before pulling back the threadbare matting and cautiously
pulling on the handle. She heard music and a fresh smell
of opium wafted through from the next room. She quickly
tied her handkerchief around her nose, hoping to reduce the
effects of the opium smoke. Her hands shook as she fumbled
with the knot, acutely aware that each second could make a
difference to their chances of escape. But it was hard to be
calm with the frenzied pounding in her head.

The trapdoor released with a suck of cold, dank air and
loose earth sprinkled down the stone steps that led away.
A squeal echoed back to Annie as an animal scuttled into
the tunnel's safe, dark depths. It smelt of rain on rotting
leaves. The trapdoor was heavy but she was afraid it would
creak if she let it drop completely open. Annie listened, the
women waited; it seemed like time hung in the air with

the cobwebs. The silence reassured Annie they had not been overheard, at least for now. She gently rested the trapdoor on the ground then, as quickly as she could, eased Chin Feng into the hole, taking her weight firmly on her side as she half carried the girl down the uneven stone steps. At the bottom they stopped and Annie returned to shuffle the matting back as much as she could, and closed the trapdoor softly. She knew it would not stop the men from discovering their escape, but at least it would slow them down slightly.

She turned back to Chin Feng who was leaning heavily against a wet, dripping wall of stone and earth. Furry tendrils of black-green moss sprung back when Annie moved her. Beneath their feet the stone was slippery with mould and Annie saw that the tunnel twisted away from them in a dark, low bend. She positioned Chin Feng against her side and wrapped an arm around her shoulder so that as she walked, Annie carried the girl's weight in her hip and torso. They moved slowly down the tunnel, following its path blindly with only the echo of their shoes wet slaps against the stony path. Annie tried to hurry but Chin Feng couldn't walk unaided and their progress was slow. She listened to their laboured breathing and wondered if they would make it out of the tunnel alive. But there was no sound of anyone pursuing them so Annie focused as much as she could on moving forward, pushing and carrying Chin Feng with her and concentrated on the next corner and finding the exit.

Chin Feng tried to speak, coughing uncontrollably as she did. The brief stop allowed Annie to rest her aching arms. For a moment she felt relief, but then her shoulders began to burn from the effort of supporting Chin Feng, and she felt the discomfort flare through her waist, down her calves, right into the balls of her feet. She wondered if she had the strength to continue.

They were standing in a straight length of tunnel that echoed with the drips and trickle of an underground rivulet. Annie moved her hand across the jagged stones in the wall and felt moisture. It had been many hours since she'd drunk anything. Hastily she cupped her hands beneath a rocky point and sucked up each drip that leached forth. Her back winced with pain as she leant towards the wall, but the sweetness of water in her throat was overwhelming. Chin Feng pushed her gently and Annie offered water to the girl from her cupped palms. But Chin Feng shook her head, instead bumping the low mossy base of the wall with her foot. Annie splashed the last drops of water over her neck, enjoying the cold wetness as she looked to where the girl was motioning.

There was a door built into the stone wall. It was wooden when Annie could see it closer, but so covered in mould and moss that it was barely visible. Annie leaned against the wall a moment longer, already feeling dry and parched again. Chin Feng grabbed onto Annie's arm encouragingly and whispered words in Chinese.

The door stuck part way open on the uneven stone floor beyond, exposing the dark passageway in a crack of light. Annie pushed again and felt the ancient wood give way as she stumbled through. Quickly she grabbed Chin Feng and pushed her forward before heaving against the door 'til it shut. Two stone steps led up to a sparsely furnished room.

Annie had to grab at her knees for support as she doubled over, light-headed with the exertion of their escape. She listened for any sound of their pursuers.

When she was sure they had not been followed, Annie stole a look down the corridor. Very quickly she recognised where they were—the back room of the gang house on Xinzha Road. The room was in semi-darkness but Annie knew the corridor Li Qiang had been dragged along. She waited for her head to settle, unsure what to do, certain they could not have escaped unnoticed. She moved Chin Feng to a chair and listened but there were no sounds. The household was asleep. Annie sank to the ground, suddenly empty of the adrenalin that had got her this far. The secret door they had just come through was camouflaged by painted characters on the wall, but it now looked like a seal had been broken where the paint was cracked around the doorframe.

'Are you all right? Can you keep moving?'

Annie knelt down in front of Chin Feng and lifted her head gently so she could see into the girl's eyes. She was frail and stared past Annie to a spot on the wall, her focus lost in a half-formed dream.

'Stop here. Wait.'

It was all Chin Feng said but it was a firm reply. Annie leant back against the wall. Her eyes ached with tiredness but she knew they had to keep moving. They were no safer here than back in the room. She looked down at her hands, which were still smudged red with Chow's blood. It had only been that morning she found him, only a few hours of her life had passed with him dead yet she felt unable to reach the Annie Brand of then. There was no future now, no one to share it with, no reason to hope, she'd lost herself along with Chow, or Chiao Chin Pao; along with the man she loved.

'We must leave now, or the Green Gang will find us.' Annie shook Chin Feng by the shoulders but she refused to move.

'I have to go, do you understand? I can't stay here, I won't.' Annie spoke urgently in a low whisper. She grasped the girl's hands in pleading and kissed them quickly, knowing it was goodbye. Then she turned and slipped silently out the front door.

Immediately Annie was in the street she felt her legs crumple and her head swam. It was a shock to be in a public place. She stood still, rebalancing herself in the moonlight. Natalia had told her so much that was impossible to comprehend. Natalia was a Bolshevik and Chow had been deeply involved with Communists. She'd been an idiot not to see any of the connections. Annie knew she should keep moving, as she turned one way, then the other, confused and disoriented.

She wandered aimlessly and stumbled over a tree root pushed through the footpath. A big American automobile moved past, close to the curb. Its shiny black bulk obliterated her view of the other side of the road. There was a light on in the interior of the vehicle and the Chinese chauffeur was smoking with one elbow resting on the open window. She wondered if she should motion for him to stop. Only she couldn't get her arm to raise enough to wave at the driver and so she just stood there, dazed. A young freckled boy in pyjamas looked out from the back seat. It was late for him to be out, Annie thought. As she watched a hand reached over and patted him, soothingly. His mother, Annie surmised, trying to get the boy to sleep. A blur of blonde curls framed the child's face as he pressed his open palms to the glass. He stuck his tongue out at Annie as he passed. The gesture was full of innocent fun and normally Annie would have laughed and waved back, but she couldn't respond; his pink fleshy tongue was all she saw in that split-second and in her confusion, it looked horrifically, unnaturally distended from his mouth. Coming up behind the car, moving dangerously fast was another vehicle.

The instant was shattered by screeching tyres and a second later a thunderous boom. The boy's door crumpled like papier-mâché as it was hit. Glass smashed out in a thousand dazzling flashes. The car swerved across the road. Annie's nose filled with the smell of hot, burning rubber. She didn't move. Her mind and body felt catatonic; overcome by the day's events. The driver's head hit the wheel as he tried to control the spin. But they kept sliding. She saw the boy in the soft leather back seat. His hands splayed out, catching at the air. His eyes were open wide with shock and his mouth gaped.

The sound of the crash buffeted around Annie, smoke rose alarmingly fast in wide swirls, but it was as though she stood inside a large, protective bubble; so much had happened that day she could not take this latest shocking sight in. She watched the car accident without flinching. It happened very fast, but she felt as though time was suspended with her in the bubble, and the accident unravelled sluggishly in thick, sticky air that slowed everything down to heartbeat after laborious heartbeat of horrifying disaster.

The boy was thrown forward. Annie saw the back of his head shiver sideways with the impact. Both his arms flapped like loose wire connections. The windscreen shattered as his neck smashed through the glass. Then he hit the bonnet and Annie lost sight of him.

Still the second car careered towards her. Annie took a step forward, looking for the boy. He lay buckled in the road, like the malformed tree root she'd stumbled across earlier. Annie saw the car swerve to avoid her, but she couldn't move. The boy lay with one crooked leg stuck out and broken forwards at a confronting angle. She'd seen a dead body already that day, and this boy was as dead as Chow, shut-off from life with the same still, inert indifference. She was reminded too of the small baby's body wrapped in a dirty sheet; the boy's leg was stiff with death like the baby's toes. But she didn't recoil from the sight as she had done earlier in the room with Chow's body. All she could do was stand there and be a witness.

The car clipped Annie as it careered past her into the wall. The bolt of power from the impact pushed all her bones from their locked places. Her stomach jerked as the breath barrelled out of her. She grabbed at herself as her legs slid out. The sound of her own body hitting the ground filled her head a moment before the pain did. Then there was no feeling at all as a dull cloud enveloped her. The chaos in the road disappeared. The panic throbbing in her ears receded. Quickly, silently, everything went black.

CHAPTER FIFTEEN

A wild current swirled and pounded in her head, crashing and churning. There was a searing pain in Annie's arm. Her back was numb. If she moved, even a little, it roared in her head again. When she closed her eyes the current was still there, dragging her under. She gasped.

'Missy, Missy?'

She tried to concentrate on the voice. It was agitated but not angry, a woman. Annie dragged herself up out of the heaviness with another gasp.

'Is okay, you okay? You very lucky.'

From where she lay, head flat against the footpath, Annie could see individual specks of glass glinting like stars. They spanned out from right beside her cheek. She tried to look around but it hurt too much. Ahead, one of the cars had stopped in the road. Fluid leaked from somewhere beneath the bonnet, running to the drain in a watery kaleidoscope of metallic sheens. But right there, where the cool stone of the footpath soothed her cheek, was restful.

A crowd huddled around something. There was noise; shouting and crying. Close to Annie the woman looked at her with concern. She was a young stranger, trying to help.

'Yes, okay,' Annie whispered.

The noise of a siren made her wince. Her head ached. She pushed herself up to sit propped against a building. One arm hurt terribly. Her back had begun to thaw, and with it another torrent of pain washed through her.

It took a moment to remember where she was. Then the local police arrived, setting up barriers, pushing the crowd back from the scene, using their whistles constantly. The noise was unbearable. Annie remembered how she'd ended up there. She had to leave, the police had too many connections, too many spies, she'd be discovered and the news would quickly get back to Natalia and her men.

As she struggled to move, a hand rested on her shoulder. The fingers were fine and long. She looked up at the face of the woman, a stranger and her protector now, who patted Annie and motioned for her to stay still, like Annie was a dog. But she hurt too much to care. She closed her eyes to it all and gave in to overwhelming exhaustion. She couldn't move, let alone run away. It was a relief to close her eyes and subside into oblivion.

The light flared and disappeared, flared and disappeared. Annie blinked awake. A minute, an hour, she had no idea how long she'd been there. Her arm throbbed horribly. But at least the pain pulled her out of the blur.

She saw the sock first. It was blue wool, with a white rabbit embroidered on the side of the ankle; a child's sock. It stuck out awkwardly. There was no shoe. The sock had been darned; neat stitches looped across the big toe area, back and forth to build up a replacement layer of wool. His mother probably mended his socks.

Then she saw the woman kneeling down beside the boy. His head fell limply forward into her chest as his mother hugged him. Her face hung in his hair. Her body shook uncontrollably. From somewhere deep within, the moan of an injured animal erupted in pitiful cries as her hands scrambled across his back, across his legs, pulling at the limbs to tuck them into her embrace.

Someone stepped in front of Annie and hands reached down to help her up. She looked around, confused, trying to see the blue sock. But she was being led towards an ambulance, led away from the small body wrapped in his mother's desolation, away from the sock so lovingly darned to keep that little foot safe as it skipped through a boy's day.

The rough hospital sheets didn't move as Annie rolled over. Her head hurt. Her wrist was wrapped in a cotton bandage. A second bandage covered the cut on the back of her head where she'd hit the pavement. She laid still, legs straight, arms resting on her thighs.

A nurse gave Annie something for the pain. She felt herself sliding out of her body, not into unconsciousness but no longer part of the pain. At last, the men had given her the opiate. She thought she was slipping through oblivion with a deathly overdose, laid on a rough bed still covered in Chow's blood. The image was thin and papery; she could walk through it like walking through the washing blowing

dry in the garden at home. Then she was swimming in the
river, struggling to breathe, fighting against the current.
It was no good, death always won, she had no choice. No
choice who to love; her sister, her father, someone else? The
other man, Chiao Chin Pao; his name felt wispy, like the
sheet in the breeze again, only this time it was a note, folded
into a soft square, telling him things she shouldn't say, helping him to die. The boy lay in the road like a tree root. His
mother knew it was death she clung to; that her boy was
already gone, into the ground with the seeds for next year's
crop. Where was the ground? Annie hovered in her mind
above her bed. Where was the girl who left the valley for
adventure? Where did she go?

A doctor approached. She latched on to his arm.

'Help me,' Annie whispered and she heard Chin Feng
talking in her ear. 'Help me.'

Annie woke feeling groggy and sore. But her head was
clear, and as the evening lights turned on, she looked
around the ward. Rows of thin metal beds were packed
tightly like finger biscuits in a tin. Beside her a small stove
was alight on the floor. Two women prepared food for the
patient next to Annie. Chopsticks flashed through green
stalks in the wok. They stared up at the misplaced foreign woman. She lay back against the pillow and took a
deep breath, wincing with pain, but she took another, and
another, expanding her chest so that heat scorched across
her back, willing to endure the pain because at least it was
a feeling, she was still breathing, still alive and still able
to hurt.

A doctor approached, and walking beside him, Annie saw Ilma. Her eyes stung with tears at the unexpected sight of her friend. She hurried towards her with such a familiar, gambolling style it made Annie catch her breath with relief. She closed her eyes.

The doctor talked in hushed, respectful tones, not wanting to wake Annie.

'Please excuse my English. We do not often get foreigners in this hospital. This lady is very fortunate; no broken bones, some bruising, very deep, and cuts. She must leave bandages on for next week. But there is something else that concerns me. May I speak frankly?'

Annie heard Ilma cough.

'Are you aware your friend is with child?'

'I beg your pardon?'

Annie heard the shock in Ilma's voice. Her fingers dug into the pillow as she listened, every fibre in her body tensed with disbelief.

'Yes, and I would like your permission to assess her to confirm that the baby was not harmed.'

'Of course, do what you must.'

Annie heard the doctor move forward, pulling a screen to the end of the bed to shield them from view. She felt his cold hands against her belly and couldn't help a shiver as he pressed gently. She went over the dates in her head to work out how long since she was last on the rag; more than two months without a doubt, maybe even three. She felt her stomach start to roll and churn.

'Pregnant?'

She whispered the word and listened to it hanging in the air.

'Annie, you're awake.'

She hadn't realised she'd said the word out loud as Ilma snuck in behind the screen. The doctor stopped his examination and smiled at Annie. His eyes were sunken with puffy mounds of tiredness suspended beneath each one. Annie concentrated on the doctor's face and the professional concern she saw in his eyes but she couldn't stop the tears that fell unhindered.

Ilma was looking at her intently.

'Did you hear what the doctor said, Annie? It's good news, no time for tears. You are going to have a baby—a baby, Annie. You've been in a terrible accident but there are no broken bones, and the baby is healthy, the doctor has checked. It's all going to be better now; I'm here and I will do everything to make you comfortable.'

Ilma bundled her into an embrace and Annie breathed in the familiar scent of Yardley's lavender soap, where her cheek pressed against the smooth cotton of Ilma's blouse.

'There you go, my dear, it's shock, that's all, let's go home. Some tea will help and then you might feel up to celebrating.' Her voice hovered in the room, soft and reassuring.

'The future will be here sooner than you think, Annie, and it's going to be grand.'

Annie rested in bed. She rolled over and faced the window where the underside of a leaf pushed against the glass, its veins pressed flat like the lifelines on her palm. Her silent tears fell onto the pillow. She closed her eyes, wishing for the blankness of sleep. Ilma appeared at her door, smiling broadly before shuffling in to smooth the blankets, leaning over Annie heavily a moment as she reached across to the far side.

'My dear, when do you want to talk about all this?'

Annie looked away. The fan's slow turn marked every new, weary moment. She thought about Natalia's men waiting for her. She didn't know if her house in the Settlement was safe from the gang; she wondered if the gang had allowed Chin Feng to return to her village. But it all seemed pointless. Chow's death eclipsed any future.

Ilma spoke again. 'This must be terribly difficult for you, but you have trusted me in the past and I ask you to do it now. There are things you must consider. Please Annie, talk to me.'

The house boy had left a sprig of rosemary beside Annie's bed to help with nausea. It slid in the small pot of water and hung precariously at the edge. Annie propped herself up against the pillows and tucked her legs into her chest, hugging her knees. She rubbed her arms, willing the bruises to disappear.

'Now you are carrying a child, you cannot avoid the future; there must be a reckoning.' Ilma's weight made the bed sag towards her when she sat. Annie reached for the rosemary and held it to her nose. She swallowed hard.

'The baby is not Alec's. This is Chow's unborn child.'

'I wondered as much. Oh my poor, dear girl.' Ilma leant over and stroked Annie's brow. 'Does he know?'

Annie's feet were cold beneath the sheets. Her voice sounded foreign.

'He is dead, Ilma. Chow was killed by the police.' She heard her friend's intake of breath but she couldn't look at her. There would be too much sympathy and it was all

Annie could do to keep speaking. 'They thought he was with a criminal gang working for the Communists. He was, actually.' She spoke slowly, as though understanding the story for the first time. 'I had no idea,' her voice trailed off. Ilma held her close and Annie didn't resist the soft rocking embrace.

A week later, Annie sat propped in a chaise longue in her garden. The house boy was preparing lunch. Small pieces of ripped-up bread scattered across the back steps and Annie watched as a bird hopped amongst them, gobbling each bite quickly before any other birds joined him. She thought of that long ago afternoon when she let her bird escape and wondered if it had survived all the freedom that Shanghai offered.

'Here you are. Now, I've finalised the ticket and you will meet Mr and Mrs Broadbent at the docks. They are a wonderful couple and you will be in good hands.' Ilma came up to stand in front of Annie, blocking the view of the garden. She spoke briskly but it didn't hide the uncertainty in her voice.

An outline of light framed her shape as Annie squinted up at her. 'I'm really very comfortable with this decision. You've no need to worry.'

Ilma had arranged Annie's passage home with Freemason friends who were returning to Australia. The two had talked about Annie staying in China; Ilma had even offered to help raise the baby. But Annie knew that would not be possible. Even though Natalia had left her alone, she could not stay. Chow's death had closed the circle of Annie's life in Shanghai.

'Sit down, Ilma. You're hovering again, and it makes me nervous.' Annie looked out across her garden but it no longer felt like home. It was mostly in shade these days under the many fruit trees whose branches spread in a ramshackle cover. They had not borne fruit as Annie hoped, perhaps next year, but by then it would be someone else's garden.

CHAPTER SIXTEEN

Karoola Private Hospital, New South Wales,
November 1925

Waking in the countryside of her childhood was always going to be hard. Annie can see the family farm now as clearly as the day she left; the old wooden house transformed by the evening light. Weather-beaten and in need of paint even back then, the sun had licked away all the freshness and rain had made the damp above the door a permanent feature. The verandah was long round the sides, enclosed with wooden lattice to keep out the flies. From the front porch where she and Judy watched the sun go down, she could see across the paddocks to the line of trees where the thick bush scrub began, spotted with cows and hazy in the evening sunlight as a dusting of flies and evening bugs rose from the grass.

Annie lets the early morning breeze fill her room with shivering gusts just to inhale that freshness; it is still such a revelation after the gutter-hot Shanghai air. There is a knock at the door and a nurse hands over a neat stack of laundered clothes. She busies herself refolding the shirts before she puts them away. The Buddha wobbles briefly as she opens and shuts each drawer of her dresser.

What else has she missed of home? Only those who no longer exist; and even then, Annie realises, being home offers her nothing more comforting than a closeness to the memories of her mother and her sister.

She closes the window. Today it will gust and billow outside if the early morning breeze keeps up, and rain will follow; that glorious pounding of water on earth that makes you shout to be heard.

It rained that hard the day of her mother's wake. She remembers the sound of it tumbling upon the roof as she occupied herself with supplying cups of tea or whisky, or both mixed together, to the small gathering of their family friends. No one saw her flinch when a teacup slipped through her fingers to the floor. She just brought out the broom and swept away the broken china, one less of her mother's to wash up in the morning. She sent her younger sister to bed early that day, so she didn't have to watch their father crumple with grief and whisky. Then Annie crept into Judy's bed when everyone had left, and held her warm sleeping body, slotting herself into the curve of her sister's back and legs, as she tried to suffocate her own sadness.

She never understood why people thought it would be a comfort to give her sentimental keepsakes after their mother died; the lace-edged card with a black silhouette of her mother's face, or the returned handkerchief her mother sewed for a neighbour as a present one year. Annie hid these things in a drawer in the kitchen, too afraid to open it and be reminded of those unbearable weeks of mourning.

She took over the job of looking after her sister once their mother died. In the beginning she held her breath when Judy needed a hug, so strong was the smell of their mother in the child's hair. But through the years, Annie learnt to ignore the ache in her chest and be strong. She loved Judy fiercely; proud that only she could make things right for her little sister, whether it was a tickle to stop the tears or an hour-long chat about her day. It was a job she loved. Those long years of hard work flew by as Annie watched her sister grow up. It was as though all the richness of their lush, river-bound farm was sucked up by Judy. Annie saw it in her bronzed skin and flushed cheeks, in the way she ran barefoot across the paddock to catch sight of the nesting owls in the crooked gum, turning to wave in huge skyward sweeps to Annie watching from the kitchen window. Annie knew Judy's contentment was due to her, which is why she never forgave herself that one moment of looking the wrong way.

Annie picks up the Buddha statue and holds it to her face, breathing in the rich smell of scented wood. He is her keepsake now, her reminder. In the bungalow in Shanghai the house boy would be rolling out the winter rugs in readiness for the colder months. The Yangtze tides would be too low by now to navigate very far north so the Club would be even busier than usual.

Outside, a group of women dash from a bus in the drive for cover from the first dollops of rain. They shake the water off their hats, laughing with the exhilaration of running, as they wait for the doors to open. Annie sees her visitor, Molly Lowe, amongst them. She wasn't sure Molly would come today but the sight of her is a pleasant surprise. At least Annie can distract herself with conversation and Molly does make her laugh. She has a dry humour that borders on rudeness, which any other patient would find offensive. But Annie knows Molly well enough to hear the pain beneath her sarcasm; an ache that is deserving of compassion. Molly told Annie she couldn't have children. Annie sensed a gritty sadness beneath the surface of Molly's confession but she said nothing further and Annie didn't pry.

In the entrance hall, Molly busily folds her raincoat into a neat bundle.

'I was worried the weather might have put you off visiting today.' Annie hugs her friend through the damp feel of her loose hair.

'Of course I'm here. Aren't we childhood friends who have some catching up to do?'

'Thank you, Molly; your visits are the highlight of my week.'

'They make my week extra special too. Now, let's move through to the lounge or we'll both catch a cold in this damp and they won't let me visit again if I make you sicker than when you arrived!' Molly's chuckle cuts through Annie's thoughts and as she leads the way to a spot in a corner of the communal lounge room she considers her friend. Here is a generous, hard-working woman who laughs more than she complains. She really does look forward to seeing Molly. Today her friend pulls out a coconut slice, sweet and juicy.

'I didn't bake this,' she explains. 'I'm good in the shop, not so good in my own kitchen. Don't laugh, Annie, I know a poor cook in a bakery is an oddity but then, Mr Lowe never married me for my cooking. I always thought I'd have a daughter to help me, maybe even someone who enjoyed baking. But there you go, wasn't to be. Poor Mr Lowe thought he'd be passing the business on to a son. His cousin arrived from Victoria last week. They say it's a family visit, but I can see he's eyeing up the bakery for his own boy. What a cheek. Mind you, we've no son to pass the business onto so perhaps we should consider it; always got to see the positive.'

Molly licks her fingers and brushes coconut flecks off her skirt. Annie realises Molly will always be 'childless Mrs Lowe' to the world, and her future will forever be defined by that one fact. There's no escape for Molly.

'That's decades away, Molly. Goodness me, I believe you can sell that business for good money and set yourselves up very nicely. Don't be bamboozled by your husband's cousin.'

Molly pats Annie's knee; it's a motherly gesture and reminds Annie of her dear friend Ilma. 'What's wrong?' Molly slides forward in her chair as Annie pulls away.

'It's been a long time since I felt genuine affection; the nurses don't often wrap you in a hug, more the cod liver oil approach. Now, tell me some news of the outside world, please.'

'Nothing really to share, Annie, business is good. The local minister cleaned up his spare room to rent it out. Always the same guests who claim they're spending the night to be closer to God, just coincidence the pub is two doors down from church. That's one way to increase your Sunday congregation! But I haven't come here to talk about my own boring life. How are you feeling?'

'One day at a time is my approach. I'm as well as can be expected, a bit uncomfortable, that's all.'

'Have you thought about the future, Annie? What are you going to do?'

'The only thing I know: get up and keep going. I can't plan more than that Molly. It might sound unreasonable to you, but at least I've only got myself to worry about, it's much easier than considering a future with a husband and a business, a home as well. I don't have any of those things.'

'Have you thought any further about seeing your father? I know how hard it is for you but he's family, the only family you have it seems to me, and that's not something to dismiss.'

'You're my family Molly, you and this godforsaken hospital.'

'Now I know you're joking. Of course you are family to me, Annie, and very welcome at our home for as long as you would like. I'd be excited to have some female company.'

'What would Mr Lowe have to say I wonder?'

'You leave him to me, there's ways to get around a man, don't worry about that!'

'I have absolute faith in your abilities. I'm lucky to have such a kind and thoughtful friend, even after I left you behind when I ran away.'

'We both had dreams, Annie. I chose to stay, but I didn't begrudge you leaving.'

'It all seems far too impulsive now.'

'Are you disappointed things turned out this way? We all want a husband and a home to go to.'

'I thought I did, for quite a long time I tried that life. But something in me wouldn't settle.'

'Don't blame yourself; it takes two people to make a marriage work.'

'You are a modern thinker, Molly. What does Mr Lowe say when you talk like that?'

'I'd never talk to Mr Lowe like this! I'm happy to be his wife and take care of him. Home and husband is enough for me, I am settled, unlike you. But I do enjoy thinking about your future, a woman on her own.'

An hour later, the bus horn sounds to tell them that its time the visitors return to town. Molly hovers a moment as she puts on her coat. She leans in close to Annie and speaks softly.

'It wasn't your fault, Annie; tragedy can be horribly random and you suffered as much as your father. Go and see him, please.' She squeezes Annie's arm with encouragement and leaves before Annie has time to reply.

The corridor is quiet after the visitors depart and the hospital's main door closes. Inside reverts to the familiar hush of the nurses' silent faith, behind which everyone is hidden.

CHAPTER SEVENTEEN

December 1925

The hospital is quiet; most of the patients have left on a day trip into town to shop for small Christmas presents. But Annie turned down the invitation, choosing instead to wander the corridors and roam through the lounge in self-imposed isolation. There is no one for whom she wants to buy a gift. She doesn't expect to receive any either, and that suits Annie. She remembers the general store on Rudder Street where her father bought tobacco—her nose came up to the counter just high enough to see the rolling forearms of Mrs Hewitt as she stuffed the leaves into a pouch. The possibility of seeing her father in town makes Annie sick with nerves. She presses a hand to her throat and feels the throb of her pulse.

Her father's farm is only a short drive from Karoola, close enough to visit. She remembers his favourite motorbike, the second-hand Invincible JAP, strong and lean, like those racing dogs stretching out to catch a rabbit. Two twist grips (throttle on the right, ignition on the left), foot clutch, foot brake and hand change, plenty to fiddle with while riding. He let her ride it on her eighteenth birthday, as a treat.

She flew straight up the fence line of the home paddock, then moved slowly through the grass and dirt of the cow yards, one foot on the ground, careful not to lose her balance. Somewhere behind, her father stood watching and waiting. *Don't dare look back*, she told herself as the bike wobbled, challenging her concentration. She bent her head low to the metal dome and let the bike roar, feeling the speed by the wind that caught at her mouth and whipped the saliva from the edges of her smile.

Cows shied and stumbled away as she rode too close to the fence. Ahead, her father's big hands waved. It was exhilarating, terrifying and fast as hell. The corner came up quickly. Her turn was overzealous. She fell sideways, and lay listening to the engine growling beside her as the bike tipped into the grass.

Her father's worried face loomed close as she grabbed his outstretched hand and hauled herself up.

'That'll do for today, missy.' The motorbike was as special as his prized bull and it made her feel special too. She'd left it to rust, abandoned in Sydney.

A sound from the hallway makes Annie look towards the door. Surely no one is back so soon? Molly rushes in the moment Annie turns the handle. Her face is flushed and blotchy from crying and she falls into Annie's arms.

'My dear, what on earth has happened? What are you doing here?' Annie helps Molly to a lounge chair and pulls one closer for herself, holding onto her friend's knees as though she will slide off the chair at any moment.

Molly wipes her face, crushing a cotton handkerchief into her eyes and nose. She breathes unevenly, sucking air quickly in a jagged, messy rhythm and then slowly breathing out again. Annie waits while Molly regains some control.

'It's not me after all, it's him, Annie. All this time I thought I was the failure, I was to blame, and he never said a word. But it's him that's got the problem, Mr Herbie Lowe himself.'

'I don't understand. What problem? What is this about?' Annie strokes her friend's hands as she speaks.

'He can't have children, it's his fault.' Annie falls back into her chair at the anger in Molly's voice.

'He's the barren one, not me,' Molly screams the words out into the empty room. Her hot breath rushes into Annie's face. 'All this time, keeping it quiet while I cried and apologised.' She talks quietly now, crying again.

'My poor, dear friend,' Annie speaks softly too. 'How did you find out?'

'He told me, finally. Said he couldn't bear to see me so unhappy, couldn't bear keeping the secret, knowing it was hurting me.'

'It's all very well to be caring now, what about these past years? How long has he known?'

'It was a childhood illness that did it to him; he was only a young boy. He said he thought I wouldn't marry him if he'd told me the truth back then, and he couldn't bear to lose me.'

'What's changed now I say? The stakes are still the same.'

'No, they are not; he knows I love him. I could never leave him now.'

'Don't be a fool, Molly. You can divorce the cad and find a man who wants children as much as you. It may not be the norm, but I can tell you it will mean a happier future and that's the most important thing, your happiness. Come and let's walk in the garden.'

For Annie, the limitless sky and familiar bird sounds in Karoola's small patch of grass give her the courage to consider alternate endings to her own predicament and she hopes the fresh surroundings might offer the same to Molly. They are not so different, she surmises; both struggling to define themselves in a world where motherhood, marriage and home are all that matters.

Molly shakes her head at Annie's outstretched hand and remains seated as she speaks. 'That's just the thing, Herbie wants children as much as I do; I know that he's torn up about this just like me. We both wish for our own little family. I could never leave him, especially now he's told the truth. We're stuck with each other.'

Annie closes her eyes and opens them again, as though the action will change what she is hearing. Molly is no longer crying. She has a whimsical smile on her face.

'I'm confused. A moment ago you were screaming the house down about this man. Now you are smiling coyly. What has changed?'

'I suppose saying it out loud sort of got rid of the anger and you telling me to leave Herbie only makes me realise I can't do that. I love him. I'm all right now, Annie, really I am. His deception is what hurt the most and I'm not denying that will take time to right itself but at least he's told the truth. I'm sorry for worrying you with my hysterics, but it's all out now.'

'I admire your courage, Molly. I don't agree with your decision but I won't say another word against it.'

'Thank you, Annie. It's simple really. I need Herbie as much as he needs me. Now I'd better get home. Herbie will be worrying.' But she hesitates, and reaches her arm into her oversized bag. 'I almost forgot these.'

Annie accepts the handful of small, waxy mandarins. 'The first of the season, thank you.'

'Now, I really must be going. It's not visiting day here either; I'll get in trouble. Thank you for helping me make sense of this.'

Annie has no idea what help she has been. She waves her friend goodbye in bemused confusion and holds one of the soft mandarins up to her nose; the citrus smells fresh and sweet.

'When the mandarins are ripe, the tailor are on the bite.' Her father's prophecy slips from her lips, making her smile. He was not a religious man and she remembers how he would hold forth on a Sunday morning while they waited patiently for a fish to take the bait, standing still and quiet in the low-tide sandbank. He could send that fishing line halfway across the river, to the deep, dark centre where the bream swam. Or if he was after flathead, he could make the line sing silently through the water, coming to rest on the sandy bottom for a moment, luring that flathead towards the bait, before skipping the line off again, until the fish's open mouth would catch the hook and he'd snagged the sweetest fish in the river for tea. Those were good Sundays.

She must look to her future now, to each new day. Could she ask for her father's forgiveness, could he be a part of that future?

The afternoons are long at Karoola, where night waits for the final rustling in the trees to end before drowning the land in a dark flood. Annie's bed is thin and high, plain white-painted metal rods form a cross in the headboard. Her fingers trace the smooth lines rhythmically and she repeats the exercise more slowly, concentrating on her control. There's only the bare hint of a tremor now as her fingers slide around the bed frame. She sighs deeply and lets her arm drop. Stars appear in the square of night beyond her window. It's the same sky her father sees from the farm, not so far away. Further still, the sky looks down on Shanghai—a world away.

There's a small table beside her bed, where the strong scent of jasmine hangs in the flowers that fill the jam jar. She closes her eyes and breathes in the sweetness, but sleep doesn't come. Jasmine grew on the walls of her garden in Shanghai, and the smell reminds her of that other life. The bedsprings wheeze through her shifting weight. The quiet rushes about in her head like a moth caught in a net. She just needs a few hours of peace, of not thinking through the next months of her life. So she gets up, rubbing the Buddha's tummy before she wraps a shawl around herself and pads quietly out into the corridor.

Beyond the doors, the cool, fresh air smells of tomorrow's rain and crushed leaves. Annie stands barefoot in the garden, looking up to the stars, and the vast blackness that swells about them, wondering if this will be her patch of sky for the future: if she will live so near to her childhood home, looking into this same night. To be so close to home, the enormity of her secret escape flares again like a freshly stoked hearth.

There's still an unexpected churn of nerves in Annie's stomach at the memory of the night she stole her father's motorbike and left. She knew the key hung by the back door and reminded herself to go carefully as the door whined so awfully. She sat a while in her sister's room that afternoon and felt some comfort in stroking the bedcover that lay untouched. She talked to Judy too, explaining her decision to leave in a hushed voice despite the fact there was no one to hear her. It didn't matter to Annie. At least she told the one person who would have missed her.

The sound of buzzing was close in her ears. Mosquitoes bit her cheeks and neck. She walked his bike further than was necessary, too nervous to start the engine. The mud pressed into the tyres like the dough she'd left to rise for the morning's bread. Her eyes winced each time the bike hit her shins. In the dark she couldn't see the potholes. She wanted to turn the key, let the engine roar and speed her away, but she feared it would let out her secret and scream *here she is, your thieving daughter, here is your blood betrayal.*

Only when her hands were sore to touch, when her shins were bloody, only when she'd pushed her father's bike as far as she was physically able did she let herself breathe.

'Bloody road, bloody mud, damn it Dad,' she muttered to herself bitterly.

She felt the sweat merging with her tears and her curses. The bike waited 'til she was ready, then she got on. It warmed up under her acceleration, heavy and wobbly. She held her legs tight against the twin tanks. The air was cold and the wind hit her face constantly. She dug her chin into the scarf wrapped around her neck, and was grateful for the gloves that were resting on the bike's seat. She wore a felt cap, tipped forward, and kept her father's riding goggles deep in her coat pocket, but soon enough decided to put them on. The fast-moving air cut into her eyes and dried them out.

Her fingers were numb under the gloves, hooked like bird's feet around the handlebars. Her back hunched into an arc over the body of the bike, her neck stretched forward.

'Goodbye Annabelle Samuels.'

The words whipped from her mouth and disappeared in an instant. The road wound through thick trees and bush and out again into cleared farmland. She thought she heard egrets rise from a swamp in one mass. But all around was still. The noise of the bike filled her ears and her head and was deep in her belly, throbbing constantly, grating into her pores, like the waves of metallic fumes in her nose.

After days of riding, she reached the wharf, and stood beside a giant of a boat, hair tangled, legs shaking, alone and lost and ready to find herself on board and sail away from home, from her father, from her life, from herself.

Something moves again amongst the bushes, turning the garden around Annie into a whispering, living thing. Like the nocturnal animals she can't see, she doesn't know who she is at that moment. No longer the girl raised in the farmhouse of her memories, married and widowed far from home and still a stranger to herself.

The night sky hangs blankly above as Annie lowers herself to sit leaning against the wooden fence. She remembers sitting with Chow on the grassy slope of hillside by the Yangtze River. Chow leaned over and crooked an elbow beside her, his hand stroked her face. She can feel the softness now, and so real is the sensation, Annie leans in to the empty night garden, towards the memory of Chow.

There's so much portent in the stars she shuts them out and as her mind relaxes, the idea of visiting her father hovers nervously. Would he agree to meet her, could he forgive her twice? In the garden around her the animal noises stay close.

CHAPTER EIGHTEEN

March 1926

When did it all start to go wrong? Was her fate sealed by that first kiss with Chow? Annie had never been in control of all the pieces or had all the information. Only now can she see this, here at Karoola, where time and distance seem to be turning her years in Shanghai into someone else's story. Here she can judge her old life and all her hopeless inadequacies. Now she can see how little she knew Chow, how much she assumed.

Lately this hospital feels less like a temporary rest and more like a permanent destination. The problem, she realises ruefully, is that she's spent too much time here already. Annie looks out of the bus window that's taking them to the picnic spot beside the Macleay. There are ten other patients seated in rows around her. No one is talking. This is the hospital's first picnic since Annie arrived at Karoola, the first chance of a social gathering for all of them; perhaps everyone is feeling introspective like her, as they travel slowly through the landscape.

It was never her intention to come home like this. But her life ran hideously out of control in Shanghai after she returned from the Yangtze; a river that covered so many miles of countryside it felt like she'd slipped into another China as they sailed. But she couldn't escape events in Shanghai. That river journey took her away from the city, but it didn't protect her.

The road is bumpy and Annie holds the seat firmly to stop her body jiggling with the movement. They are so close to the river; she can see a ripple run across the water's surface as a school of small fish swim by out of sight. The patients' picnic is a welcome distraction from the boredom at Karoola, but none of the nurses know the significance of the river for Annie.

They were canoeing, taking the shortcut home. Annie and her sister had taken off their shoes and hitched their dresses up to their thighs as they struck out through the familiar water. But somewhere in the middle between the blue-black deep and sandy shallows, the canoe tipped sideways and as they struggled in the water, Judy flung out a hand that Annie didn't catch. The current caught them unawares, moving so swift and strong in the dead centre of the river. Annie remembers the small boat approaching and her glorious relief. But it passed the girls as Annie waved and called frantically. She kept her eyes on the boat, on their chance of safety, and watched as it turned and drifted back towards them in the current's passage. She turned to Judy, grinning and whooping with glee, but she was gone. A hand reached down and grabbed Annie by her dress, dragging her out of the water. She pushed it away, trying to get back to the water and her sister, but they held her tight. A man dived in to look for Judy and she heard the fathomless echo of his splashes and hopeless gasps through the hollow tin floor of the boat where she lay exhausted and empty.

She sighs deeply as the bus pulls up beside a patch of grass that runs down to the riverbank. In front of her the Macleay stretches across a vast reach of muddy water. This is the first time she has looked at it for years. Even before she left the valley, Annie stopped going near the river. It overflowed with the horror of death and loss and it was impossible to look at it and not feel her chest fill with suffocating guilt. She stares out into the fast-moving current, breathing deeply. A fishing boat sails smoothly past with a pelican trailing in its wake. She remembers watching the birds that circled above Alec's ship as they sailed along the Yangtze. There's the same sense of lazy journeying in this river's view, but Annie knows the moving waters are not as placid as they seem. Would the years make Chow's absence more bearable too? Rivers, for Annie, will always be about loss.

Someone calls to her to join them before the ham sandwiches are all eaten. She turns away from the river and sits down with the group. The smell of dried oyster shells carries on the breeze off the water and makes her think of days spent exploring the uneven rocky banks while her father fished. It feels right to be back; despite her circumstances, this is home.

'Why the sad face, Annie?' a woman asks her pleasantly.

'I'm not sad, just thoughtful. This place does that to me.'

'You've heard the story, then, of the young girl who drowned near here, a few years ago now? Such a tragedy; they say her sister up and ran away afterwards and died too.'

The woman relays the story with the easy impunity of someone disconnected from the tragedy. There is no reason for her to be otherwise, except were she to notice the stunned look on her fellow picnicker's face. But Annie doesn't socialise with the other patients, and her discomfort goes unnoticed today just as her presence has been ignored in the preceding months.

'How did the sister die?' Annie hears her own question like an echo from within the cavernous well into which she's fallen at the mention of her past. She knows every intimate detail of this story but its unexpected retelling, here, as she looks over the very river of her sister's demise, unnerves her utterly.

'Threw herself off a ship in the middle of the ocean, so her father said.'

Unaware of the impact of her words, the woman picks at bits of food stuck in her teeth, sucking and smacking her lips with enthusiasm.

'Do you know her father?' Annie tries to steady her voice as she asks.

'No, never met the man. I heard it from my sister who had a friend who knew the family.'

Annie leaves the ham sandwich untouched in its paper wrapping. She wanders back down to the riverbank and stumbles in the mangrove roots where the grass turns to dirty sand. Behind her, the woman calls out again—her sandwich will be eaten if she leaves it too long. Annie ignores their laughter.

Now she knows how much leaving home hurt her father. It was her only chance of a future, that's what she told herself. How easily she managed to crush any thought of her father's desperation at finding his only remaining child gone that morning as her silhouette dissolved into the quiet of the pre-dawn paddocks.

Now she is back, and standing beside the river, with home so close, she understands in that moment how deeply she betrayed him. She pictures her father angry and ashamed, pretending his daughter is dead to anyone who asks. It makes her heart contract with sadness and her eyes sting with the emotion of holding back tears. There is no chance of explaining why she left now, or apologising for stealing his motorbike. Her father's already decided her fate; Annabelle Samuels drowned two years ago. She can never be that girl again.

The flies are beginning to annoy Annie. She brushes them off her face. There is no point staring at the river any longer. There will be no reconciliation with her father. There is no one now who cares about her fate. She will waste no more time on notions of hope which are as flighty as one aimless cloud. She must make a new start. It's a necessary decision. Her job is to simply keep going, no faith required.

Annie fingers her gold wedding band. The ring rolls silently through the grass as she throws it: a glinting circle of security for someone else. If she is to focus ahead, she must do so with honesty, and hope that others accept her because of it; there will be no more deception, just as there is no more running.

CHAPTER NINETEEN

April 1926

Annie pushes herself up to sit so that Molly can massage her swollen ankles. She slept poorly the previous night; a dream of Chow with her on the boat trip up the Yangtze woke her and now she can't get rid of the image of him drowning; sucking air frantically as his arms splash each time his head rises above the water.

'You're a good friend,' Annie sighs, leaning back as she tries to shift the baby's weight off her bladder.

Molly smiles through her industrious kneading. The pressure sends pleasant waves of warmth through Annie's calves.

'I'm lucky you found me again, Mrs Molly Lowe.'

'I've not done badly out of the friendship either, Mrs Brand.'

'Remember how surprised I was to see you? We must look an odd couple—the unhappily pregnant vixen with kindly

Mrs Lowe who longs for the child she cannot bear. Sorry, Molly, sounds so harsh.'

'It's the truth Annie; I've come to terms with it so it doesn't hurt anymore, and as you say best to be straight. Mr Lowe and I do just fine.'

'Maybe it wasn't coincidence, Molly. Maybe our reunion was meant to be.'

'Always see the positive—remember?'

'Yes, yes, I remember your husband's catchphrase, how could I forget it when you say the words almost every time we meet!'

'Some days I need to remind myself.'

Annie reaches for the Buddha statue on the table beside her bed and rubs its stomach tenderly with her thumb a moment before handing it to Molly.

'I want you to have him, as a thank you for putting up with me.'

'Annie, I can't take this; I know how precious it is to you.'

'I insist. After all these months you deserve it. I was hopeless with Christmas gifts anyway. Please Molly, you can't say no.'

'What on earth will I do with a Buddha statue?'

'I'm sure you'll find a home for him.'

Molly reaches over and hugs Annie. She smells of flour and salt, of pre-dawn kneading in a hot, sticky kitchen. Her thick arms hold Annie only a moment.

The tightening around Annie's groin intensifies, hard and sharp. The baby shifts inside and it feels like a huge glug of water trying to find space in an already full bottle. Deep, flushing breaths push her through the pain. Molly runs for a nurse.

'I'll be back when you're done.' Molly strokes Annie's brow before she is ushered out. 'I'll bring some things for the arrival and we'll celebrate. Don't be afraid, it will all be over soon and you'll have a beautiful new bub to show for it.' Her words fade away as Annie is taken to the surgery.

She grips the metal bed frame and groans. It's like a horse kicking her on the inside. Each wave of pain sinks so deeply in her bones that it feels like her tongue will rip from her mouth. The sound is guttural; Annie grunts and pushes. Her legs are locked into stirrups, so she can't move. Something cool and wet on her forehead gives momentary relief. Then she's in the pit of her body, the dark, suffocating hole where the pain smothers her mind. She pushes at the stirrups, screaming. Hands hold her, soothing hands that don't help. Panic rises out of her, like a terrifying monster. She rides on it, holding to the pain and the terror of this thing that keeps pushing at her to escape.

There is one last moment, tipped into her baby's birth, the moment when light touches the unopened eyes. Her mind is down with the crowning head in that moment, down feeling the shaft of that light piercing her, the weight of his shoulders ripping, down being the light and the pain, being flushed with the light and the pain of his body as it slips from her. And then gushing, exhausting relief.

A nurse lifts the newborn clear. Hands rub him over and wash away the birth. Muffled noises of wrapping reach Annie. A glorious feeling of sweet nothing consumes her. No pain, no weight, just her own tired body.

'It's a boy,' she hears someone say.

Then her son cries. It's shaky and pitchy, demanding and pointed with the first flush of hunger. The sound reaches down and attaches to Annie's core. It drags her, gasping, out of the exhausted emptiness that has set in. She wants to feed him. This is no small desire. She pulls herself up to sitting.

Where is he? The nurses have the bundle open, inspecting her son like one of those horrid, mummified museum exhibits. She can see their frowns at his exotic features. How dare they judge her boy. Annie's body tingles with the overwhelming physical need to feed him. It is utterly unexpected. But the feeling is absolute and intoxicating.

A nurse looks towards her, frowning. Annie sees a foot, so small it looks like a doll's, but pink and waxy as a peeled potato. The nurse is putting socks on her baby. They are blue wool, the sort of clothing a mother would knit. He cries again, wailing like the long-arced call of the magpies outside.

Annie reaches for her son, wrapped in white muslin and blue socks. She ignores the hushed approval at her mothering instincts from the nurses as they fuss about. He is small and light but solid and warm as a newly baked loaf of bread. He smells dusty and sweet, of talcum powder and the fledgling vapour of his very first breath.

'Feed him up,' the nun says. 'He's come a long way to get here. You both have.'

Molly arrives the following morning, a sheen of sweaty excitement visible on her brow and carrying a bag of newborn clothes she's been knitting for the past three months. Annie sits up tiredly as her friend enters the room, immediately surprised by how easily she can move now the baby's bulk has left her.

'How are you?' Molly looks around the room expectantly, then back to Annie when she can't see a baby's bassinet anywhere.

'I'm as well as can be expected. How is one supposed to feel?'

'Like a mother I guess, though you're the expert in that category now!'

'Honestly, Molly, I'm too tired to care. It was utterly exhausting.'

'Do you mind if I go and see the little man?'

'Of course not, off you go.'

Molly disappears down the corridor, leaving Annie to look through the bag of knitted gifts. There are three cardigans, in green, cream and red wool, all beautifully finished with matching buttons. There's a cream cap with silk ribbon ties, soft as new grass, and little grey booties. Hours of careful work have gone into producing these miniature clothes. Annie wonders at Molly's patience as she holds up the ridiculously small booties, and then remembers the nun putting socks on her son last night and how tiny his feet were. They will fit perfectly.

Molly returns with the baby bundled in layers of muslin and a shawl. She sways slightly from foot to foot as she holds the boy, rocking him gently to soothe the fretting sounds he makes. The sight is reassuring and Annie feels comfortable watching her friend, shaking her head as Molly motions to hand him over. She's made the right decision, no turning back now.

'You're a natural, Molly.'

'This is the easy part. It's bearing children we can't seem to master. He's got your cheekbones Annie, but I'm not sure where the rest of his face comes from?'

There's nothing to see of the baby except pale blue cotton and trailings of scallop-edged blanket hanging over Molly's arms. But Annie knows Molly is referring to Chow's eyes which her son has inherited. Molly gently places the bundle into Annie's arms.

'I don't mean to sound rude—he's a darling, Annie. Well done.'

'He's got his father's eyes, Molly; warm and friendly, alive with light. Just like this little chap looking up at me now.' Annie unwraps her son and strokes the thick tufts of soft, dark hair. Molly leans over and holds one of his little feet.

'I can't get over how tiny he is. I'm afraid I might drop him, Molly.'

'Don't be silly, he's a perfect size, a cherub if ever I saw one.'

Annie smiles at Molly's compliment, relieved that her friend accepts the baby without judgement. The nurses were right when they said she'd come a long way to get here. A wave of melancholy floods Annie as she looks at her son and remembers Chow in the reeds on the banks of the Yangtze, motioning with outstretched hand for her to join him. How full of hope she was during that final summer in Shanghai; when she moved out of widowhood and into being someone else altogether, living only for that moment, with no past, no tomorrows. The baby cries and squirms about, clinging to the shawl with tiny, firm fingers. She'd thought the version of herself with Chow was truer, more honest, and that a life with him would make her happy. Only now does she see how foolish she was, how cavalier. She can't escape her past; the loss and the pain will always be a part of her. And who is she if not the failed sister, the broken widow, her father's disappointment? Together they form the woman she's become and Annie accepts now she'll always struggle to settle the failures that haunt her. But she's stronger than the girl who arrived in Shanghai, and more honest with herself, and that's what makes Annie able to offer her son the chance of a better future, one of hope. The baby's fingers are cold so she tucks them into the shawl and tightens the wrap. She was once like this baby, freshly born with no mistakes to count, full of the possibilities of life.

She must think about the future, even though she can barely face the next days, she knows she must. The only way to move forward now is with no expectations, no hope, and that is the end to it. Her job is simply to keep going.

Annie waits at the turn-off to the river road. It's dusty standing in the verge of grass. She rocks her son to keep him quiet. His gummy mouth on her knuckle feels hard and wet but she doesn't mind him sucking if it keeps him happy. He is only a week old, after all. There is no shade and the small woollen cap propped over his head does little to protect from the morning sun so she slips it into her pocket.

The pair do not have long to wait. Shortly before five, after the bullock dray passes and upsets the baby with all its grunting beasts and cracking whips, the Lowes arrive. Molly hangs back on the other side of the path up by the line of poplar trees, pressing down her skirts nervously. She grips the high handle of the baby buggy beside her, expectantly. Annie wonders if she will at least wave, as she waits for Mr Lowe to reach her, but Molly doesn't move. Mr Lowe walks purposefully towards Annie, his large hat pulled down low, fearful of being recognised when there is only the three of them within twenty miles.

Annie pockets the notes. It will be enough to leave the valley and set up somewhere new. She gently prises her finger from the baby's mouth. His lips keep moving in that sweet way she's come to know, sucking on a memory. She kisses his cheek and stays close to him a moment, burying herself in the overwhelmingly good smell of his milky clean skin.

'Take care of him; he'll be a good son for you.' She can barely hear her own voice. Her hold tightens around the bundle in her arms. Mr Lowe digs his hands in under where Annie cradles the baby and scoops him up in one swift, firm movement. For a moment he stands there in front of her and Annie has to steady herself. A gentle smile of wonder creases Mr Lowe's eyes as he looks at his new baby. But it's not the heart-wrenching decision to give the Lowes her son which makes Annie stumble in that moment, but the resemblance to Chow she sees so clearly in this man's eyes.

Then he turns towards his wife. Molly raises her arm, not a wave so much as a request, like she's putting her hand up in class to claim her turn, her child. Annie lifts her hand in response, stamping her feet as she watches her friend in the distance. Mr Lowe is already walking back to Molly and the only sign he is carrying her boy is the slight stoop in his back. She waits until the baby is safely in the buggy, watching Mr and Mrs Lowe as they tuck him in; Molly holding firm onto the pram while Mr Lowe locks his arm through hers.

Then Annie turns away down the dirt road to where it opens out beside the Macleay, unable to watch the new family any longer. She digs her hands deep into her pockets as she walks, looking out across the channel that dips and swells with the current. She feels something soft in her pocket, her son's cap. The discovery makes Annie catch her breath and stop. The silk ties slip through her fingers as she breathes in his smell. In the quiet she thinks she hears him cry, but it's only a magpie, calling into the wide-open sky above.

HISTORICAL NOTE

Shanghai in 1925 was divided into three distinct administrative areas: the International Settlement, which was made up of the earlier separate British and American concessions; the French Concession; and the original walled city under Chinese control. The International Settlement was ruled by the Shanghai Municipal Council (SMC), a body of nine men weighted in favour of Britain and without any Chinese members until 1928.

The boundary between the underworld of Shanghai in the 1920s and the legal activities of the SMC and its police force, the Shanghai Municipal Police, was very grey. The most influential criminal organisation was the Green Gang; a confederation of small bands of gangsters, originally formed by river boatmen. The power of the Green Gang was fuelled by its control over the opium smuggling networks. Green Gang members could be found in the police forces

of the French Concession and the International Settlement
as well as the Chinese jurisdiction. This was helped by
the foreign authorities' longstanding policy of deliberately
recruiting gangsters into their Chinese detective squads.
Middle-ranked gang members were officers in the local
military garrisons, and minor politicians, factory foremen,
labour contractors and merchants. The top ranked members
were bankers, rich businessmen and important politicians.

Labour activism in Shanghai in 1925 was alive and
growing. The Chinese Communist Party had been formed
in 1922 and it was involved in unionising and educating
workers to their rights. In May 1925, a Chinese worker was
killed at a Japanese-owned mill in the Pooto Road district
of Shanghai during a labour demonstration. At a memorial
service for the victim, a group of students was arrested for
distributing illegal leaflets and their trial date was set for
30 May.

A day of action on 30 May was organised by the students' union and more students were arrested on that day
for protesting on Nanking Road, within the International
Settlement. They were gaoled together in the Louza police
station. By mid-afternoon their number had swelled as
the police broke up more impromptu meetings in nearby
streets. A huge crowd followed one of these parties back
to the station, and forced their way into the charge-room.
They were pushed back out onto Nanking Road by Inspector Edward Everson and the small police force manning the
station. But within an hour, the crowd had grown and Everson gave the order to fire. Four young men died instantly
and another eight died later. Those in the front ranks stood
no chance. Everson claimed the station would have fallen

to the bloodthirsty anti-foreign mob if he had not given the order to fire. But witnesses agreed the crowd had remained good-humoured almost up to the last. Photographs of the torn white shirts worn by two of the dead were used by the Chinese Ministry of Foreign Affairs to show they had been shot in the back.

A day later, on 31 May, the Chinese Communist Party founded a General Labour Union that co-ordinated a triple strike of workers, students and merchants. The strike lasted until September and riots and violence in the streets of Shanghai during this time were common. The Shanghai Municipal Council declared a formal 'State of Emergency' and blamed the Bolsheviks for funding the disruption. At least twenty-two Chinese were killed during what became known as the May Thirtieth Movement. It was a major international news story, damaging to the Shanghai Municipal Council, and it resulted in a public exploration of the workings of the International Settlement regime. Membership of the Chinese Communist Party leapt from about 1,000 in May 1925 to 11,250 a year later.

ACKNOWLEDGEMENTS

Through the years that it took me to write this, my first novel, I have been blessed with so much support. Thank you to my mentor and teacher at the Faber Academy, Kathryn Heyman, for her invaluable help during the early drafts of this book and her continued faith in my abilities. I was also fortunate to work with Tom Keneally in a masterclass series during which he gave me some gems of writing advice. Claire Corbett, who taught the masterclass with Tom, was a fantastic tutor. Tom Flood of Flood Manuscripts reviewed a later draft and his input was spot-on and a wonderful invigoration at a time when I had flagged. Thanks must go to the other people who gave up their time to read drafts of my novel and offered precious feedback and advice; Petra Fowler, Kevin Ralphs and Will Berryman. This book would not be here if it weren't for my wonderful agent Pippa Masson at Curtis Brown Australia, who saw the possibilities of my manuscript. I am extremely grateful to my publisher Harlequin, to Jo Mackay and the editorial team who have welcomed me with warm enthusiasm and professionalism. A special thanks to my editor Alex Craig for her marvellous and insightful work.

To my dear friends who listened to me, who offered me a place to write, sometimes whole houses, and who kept me sane, I say thank you for the distractions of laughter, dinners and wine. I'm especially thankful to Sunara Fernando who listened patiently through endless discussions of plot and character and embraced this story as much as I did.

Finally my love and gratitude to my mother Karen, my sisters Phoebe and Rebecca and to the big family brood who hold me close. How dearly I wish my father were alive to see this book come into being. Above all, and for always, my love and thanks to my dear children: my son Oliver whose own journey inspires me every day and my daughters Clare and Zoe who ground me with their curiosity and dance with me for pure joy.

talk about it

Let's talk about books.

Join the conversation:

facebook.com/harlequinaustralia

@harlequinaus

@harlequinaus

harpercollins.com.au/hq

If you love reading and want to know about our authors and titles, then let's talk about it.